Tabitha lowered her head and shrugged. "He said that a few nights ago he dreamed he killed a homeless man in an alley. He was highly agitated and his clothing was a mess. I got the impression that he hadn't slept since then."

"Dreaming of murder isn't a crime, Ms. March. But assault is. If I find—"

"No matter what you find, he didn't intend to hurt me, and I'm not pressing charges."

In what was becoming a familiar gesture, Darling jammed his hands into his pockets and scowled at her. "Pardon me, ma'am, but that's the stupidest thing I've ever heard. Griffin had his fingers wrapped around your throat. You have absolutely no way of knowing what his intentions—"

"I do so," she snapped. "When he grabbed me, I saw into his mind for a moment. He doesn't know what's happening to him. He's terrified—"

"*Inside his mind?*" Darling barked. His eyes narrowed on her. "You saw inside his *mind*? Great! Did you happen to catch his name and address while you were in there?"

By Marianne Stillings

Arousing Suspicions

MARIANNE STILLINGS

AVON BOOKS
An Imprint of HarperCollinsPublishers

AVON BOOKS
An Imprint of HarperCollins*Publishers*
10 East 53rd Street
New York, New York 10022–5299

Copyright © 2007 by Marianne Stillings
ISBN: 978–0–06–085009–8
ISBN–10: 0–06–085009–4
www.avonromance.com

First Avon Books paperback printing: March 2007

Avon Trademark Reg. U.S. Pat. Off. and in Other Countries, Marca Registrada, Hecho en U.S.A.
HarperCollins© is a registered trademark of HarperCollins Publishers.

Printed in the U.S.A.

10 9 8 7 6 5 4 3 2 1

To Bina—
This one's for you, duckie.
Sweet dreams.

 **Chapter 1**

If you dream the same dream three nights in a row, it will come true.

FOLKLORE

She took his hand and turned it over, settling it gently into her palm. His fingers curled as though he were cupping water. His skin was smooth, cool.

Awareness surged through her like the aftershocks of a deep earth tremor. She struggled to center her emotions, allowing him in on one level, on another keeping him out.

His brown eyes smiled, suggested, connected.

"Close your eyes, please," she said.

He stared at her for a heartbeat, then his lids drifted down.

"Good. Now take a deep breath. Relax. When you're ready, tell me your dream."

He was a new client and, judging from his hesitation, uneasy about putting words to personal, private, *possibly intimate thoughts. She was not only a stranger to him, but a woman. Would he be able to move past his defenses and allow her in? Was he prepared for the consequences of raw honesty?*

She tried to get a sense of how important this was to him, how badly he needed to know, but his energy seemed to be turned in another direction, and she came up empty.

His eyes were closed; she studied his face. Strong bones, handsome features. Early thirties. Light brown hair streaked golden by the sun, dark lashes, strong jaw. He wore glasses, and even though his eyes were shut, he'd kept them on.

She let her own lids drift down as he began to speak. His voice was deep, interesting, boyishly sexy. She focused on his words—and the pictures materializing inside her head.

A sense of uneasiness skittered across her skin, prickling the nape of her neck. Where she had felt comfortable a moment ago, now she felt . . . exposed.

His voice changed, deepened, roughened. Impressions formed behind her closed lids, but they were as fragmented as his words, as though he were forcing a puzzle together using the wrong pieces.

She tried to remain calm, to listen, to see, but her nerves were beginning to fray, and when she lost hold of the bizarre images, she felt relief.

She opened her eyes to study him. Blinking in shock, she jerked her hand away, holding it to her as if she'd been burned. His hand remained in the air, frozen, fingers curled grotesquely. He slowly opened his eyes, stared into hers, then let his knuckles hit the table with a dull thud, as though his hand had no life in it at all.

Swallowing, she stared back at him.

Gone were the light hair and glasses, the handsome, youthful features. His hair was dark now. His eyes, black and empty as night, transfixed her. He continued speaking, his thin lips forming words, but what she heard made no sense.

Terrified, she pushed her chair away, but before she could stand and run, he lunged, grabbing her throat with one hand, tearing her dress with the other.

She choked and gasped, clawing at his fingers, fighting for breath. He shoved her down to the floor, tightening his grip, his eyes telling her what he intended to do to her. . .

Tabitha March struggled with her twisted bedsheet as though it were a pink muslin anaconda eager to squeeze the life out of her. Finally throwing it off, she sat up and gulped for air, raising her hand to her neck, making sure the fingers around her throat had dissolved along with the dream.

Her heart pounded in her ears; perspiration beaded her forehead. She reached for the water bottle on the bedside table, twisted off the cap, and downed its contents. Wiping her mouth with the sleeve of her coral sleep shirt, she used a wad of bedsheet to dab at her brow and rub the back of her sweaty neck.

Finally, after taking ten or so deep breaths, she felt her shoulders relax, her heartbeat slow to normal. In her head, the terrible images faded.

From the foot of her bed, two pairs of eyes stared warily at her.

Obviously awakened by Tabitha's abrupt movements, Winkin looked at her like he wanted to offer her comfort, while Blinkin just looked peeved. The difference between dogs and cats, she mused.

"The next time I feel the urge to munch on pepperoni pizza before bedtime, stop me, okay?"

She was fairly sure the Jack Russell terrier and the green-eyed Siamese agreed, but it was hard to tell, what with Winks licking his haunches and Blinks scratching an itch behind her ear.

"You guys are some comfort." Her sarcasm was wasted on the pair.

She looked over at her bedside clock. Seven-fifteen. Scooping up her daytimer, she flipped to Tuesday, April the tenth. Nothing at eight, but . . .

Oh, right, right. She had a new client coming at nine. Nathan Damon. On the phone, he'd sounded a little shy. He said he'd never consulted a psychic dream interpreter before, so that could explain his hesitation.

Tabitha always felt a little apprehensive before

seeing someone new, though she had little choice but to take on new clients since her livelihood depended on expanding her client base.

Her part-time legal transcribing service didn't come close to providing the income she needed. The Victorian she'd inherited from her grandmother was so expensive to maintain, the repairs so constant, the taxes so outrageous, it took every penny she made each month just to stay ahead of her creditors.

Most people who sought out her services did so because they understood how psychic dream interpretation worked. But there were the occasional clients who reacted badly to her revelations, either because they didn't get what they wanted from a reading or got too much.

Three weeks ago, Ed Figueroa had been just such a man. After his reading, his round cheeks had become flushed, his bald head damp with perspiration.

"Mr. Figueroa," she'd said, quickly releasing his hand. "Please understand, everything you say, everything that happens in a session, is held in strictest confidence. If you want an honest interpretation, however, you're going to have to open up and—"

"You're a fake!" he'd snapped, slamming his doubled fist on the table. "*And* a liar. I've never cheated on my wife!"

"I did not accuse you of infidelity," she'd replied, in as calm a tone as she could. "In any event, your personal life is no concern of mine. I make no judgments, Mr. Figueroa. I'm simply trying to interpret your dream accurately. That is why you came to me, isn't it?"

He'd rubbed his chin with one pudgy knuckle. Flicking nervous glances at her, he said, "Yeah."

The odds were that Ed Figueroa really was cheating on his wife and it had shocked the man that Tabitha had picked that up. And now he was afraid.

She smiled, trying to put him at ease. "What I meant was, your dream indicates to me that you may be experiencing some, um, unresolved issues over something going on in your life right now. And you may possibly be feeling a little, um, guilty. Your subconscious is trying to cope—"

"I never cheated on my wife, and if you tell anyone, I'll sue your ass!" He shoved himself away from the table and stood. "You're a fraud, lady. Taking people's money and telling them lies. Fraud!"

Tabitha rose slowly, clasping her hands in front of her. "I'm sorry we didn't have a more productive session. There will be no charge for today, Mr. Figueroa."

He gave her a curt nod, called her a shocking name, and mumbled defamatory remarks about her ancestors all the way out the door. She hadn't heard from him since, thank God, and prayed she never would.

But clients such as Mr. Figueroa were rare. Hopefully, Mr. Damon would see reason, understand how the process worked, and they could have a successful session.

Now, as she tossed aside the damp sheet and walked to the door, Winkin and Blinkin leapt off the bed to race each other down the stairs, sounding more like a herd of buffalo than a dog and cat. When the slap-and-bang of the doggy door in the kitchen echoed up the stairs, she knew they'd hit the backyard at a full run.

Meandering over to her west-facing window, she pulled the curtain back and gazed out into the side yard at the eucalyptus tree her grandmother had planted fifty years ago. Its long, scythe-shaped leaves rustled in the morning breeze as though warning of more wind to come.

Of course, San Francisco could be very windy; everybody knew that. The turn your umbrella inside out, blow your hair all over your head, and lift your skirt up to your thighs sort of wind. Men didn't seem to complain about the latter, though. And the rain, when it came, splashed all over everything in big, fat drops that burst like tiny water balloons when they hit your windshield. Water sluiced off canvas awnings to ping pedestrians on the head. The black streets became shiny, their painted lines distorted and hard to see. Driving in San Francisco rain could be a real bitch.

But she loved it. She loved all of it.

She lifted her gaze to the slate-colored clouds pressing down on the city. It might rain today. She tried not to view that as an omen.

Suddenly irritated at herself for making an appointment with a new client so early in the morning, she resigned herself to get it in gear, shower, dress, and head downstairs and make coffee. Better have some hot water ready, too, in case Mr. Damon preferred tea.

Twenty minutes later, as she slipped into her denim skirt and lacy white top, the images from the nightmare formed inside her head once more. For a psychic dream interpreter, she was lousy at deciphering her own dreams. In her entire life, she'd never had a prophetic dream, but then, many psychics didn't.

Rising, she walked to the head of her bed and looked up at the dream catcher dangling from the ceiling, high above her pillow. Except for a hole in the very center, the large willow hoop had been filled with a delicately woven spiderlike web. From the bottom of the hoop hung three long strings decorated with shiny beads and soft white feathers.

According to Lakota legend, the web caught

a dreamer's good ideas and omens, while the hole in the center let evil or malevolence pass through and away. She sure hoped it worked, especially after the dream that had awakened her this morning.

The nightmare had carried with it a feeling of importance she had never felt before. It had been frightening, but more than that, it had been solid, real in some way. An indicator dream.

An indication of what, though?

As she slid into her sandals and closed the bedroom door behind her, she couldn't help but feel the dream was a warning that her life was about to change.

Uneasiness settled deep into the pit of her stomach. Lately, one day had been pretty much like the next, but now she felt a tug of expectation. Not the kind of expectation when you buy a lottery ticket and just *know* you're going to win. More like when you stare at the phone because you know somebody's going to call you—with very bad news.

Inspector Nate Darling of the San Francisco Police Department stood across the street from the suspect's house, checking out possible points of entry and exit. One door in front, probably one in back, and maybe a side door, as well. Hard to say from this angle.

The somewhat run-down Victorian was of a basic Queen Anne design, and featured a gabled roof and decorative trim. The narrow house rose up three stories and boasted a turret with arched window frames. While the clapboards were painted a sort of peachy apricotish color, the Palladian windows, balcony rails, and window frames were contrasted in faded blue and green.

Next to the turret stood an enormous eucalyptus tree, its overgrown branches brushing the side of the house with every gust of wind. He'd be willing to bet that decaying eucalyptus leaves clogged the gutters; they'd be a real pain in the ass to clean.

The house belonged to one Tabitha March, who lived there and rented out rooms to boarders. She also conducted business from her parlor office on the first floor.

But just what kind of *business* did Ms. March *conduct*? That was the question, and the reason for his visit.

The citizen who'd lodged the complaint had been very specific—Tabitha March bilked her clients, took money under false pretenses, tendered bad advice, and offered more "personal" services on the side—for a hefty fee.

Even though there had only been the one complaint, Ed Figueroa was a well-respected and prominent San Francisco businessman who had friends in the upper echelons of local law enforcement. As a result, his accusations of fraud and solicitation could not be ignored.

In the time Nate had been standing under the magnolia tree that shaded this brief bit of Larkin Street's sidewalk, nobody had entered or exited the house. He checked his watch. Nearly nine. "Nathan Damon" had an appointment at the top of the hour with Tabitha March, dream interpreter.

Dream interpreter, my ass. He nearly scoffed out loud. Well, there was no law against such a vocation, especially in California. Though he'd been away for nearly twenty years, he'd never forgotten how differently people viewed the world here. They were all so touchy-feely, so open to new things, some of them were borderline nutcases, as far as he was concerned.

Pursing his lips, he wondered how he'd have turned out if he'd stayed in the Bay Area instead of moving to Olympia with his dad when his parents had split. A year after his return to San Francisco, Nate still missed the Northwest—and the woman he'd loved there—but when the relationship had ended, he'd decided it was finally time to return home. There were lots of fences to mend here. Almost two decades of neglected, broken fences.

His watch gave a quiet bleep. Nine o'clock. Showtime. He glanced at the car parked down the block and gave a subtle nod to his partner. Inspector Bob Stocker would hear and record every word Nate and Ms. March said.

Adjusting his wire-rimmed glasses, he crossed the street, taking the ten porch steps two at a time. When he pressed the doorbell, a musical trill sounded inside. Nice, like cascading chimes.

A moment later the door opened, and Nate's heart skidded to a stop. His mouth went dry. His brain shut down, and . . . well, he'd have to have a talk later with his testosterone.

Tabitha March didn't look like a con artist or a hooker. No sirree. More like some farmer's fresh and pretty daughter.

Her strawberry blond hair fell to just below her shoulders and had a slight curl to it. Clear skin accentuated the bluest eyes he'd ever seen. Her cheeks were soft and rosy, and just the right amount of freckles dashed across her straight nose. Totally cute.

Those big baby blues widened as she looked him up and down, a little frantically it seemed to him.

"Mr. D-Damon?" she stumbled. Her words were spoken as though she were hoping he was somebody else.

"Yes, Nathan Damon," he said, and smiled. "We have an appointment at nine."

Why in the hell was she gaping at him like

she'd just seen the Grim Reaper? Had she made him as a cop already? If so, this whole deal was a waste of time.

"Are you the one I spoke to on the phone?" he ventured.

Her dark lashes fluttered and her eyes clouded with confusion. Swallowing, she stared at him for a moment.

"Yes," she finally said. "I'm Tabitha March. Sorry. I, uh, you look like somebody I met once. Sort of. Recently."

Stepping back, she swung the door open and gestured for him to enter. "This . . . there . . . office." She stopped speaking and pointed to an open doorway. When he gave her a questioning look, she smiled shyly. "Probably just a coincidence."

"What is?"

Her smile brightened and she shook her head. "Nothing."

She walked past him and he followed her through the oak double doors into her office. Warm sunshine filtered through the curtains, giving the small room a cozy intimacy. Faded floral wallpaper, lace curtains, a tiny fireplace, and an elegant crystal chandelier lent the room an Old World charm.

In the far corner, an antique desk held a modern computer and printer, a phone, various ledgers, and stacks of papers.

Shutting the doors behind them, she indicated he should take a seat at an oval mahogany table in front of the fireplace.

While he made himself comfortable, she moved around to take the seat opposite him.

"So," she said on a long exhaled breath. Clasping her hands in front of her on the table, she said, "On the phone you mentioned you've never consulted a dream interpreter before."

"That's right." *But if I'd known they looked like you, I'd've given it a shot years ago.*

She absently curled a lock of her hair behind her ear. The gesture brought his attention to the delicate bones of her face, slightly arched brows, full mouth.

Without thinking, he licked his lips.

If she was soliciting, she must have caught on that men liked to see a woman in scooped-neck tops and little diamond dangle earrings.

Though her clothing wasn't obvious at all, her curves would be very hard to hide, and he wondered how she managed to look both hot and sweet at the same time.

But it was the doe-in-the-headlights look in her eyes that interested him the most. If he didn't know better, he'd swear she was terrified of him.

"How did you hear about my services, Mr. Damon?"

Her *services*. Yeah. Here we go.

"I have a friend who's a client. You came highly recommended."

"One of my regulars?"

"I believe so."

"Would you be comfortable sharing his name?"

Nate pretended to give it some thought. "I'd like to keep his name out of it, if that's okay."

That seemed to disturb her, but she didn't press the issue.

Fiddling with her hair again, she cleared her throat. "Have you been having difficulty sleeping?"

"You might say that."

"Bad dreams?"

"Yes."

She nodded. "Many clients have thanked me for the enormous relief I've given them. They've felt comfortable enough with me, even first-timers, to strip away all their inhibitions and get down to raw honesty. It's very freeing to unburden yourself in this way, get right to the bottom of things."

"Yeah, that's what my friend said." Nate swallowed.

She perked up. "I'm happy to hear your friend was satisfied enough to recommend me to you."

Relaxing into his chair a little, he said, "So, how does this work, exactly?"

Her lashes fluttered and she got that nervous

look about her again. "Okay, well, basically, I'm tactile. That is to say, I do my best when I'm in physical contact with a client. Generally speaking, if we touch during the session, the results are much more satisfying for us both."

No doubt about it, baby.

She smiled sweetly. "Would you have any problem with me touching you, Mr. Damon?"

Hey, it's one of the perks. "No." ·

"All right, then."

She slid one hand onto the table, palm up. With her other hand, she reached for his, turned it over, and rested it in her own. His knuckles nestled into her palm, his fingers relaxed into a slight curl as though he were cupping her breast. She stared at their hands for a moment, and seemed to grow more agitated.

"*Oh* . . . I, uh . . . oh . . ." she mumbled. Flicking a quick look into his eyes, she glanced away again, then inhaled sharply, like somebody had just jabbed her in the ribs.

"Okay, we're c-connected." She ran her tongue over her lips, then swallowed. "Please close your eyes and tell me your dream. As you speak, I'll be able to see the images. Then we can talk about what your dream means."

Her palm was warm, damp. She was definitely nervous as hell.

So now he was supposed to relate a dream to

her? He didn't dream very much. At least, he didn't remember them. Since this whole thing was utter BS anyway, she'd never know the difference if he made something up. Besides, any minute she was going to stop beating around the bush and offer him sex for money.

And then the game would be over.

Nathan Damon was tall, and big. Broad shoulders, athletic. He appeared about her age, maybe a year or two older. He had light hair, dark blond with steaks of gold. And he was handsome. Very. When she'd looked into his eyes, she'd felt something heavy grow and twist in her stomach. His eyes were brown and he wore wire-rimmed glasses, exactly like the man in her nightmare.

She'd never had a prophetic dream in her life, and now here was the man she'd dreamed of just a few hours ago, the man who had been trying to strangle her. When she'd first seen him standing on her porch, she'd wanted to slam the door in his face—and run.

Had she somehow picked up what he looked like when she'd heard his voice on the phone? Was the dream a good omen or, as it had played out, a bad one? Did this man mean her harm? If she closed her eyes, would he morph into a demon and try to choke the life out of her?

Dreams of being killed didn't mean someone

was actually going to murder you. They generally symbolized an end of some kind, an abrupt halt to a dilemma you were facing in your waking life. But the nightmare had frightened her so, and now sitting across the table was the very man whose fingers had been wrapped around her throat.

No, that wasn't quite true. It had not been this man, but the darker, more evil figure he'd become who had tried to kill her.

Regardless, the prophetic nature of the nightmare couldn't be ignored. *Demon? Damon?* It was too close, it couldn't be a coincidence.

Maybe she could press him to reveal the name of the client who'd referred him. That would help. She could contact the client and ask about Mr. Damon and whether he was telling her the truth about himself or not.

To add to her confusion, the moment she touched him, images had begun to bombard her senses, completely throwing her for a loop.

She'd seen him, *them*, together . . . *very* together. Intimately together. Pleasure wound through her like a silken ribbon; excitement teased her skin.

"Do you want to do it now?" His voice was low, suggestive.

Startled out of her trance, she searched his eyes.

"Do? It?" The lightbulb went off. "Oh! Your dream. Yes, please tell me about your dream."

In her hand, the weight of his felt hot, heavy, perfect.

What was wrong with her? After the way she'd been behaving and stuttering and hemming and hawing, he must think she had the IQ of an emotionally unstable gnat.

Squaring her shoulders, she took a cleansing breath, focused, and said, "Let's close our eyes, and we can begin."

As soon as they did, stronger images began assaulting her senses. People, their faces blurred at first, then coming into sharp focus. Noises, voices, the deafening explosion of gunfire, a scream, laughter, a moan.

Damon cleared his throat. "I, uh, I dreamed I was with a woman. Someone I'd never met before. She was very attractive and I wanted to sleep with her. But she, uh, kept giving me the runaround. She was wearing a green dress and kept telling me how much she liked green. Finally, I figured out it meant she wanted money." He stopped for a moment, cleared his throat again. "So, I paid her and we had sex."

Tabitha frowned. Slowly, she pulled her hand from underneath his. Opening her eyes, she said, "Mr. Damon. I'm sure you're uncomfortable with revealing your innermost thoughts to a stranger, but unless we have complete honesty between us, I won't be able to help you."

His eyes opened. Brown, smoldering, warm. The kind of eyes a woman could get lost in first thing in the morning or last thing at night. Lunchtime, dinnertime, coffee breaks, weekends, national holidays, Christmas Eve, St. Patrick's Day, weddings, bar mitzvahs . . . just looking at him made her want to flop down on a bed somewhere and let him have his way with her.

But he had lied.

"I told you my dream. Can't you interpret it?" Those intelligent eyes challenged her.

"No, I can't. The dream you related to me was *not* the dream I saw, not in the least."

He shrugged, adjusted his glasses as she'd seen Clark Kent do in the movies countless times. Sigh.

"What *did* you see?" His tone was flat.

"Frankly, a mess." She crossed her arms under her breasts. "Assuming you really had the dream you just related to me, what do *you* think it means?"

He crossed his arms over his chest. They sat there, eyeing each other.

"I think it means I'm willing to pay a woman I don't know to have sex with me."

"Why do you think that is?"

His sensuous mouth flattened. "Men think about sex, on average, every time they blink. The dream most likely means I want to have sex."

She felt her skin flush, but maintained eye contact with him. "Then why don't you go have it, Mr. Damon? You look to be the kind of man who doesn't have any trouble getting women."

"I came to you so you could interpret my dream. I'm sure it has a deeper meaning."

"Some dreams are exactly what they appear to be."

He blinked.

She lifted a brow. "Was it good for you?" she said dryly.

As he leaned forward across the table, Tabitha automatically eased back in her chair.

"Okay," he admitted. "Maybe there is no deeper meaning. I'm a guy. I'm shallow. I can live with that. What other services do you offer?"

Confused, she scowled. "Other services?"

His lips curled into a suggestive grin, and she figured he could melt most any woman's resistance with that smile.

"Yeah, other services." He sat back in his chair. Rubbing his jaw with his thumb, he said, "I understand you provide your clients with a variety of services."

"Oh, yes, I *do*." She relaxed a little. He obviously meant her part-time legal transcribing job. She kept a running ad in the newspaper and sent out flyers occasionally to law firms in the area. "Would you be interested?"

"Definitely."

She lifted a shoulder in a half shrug. "Then I'm sure I could accommodate you."

He flicked his gaze over her. "I'm sure you could. How much do you charge?"

"It depends on how much there is, and how long it takes me."

He pursed his lips and looked modest. "Well, I've never had any complaints, and if you took your time, that would be okay. The longer it takes, the better."

She tilted her head. "Oh. Well, actually, I'm known for my quick turnaround."

"Are you, now? Well, what if I wanted a slow turnaround instead?"

With a little shrug, she said, "Sure. In that case, though, I'd charge you by the brief. That way you'd get the best rate."

His brows shot up. "By the brief?" He thought for a moment. "Nylon tiger stripes or plain white cotton?"

"Excuse me?" Confusion fogged her brain.

"Excuse you?" Confusion fogged his glasses.

"Are you a lawyer?" she asked.

He took off his glasses, wiped them, put them back on. "No."

"Then why would you want me to transcribe legal documents?"

"Trans—" His eyes widened in shock. "Is that the service you provide?"

"Yes," she said, tension tightening her stomach. "What did you think I was talking about?"

Pushing away from the table, he stood and began backing away. He reached into his pocket and pulled out a wad of bills. "How much do I owe you for today?"

"Mr. Damon, I—"

"I have another appointment. I'm late. Will fifty cover it?" He slapped the money down on the table.

She stared at the bills. "Um, sure. Do you want to schedule another—"

"No," he rushed, as his back collided with the door. Fumbling behind him for the knob, he mumbled, "Uh, no. Thanks. No. I'll see myself out."

Turning, he yanked the door open and hurried down the hall. When she heard the front door close behind him, she put her hands to her temples.

What in the world had that been about?

Giving her head a little shake, she reached for the money. As soon at her fingertips touched it, images began filling her brain. Her lids drifted down.

Them again, together. Naked. Her neck arched back. His hands, all over her. Pleasure. Then darkness. Loss. Her heart ached.

She crumpled the bills in her fingers.

Pain. A man she knew. A woman she didn't. Death.

Her eyes flew open and her breath snagged in her throat.

Dear God. Whoever Nathan Damon really was, he was bad news. For some reason, he'd lied to her, and she'd had it up to *there* with men who lied.

Anger warmed her cheeks. "Jerk," she mumbled.

Shoving the money into her desk drawer, she slammed it shut and let out a long breath. So much for Mr. Damon. With any luck, she would never have to see the damn man again.

Chapter 2

To dream of someone removing his clothes means you will soon solve a mystery.

FOLKLORE

"Yoo-hoo! Darling! I got a love letter for you!"

Nate watched as the sergeant made his way through the sea of desks and people like a walrus navigating a crowded beach.

From day one, the sergeant had taken a dislike to him, hassled him at any opportunity about his name, and assigned him every weirdo and derelict who stumbled in off the street.

"Interview Room Three ... Darling," the sergeant drawled, tossing a piece of paper onto Nate's cluttered desk. He adjusted the belt that fought a losing battle to gird his obtruding gut. "Lady with a problem, my Darling boy."

Nate let his pen drop to the report in front of him. Smiling up at the uniformed officer, he adjusted his glasses and said softly, "It's obvious you find my name amusing, Sergeant, but I'll take Darling over Butt-kiss any day."

"That's Butkus!" the sergeant snapped. Titters and chuckles competed with the sound of ringing telephones, the click of computer keys, and heavy footfalls across the wooden floor. Gesturing at the paper, Butkus snarled, "Room Three. She's waitin'."

With that, he did a lumbering one-eighty and stomped out of the room.

Nate shook his head in bemused silence, then picked up the paper. Butkus's scrawl indicated one Thelma Marx wanted to talk to a detective about a possible homicide. No further details were given.

He stood, straightened his tie, and slipped into his navy suit jacket. Paper in hand, he headed for Room Three.

Pausing at the interview room window, he studied the woman for a moment.

She was seated at the small table in one of the four metal chairs, her back to him. Her outfit was simple, a denim jacket, floral skirt, and boots. On her head she wore one of those knitted tam things in a pretty shade of blue. She held her delicate hands neatly folded on the Formica tabletop in front of her. The line of her back and set of her shoulders told him she was tense.

Opening the door, he stepped inside.

"Good morning, Ms. Marx. I'm Inspector D-Duh-uh—"

The words jammed up behind his teeth when she turned to face him.

Her smile of greeting faded and her jaw dropped. Bluer-than-blue eyes widened in shock. She jumped to her feet, nearly knocking over the chair.

"You!" she accused. "What are you . . . how did you . . . You're a *detective*? I . . . I . . . why . . . I . . ."

Her words trailed off as Nate closed the door. Goddamn that Butkus for having such lousy penmanship.

Nate put his hands up in a defensive gesture.

"Ms. March," he soothed. "Please have a seat. I can explain everything—"

"Oh, *now* I understand," she said, her hands balled into fists on her hips. "No wonder nothing made sense. You *lied* to me. You made up that dream, *didn't* you? Were you testing me to see if I was competent? We could have discussed it, you know. I would have told you—"

"Ms. March," he interrupted. "Please calm down. We had a complaint. I was sent to check it out."

She appeared even more shocked than before. "A complaint?" she squeaked. "From one of my clients? Listen, Detective Damon—"

"Darling."

She looked startled. *"What?"*

"Nate Darling," he enunciated slowly, in the hopes she'd take the hint and not do what everybody else in the frigging world did when they heard his name.

She lifted a brow and gazed up at him, her lovely mouth tilting in a slow, sardonic grin. "Darling?"

Sending her a meaningful look, he warned, "Don't go there, ma'am."

She crossed her arms over her stomach and looked him up and down, her eyes speaking volumes.

He flipped back the edges of his jacket and rested his hands on his hips. "I can understand why you'd be upset, but as I said, we had a complaint—"

"If one of my customers isn't happy, why didn't he just tell me? Why did he involve the police?" She looked thoroughly dejected. "I don't understand."

Nate moved forward and held the chair for her. "Please sit down."

She flicked a glance up at him, then dropped into the chair, pulling the tam from her head. A glorious tumble of strawberry blond hair fell around her shoulders. He caught the scent of her floral shampoo, sweet, evocative, and he fought hard not to reach out and feel for himself if the strands were as silky as they looked.

"The good news is," he said, taking the seat across the table from her, "you've been cleared and the complaint has been closed."

Her gaze lifted to his. "Who filed it?"

"I'm not at liberty—"

"It was Mr. Figueroa, wasn't it?"

"The important thing to remember is . . ." *That you have the most incredible eyes I've ever seen.* "Uh, that the charges were unfounded. I'm sorry it was necessary to deceive you, but we had to determine whether the complainant's, uh, complaint was valid." Cripes, where in the hell had his brain gone?

She nibbled absently on her full bottom lip. Nate watched for a moment, then forced his eyes away.

"So," she said, cocking her head and assessing him. "You're not regular-guy Nathan *Damon*, you're a detective named *Darling*." He could almost see the wheels turning inside her brain as she made the mental adjustment from the client who'd visited her house to the cop who sat before her now.

"Yes. Inspector Nathan Darling—"

"Inspector? Are you a detective or not?"

"I am. In San Francisco, a detective of my grade

is referred to as Inspector, like in England. But senior detectives are called Detective or Detective Lieutenant and so forth. It's a little confusing."

Clearing his throat, he took a deep breath and straightened in his chair. "Now, what brings you—"

"Oh, hell," she growled suddenly, looking away. "Never mind. Just . . . never *mind*. This was a stupid idea."

Clutching her hat in one hand, she grabbed for her purse on the chair next to her. But before she could stand, Nate reached across the table and curled his fingers around her wrist. Her skin was soft, warm. She tugged on her hand. He tugged back.

"You're restraining me?" She stared at him in obvious amazement.

"No. I'm encouraging you to remain seated and tell me why you're here. Something important must have happened, for you to come down to the police department. I want to know what it is."

He let go of her wrist slowly, and she settled back into her chair warily.

"Your powers of deduction are brilliant," she drawled. "I can see why they made you a detective."

"Sarcasm won't get us anywhere."

"I want a different detective."

"Why?"

"I don't like you. I don't trust you. You lied to me."

"In the line of duty, a police officer lied to a possible felon," he corrected. "That's different from *me* lying to *you*."

"So you admit that ... Felon?" she choked. "Just what did Mr. Figueroa tell you? What did he accuse me of?"

Nate looked her in the eye. "A charge was made of fraud and solicitation."

"What!"

He thought she might leap up and run out the door, or smack him with her purse, but she stayed put, her cheeks flushed with rage. Attractively. He'd be willing to bet her cheeks flushed in exactly that same way when she—

" ... came in here and accused me of being a ... That's *outrageous*," she growled. "Just because I found out—"

She stopped herself, then lowered her lashes.

Aha. So the truth comes out.

"Ms. March," he said. "If Mr. Figueroa is using the SFPD as a tool for personal vengeance, you can file harassment charges against him. But I have to warn you, it would be hard to prove he simply intended to hassle you. It's a he-said-she-said kind of deal, and he would swear he thought he was doing his citizen's duty by reporting a possible crime."

She seemed to calm down a bit. Shaking her head, she smiled—a little too sweetly, if Nate was any judge.

"No problem," she said in a light, dismissive tone. "What goes around comes around. He'll get his in the end."

Nate blew out a short breath.

"I hope you're not contemplating retaliation against Mr. Figueroa."

She smiled again. "Don't need to. Karma will take care of him."

"As long as Karma isn't a hit man from New Delhi, we're good."

Again with the Cheshire Cat grin. Wow. She was beautiful.

Clearing his throat, he turned his attention to the form Butkus had handed him.

"Okay. Now that that's settled, can we continue with the reason you came in today?"

Her eyes grew serious and she shifted in her chair. Reaching into her handbag, she pulled out a newspaper clipping and handed it to him. It was dated two days ago.

BODY OF SLAIN WOMAN
FOUND IN GOLDEN GATE PARK

His eyes sought hers. "You have information regarding this homicide?"

She paused, almost as though she were assessing him, judging whether or not to trust him with the information. Finally, her shoulders relaxed a fraction and gave a quick nod.

"I . . . I think I know who killed her."

There. She'd said it. No going back now.

Instead of continuing to look at the disturbingly handsome Inspector Darling, Tabitha averted her eyes to the newspaper clipping in his fingers.

At her words, he'd lifted his chin and straightened in his chair. Adjusting his glasses, he leaned forward.

"Are you saying you witnessed this crime?"

She shook her head. "No."

"Did the killer confess to you?"

"No."

"Did you see who dumped the body in the park?"

"No."

Pursing his lips, he watched her for a moment. Finally, "Okay, you want to help me out here? The twenty-questions thing is fun, but I'm really lousy at it and—"

"I have a client," she rushed, before she could change her mind. He wasn't going to believe her; skeptics never did. It didn't take a psychic to see Inspector Facts-and-Data was probably going to laugh out loud as soon as the words were out of her mouth. Still, she'd come this far.

"You have a client," he repeated. "Go on."

"He came to me several weeks ago. He described a dream where he killed a woman in Golden Gate Park. I think he's the one who may have killed this woman." She flicked her finger in the direction of the newspaper clipping. "When he described the dream, I saw . . . um, I saw . . . it. The murder."

Darling set his pen down and closed his notebook.

"That's your evidence?" he said. "You think your client is possibly guilty of murder because of a dream he had? Do you have any other reason to believe this man committed a homicide?"

"No."

There was a moment of silence, then, "Thank you for coming in, Ms. March. The city of San Francisco is grateful for your—"

"I *knew* you wouldn't believe me," she groused. Why, oh, why had she put herself in a position, yet again, to be doubted and dismissed?

Over the last few years, Tabitha had tried to use her psychic abilities to help the authorities, but the police rarely let her. Since her particular strength was tactile, if she didn't have something to touch, she couldn't get a clear image. As a result, her best efforts often failed and she came off looking like an incompetent, or worse, a fake.

But dream interpretation in conjunction with touching the client was her strength; her success with people who sought her services proved that. The images she saw could be trusted nearly a hundred percent, but trying to convince the police of that was a different matter.

Coming down here had been a huge mistake. Despite his sexy voice and soft brown eyes, Inspector Darling was no better than the rest.

"Fine," she sighed.

Darling rose, eased back the edges of his jacket, and put his hands on his hips. With a build like his, she'd bet anything he'd played football. Quarterback. Yeah, he was arrogant enough to have been a star quarterback. The sexy jerk.

With a look of profound displeasure on his face, he said, "You've just wasted my time and the taxpayers' money, Ms. March. I hope you're happy."

"I'm not happy, you closed-minded ass," she huffed. "I came down here out of a sense of duty and felt I had knowledge that might help in an investigation."

"Did your client *tell you* he'd killed this woman?"

"No."

"Dreaming of committing a murder is not a crime, Ms. March. What *evidence* can you provide? Evidence," he added, "that would stand up in a court of law?"

She held her purse to her bosom like a warrior holds a shield. "None," she said. "But I know what I saw, and judging from that newspaper article, the similarities to the actual murder and my client's dream are stunning."

"*Stunning*, Ms. March?" He grinned. Now he was laughing at her. But that was almost okay, because he had the most incredible smile . . .

Heat radiated between them as they glowered at each other, then his grin began to slowly fade. She knew the moment he became aware of her, not as a citizen, or even as a crackpot, but as a woman. Something in his eyes changed. His stance shifted. His gaze drifted down her body and back up again. His breathing altered slightly.

"On behalf of the San Francisco Police Department," he said quietly, "thank you for taking the time to do your civic duty, coming in, and reporting your, uh, suspicions." *As loony as they are*, his eyes mocked. "But without solid evidence or an eyewitness account, there's nothing I can do."

Reaching into his breast pocket, he pulled out a business card and handed it to her.

"If anything more solid presents itself, you can reach me here."

As she took the card, her fingers brushed his, and in that split second she saw them again. Together. Naked. In a passionate embrace. This time she felt him, too. His hands on her bare breasts.

She could hear music, a mellow tune sung in a deep and melodic voice. And all around them the scent of pink jasmine . . .

She must have made some kind of noise, because he frowned.

"You okay?"

Snatching the card from his fingers, she slipped it into her purse and headed toward the door. With her hand on the knob, she bit out, "The article said the woman had been strangled, her body left near the Conservatory of Flowers."

"Yes."

"That's pretty specific."

"I guess so. Are you saying the dream you're referring to involved a strangled woman whose body was found near the conservatory?"

Her back still to the detective, she said, "Yes. But the article doesn't say what color outfit she was wearing."

There was a momentary pause. "It doesn't mention type or style of clothing at all."

She nodded, turned the handle, and opened the door.

"It was a dress. Red. With white polka dots. Good day, Inspector."

Chapter 3

*To rid yourself of bad dreams, place your shoes
under the bed with the toes pointing outward.*

FOLKLORE

"*What* red dress, Ms. March?"

Tabitha stood with one hand on the doorknob,
the other holding her fully loaded toothbrush. Ignoring the minty freshness beginning to ooze off
the bristles and onto her fingers, she assessed her
early morning visitor.

"What took you so long, Detective?" The best
defense was a good offense, she'd heard it said,
especially when one was greeting a fully clothed
police detective in your jammies and bare feet.

"It's *Inspector*," he muttered, giving her the
once-over.

"I know, but it's sad." She puckered her lips in
an exaggerated pout. "*Detective Darling* is so ador-
ably alliterative."

"I can live with the disappointment."

She scowled. "It's seven o'clock on a Monday morning, *Inspector*. It's been three days since our rather pithy conversation. This couldn't wait until after I'd had my coffee?"

"You drink coffee?" He gave her the once-over again, making it a twice-over, she supposed. "Somehow, I'd pegged you as the herbal tea type. Bland, like ground-up redwood bark or dried pomegranate seeds or something."

She defiantly edged her chin up a notch and snared his gaze. "If you think anything about me is bland, you are mistaken."

His attitude suddenly all business, he said, "I'd like to ask you some questions. About a red dress with white spots. May I come in?"

"What can I possibly tell you that you don't already know, besides the fact that the fabric is called dotted swiss?" Toothpaste dribbled into her palm, but she stood her ground.

"I want to know how you know about that dress."

He was as handsome as before, except today he wore a dark gray pin-striped suit and charcoal tie. Standing on her porch, his legs braced, his hands in his pockets, he looked cool and hot and rough; a little charming, a little dangerous. His wire-rimmed glasses added a dimension to his appearance that just about drove her nuts.

Tabitha was a complete sucker for a good-looking guy with weak eyes. However, she sternly reminded herself, he was a skeptic and a *cop*, and everybody knew what jerks they were. Their divorce rate was astronomical. They were controlling and pushy and egocentric and . . .

Darling's lips curved slowly into a smile, and Tabitha's thoughts hit the wall like an unrestrained crash test dummy.

"We obviously got off on the wrong foot," he said. "I apologize. I'm conducting a follow-up on a possible homicide and need some information. Can we start over?" His perfect smile slid from charming to mesmerizing.

Without words—because her brain suddenly couldn't form any—she swung the door open, and he stepped into the foyer. Shoving the gooey toothbrush into her mouth, she wiped her hand on her JCPenney blue cotton chenille robe, then pointed to the office. She held up her hand, displaying five sticky digits. "Gib me fibe minufes," she said past the toothbrush in her cheek. Turning, she raced up the stairs to her room.

Fourteen minutes later, hands, face, and teeth clean, hair brushed, and wearing jeans and a rose-colored sweater, she bopped on down the stairs and into her office.

Instead of sitting at the table like when he'd been her "client," Darling had taken a seat on the burgundy velvet sofa in front of the bay window.

To ensure she wouldn't accidentally touch him, Tabitha took a seat in the matching wing chair on the other side of the coffee table.

When she'd settled herself, he leaned forward, rested his elbows on his knees, and flipped through a notepad.

"FYI, Ms. March," he began, his attention focused on the notepad, "I work out of Metro Central. The homicide in question occurred in Golden Gate's jurisdiction."

She folded her hands neatly in her lap. "So why are you here and not a detective associated with the case?"

He gazed into her eyes. She wanted to look away, but didn't.

"After you left the station the other day," he said, "I contacted Lieutenant Yardley, the detective in charge of this homicide. Ran your story by her. She thought it was fascinating, but hardly viable. Still, she asked me to speak with you further."

"Did she use the word fascinating?"

"Uh, no."

"What word *did* she use?"

Before he could reply, the office doors squeaked open a couple of inches, revealing two pairs of curious eyes. As soon as Winkin spotted Darling, he began to bark in sharp staccato notes, while Blinkin yawned. It took a lot more than a strange man in the house to get a rise out of Blinkin.

The detective's mouth flattened as he sent her a look that said, *Lose the fan club.*

"Hush, Winks," she admonished. "Listen, you two. Go on out in the yard and chase your own tails."

Winkin was still barking as she closed the door. A few more muffled woofs, then a scramble of doggy nails on hardwood as he took off down the hall and out his door into the yard. Presumably, Blinkin went with him.

"I'll bet you have a really big dog, don't you, Inspector? A loyal German shepherd or a stately Great Dane. Some kind of proud, heroic, manly canine, right?"

For a moment the detective said nothing, then sent her a grin designed to melt the heart of any female between the ages of birth and death.

"Just to set the record straight," he said, "I have an aquarium. No macho dogfish, though. Just cichlids, some tetras, a couple of angelfish, and a plecostomus named Oliver."

"You name your fish?" Oh, how sweet!

"Just Oliver," he said, then shrugged. "He's one of a kind."

Tabitha sat back in the chair and clamped her mouth shut. Well, he couldn't be a total loser. After all, a man sensitive enough to name his favorite fish . . .

Glancing once more at his notes, the detective said, "What's the name of the client who had the dream?"

Returning to reality, she stumbled, "Oh, um, Jack Griffin."

"Are you sure that's his real name?"

"The name he gave me was Jack Griffin."

The detective's eyes narrowed as he wrote down the name. "Did this Jack Griffin fill out any kind of paperwork? Show you any ID? Are your sessions covered by medical insurance?"

Tabitha swallowed a laugh. Where did Inspector Darling think he was, the Mayo Clinic?

"No," she said. "He told me his name was Jack Griffin and I never questioned it."

More scribbling.

"Address?"

"Don't know."

He pursed his lips.

"Phone?"

"He calls me. His number's blocked."

Darling tossed his notepad onto the coffee table.

"Okay," he sighed. "Let's try something else. How many times have you seen him?"

"Six."

"A real answer. Now we're getting somewhere."

Tabitha set her jaw and crossed her arms under her breasts.

Tapping his pen on his knee, he said, "Six visits. Over what period of time?"

She thought for a moment. "The first session was just after Christmas, so that would be a little over three months. Why are you asking these questions when you obviously think you're wasting your energy and the taxpayers' money, and the SFPD's—"

"Because a woman was strangled in Golden Gate Park near the Conservatory of Flowers. Because she was wearing a red dress with white dots. Because right now a loony dream interpreter with a loony client is as close as we've got to any kind of lead."

Tabitha's heart tripped inside her chest. "She *was* wearing a red dress with white dots?"

"Affirmative."

"Can't cops ever simply say yes?"

"Negative. Why did Griffin say he wanted his dreams interpreted, anyway?"

Tabitha's fingertips covered her mouth as she remembered the day Jack Griffin had told her about this particular dream. At the time, his words hadn't had much impact. Dreams were symbolic. To dream of killing someone didn't mean you really wanted to kill that person, or any person. It usually meant the dreamer wanted to do away with certain waking behaviors or bad memories.

"Dreams have been studied by all cultures the world over for thousands of years," she explained. "In the Bible alone, there are over a hundred references to dreams and dream interpretation. The Egyptians had special priests to help decipher dreams and their meaning. People are always trying to figure out what their weird dreams mean. Don't you?"

He didn't look at her. "At the moment, the only dreams I'm interested in knowing about belong to Jack Griffin."

She licked her dry lips. "Well, he said that he'd started having violent dreams, sort of out of the blue, for no reason at all. He felt he was being sent some kind of message but didn't understand what it was." Leveling her gaze on the detective, she said, "People come to me because they need to understand. Dreams can be confusing, and if you misinterpret them, you can panic or think something's wrong with you, when it's simply your psyche trying to work things out. It's why I do this, to . . . help . . ."

She let her words trail off without further explanation.

Darling seemed thoughtful for a moment, then said, "What did you tell him?"

"I held his hand while he related the dream," she whispered. "I saw it clearly. He described it, and I saw it unfold. Even so, I didn't think it was a prophetic dream. It seemed more like a kind of release dream, where he was letting go of some long-held belief or anger or sorrow. I told him to keep a dream log next to his bed."

"What's that?"

"When you wake up in the middle of the night after a dream, or at the very least first thing in the morning, you write down as much of your dreams as you can remember. Details are important. Colors, numbers, smells, sounds. Those are especially telling. Mr. Griffin agreed to keep a diary, and the next time he visited, he brought it with him."

Darling seemed to perk up at this news. "Did you read it? Did he leave it here? Did you make a copy?"

She smiled and Darling's eyes flicked for a moment to her mouth.

"He read parts of it to me," she said. "The parts that pertained to the dreams he wanted to discuss, but when he left he took it with him. I never actually got my hands on it."

The detective stood and walked to the far window. Light from the early morning sun grazed his hair and, though it was short, it looked soft to the touch. She imagined what it would be like to have her arms around his neck, her fingers entwined in his hair, her mouth pressed to his . . .

Unaware of the direction her thoughts had

taken, Darling said, "What kind of man is this Jack Griffin? Describe him."

She let her attention linger on the detective's body for a moment longer. She was a woman, after all, and he was a man, an enormously attractive one. Her gaze drifted across his broad shoulders, lean hips, long legs. Under those civilian clothes, she'd bet anything his body was perfect, well muscled and strong.

She didn't fool herself for a moment. She knew part of her attraction was based on the fact she hadn't had a steady boyfriend since she'd split with Cal, and the presence of an interesting man sent her desires into a dither.

"I'd guess he's in his mid-thirties," she said, forcing her attention to the matter at hand. "Taller than I, shorter than you. Brown hair, blue eyes. Very attractive. Oh, and I think he's rich."

"What makes you think so?"

She shrugged. "He dresses casually, but in expensive stuff. Wore a Rolex, and not a knockoff, either. Parking's tough to get around here, so I'm not sure I saw his car. Once, though, after our session, a Jag zoomed past and I got the impression it was him."

"What color? What year?"

"Black," she said. "What *year*?" She snorted. "Do I look like a high-end import auto mechanic?"

Rubbing his jaw, Darling seemed to turn inward

for a moment, then looked over at her again.

"Was that the only dream where he killed someone?"

"There were one or two others, but I didn't see anything in the newspaper about them."

Darling walked toward her and stood next to her chair. She could feel the heat from his body and worried it would be enough to create the images in her head of the two of them together again. Bracing her mind against it, she scooted as far away from him as she could.

"Does he have a regular appointment, or does he just call you?"

She shook her head. "I never know when he's going to call, but he seems to pop up every couple of weeks."

"How long since the last—"

"Ten days. If he holds true to form, he should call again this week." Sliding him a wary look, she said, "Why do you want to know, since you don't believe in what I do?"

He glanced around the room, apparently considering her question. Lifting one arm, he let it drop to his side in a gesture of obvious frustration.

"I don't know what I believe. I know a woman is dead. I know certain details of her murder match things you claim you picked up psychically from a man who told you about a dream he had." He looked at her. "Just think of how that sounds to a logical person, Ms. March. If this guy did commit a murder and felt the need to tell somebody about it, pretending it happened in a dream would let him get it off his conscience without being accused."

"But I *saw* it. He did dream it just the way—"

"Maybe he *used* you, Ms. March. Maybe you're sweet and kind and gullible, and he knew it, and he *used* you."

Pushing herself to her feet, Tabitha took two giant steps backward, separating herself from the detective's powerful presence. He was too ... magnetic or something. He disrupted her thoughts, invaded her senses. God forbid he should touch her again.

"I know what I saw," she insisted. "It was a dream and not reality. Dreams and real events show up differently, I see them differently inside my head."

He raised his voice. "Okay. Okay, then. Let's just assume for a moment that it *was* only a dream. That it was not an actual recounting of Jack Griffin murdering a woman in a polka-dot dress. Try this." He took a deep breath. "The population of San Francisco is roughly eight hundred thousand. How many dreams is that per night per person for the last ninety days?"

"I don't like questions that require the use of a calculator."

He closed his eyes. "Um, yeah. At three dreams a night, that's over two million dreams. Times ninety days is, uh, roughly two hundred million dreams."

Tabitha pressed her lips together. "Okay, Inspector Math Whiz, tell me this. If a train leaves San Francisco traveling east at eighty miles per hour, and a train leaves New York—"

"What I'm saying is, in two hundred million dreams, only one involved offing a woman in a red dress?"

"I can't begin to imagine what other people—"

"Okay, so maybe in those two hundred million dreams, one or two other men envisioned similar scenarios, but only this Griffin guy goes to a psychic voodoo woo-woo dream interpreter."

"What are you saying?"

"Hell, I don't know!" he snapped. "You've got me all turned around. I don't know if you really saw a dream and it's just a coincidence that a homicide matches the details, or if this guy related a real murder to you. I don't believe in dream interpretation, so if Jack Griffin came to you and in one way or another, related details of a homicide, I have to assume he is somehow involved in this murder."

"Your argument is practical," she accused. "But this situation is emotional. Don't make me doubt myself, Detective, or Inspector, or Officer, or whatever in the hell you want to be called. I know my business. I know what I saw, what I experienced. Just because you're a closed-minded nincompoop doesn't mean I'm wrong. The truth is, you don't *want* to believe I can see other people's dreams. Jack Griffin didn't say a thing about a red polka-dot dress—I *saw* it when I touched him!"

The air crackled between them and Tabitha fought to control her breathing. Damn, she hadn't been this mad since she'd walked in on Cal that wretched day.

Darling nodded a couple of times. "Okay, Ms. March. But red dresses are common. Could be a coincidence. Give me something else. Another detail, something that wasn't in the newspaper and something only the killer would know."

In frustration, she turned away from him and pinched her eyes closed. Calming her frayed nerves, she forced herself to remember the session with Griffin—his words, and the images they'd conjured inside her head.

I'd noticed her earlier, but she hadn't so much as looked my way. Everyone had gone. I crept up behind her. She was admiring the roses outside the conservatory. It was just past dark and she'd wandered off the lighted path to bend and smell a blossom. I did it then, grabbing her from behind, my arm around her neck, choking her. She fought, but I was stronger. It hadn't taken much after that to squeeze the life out of her.

When I was sure she was dead, I let her fall to the ground. She looked just like a doll some careless child had tossed aside. Very sad. Then I shoved her under the bush until only her feet were visible. I . . . I couldn't resist. I crouched and . . .

"Her shoe," Tabitha mumbled. "He . . . he took her shoe. A memento. A trophy. Killers do that, don't they?"

She turned, seeking Darling's eyes, wanting the acknowledgment, the recognition that she really *had* seen, really *did* know. He was staring at her, all right, but it wasn't with the look of appreciation and apology she deserved.

"It occurs to me," he said slowly, "there is one other distinct possibility here."

She shifted her weight to her left leg and assessed his words, while some emotion she couldn't define oozed into her stomach.

"And what's that, Inspector?"

He locked eyes with her. "Let me put it this way. Do you want to confess now, or do we need to go downtown?"

Chapter 4

To dream of dying your hair means you will nar-rowly escape imprisonment.

FOLKLORE

Nate watched Tabitha March's jaw drop. She blinked up at him, fear and confusion plain to see in the depths of her eyes.

Knowing he was a big guy and his size could intimidate, he took a step closer, invading her personal space . . . and instantly regretted it.

He caught the scent of her perfume. Sweet, spicy, warmed by her skin. It reminded him of things he absolutely should not be thinking about.

"So," he said. "You want to confess or do we stand here all day?"

He'd expected her to back up, or, best-case scenario, blurt out something incriminating. Instead, she put her hands on her hips and scowled.

"You're out of your mind," she snapped. "First

of all, what possible motive would I have for killing a woman I didn't even know? Second, I probably don't have the physical strength to strangle
so much as a geriatric earthworm, let alone a
grown woman. Third, if I really were the killer,
why would I draw attention to myself by going to
the police? Fourth—"

"Is this a long list?" he drawled. "Because if it
is, I'd like to pull up a chair."

Her eyes flared like blue fire. "I was only going
to add that I have an alibi for the night of the
murder."

"What night was that, Ms. March?"

She shifted her stance. "The eighth. I was babysitting my best friend's two little—"

"Iris Reynaud was murdered on the ninth."

There went that jaw again. And those eyes.
Blink, blink, blink. Like a baby bird who'd just
fallen out of the nest and landed on her noggin.

"That was her name? The woman in the polka-
dot dress?"

"Yes. Did you know her?"

She slowly shook her head. "No. You say she
was killed on the ninth? But the paper said—"

"The coroner set time of death between seven
and ten o'clock on the night of the ninth. Were
you babysitting that night, too?"

"Oh. Uh, no." She slid her hands into the pockets of her jeans and lifted her shoulder in a small

shrug. "That was Sunday. I had my hair foiled at five, got home at about six-thirty."

He let his gaze wander over her tumble of hair. It was that burnished red-gold color with streaks of blond, like ribbons of sunshine, running through it.

"Foiled?"

When she smirked at him, he realized he'd just made an I'm-obviously-a-buffoon-when-it-comes-to-women remark.

"They use aluminum foil," she said with over-stressed patience, "to keep the strands separated from the rest of the hair while they add highlights."

Nate checked out the strands in question. He wiggled his index finger. "That's not natural?"

"No, Inspector," she said, as though he were an idiot. "It's fake. Dyed. Chemicals have been added. My hair is one big lie."

"Hmm," he said, appreciating the deceit. "Looks natural."

"It's supposed to. That's why it's so expensive. Is there some *point* to this? Does the fact I highlight my hair indicate I have a penchant for murder?"

"No. But I would never have guessed." He looked into her eyes. "What did you do after you got your hair boiled?"

"Foiled. I came home, ate dinner, watched TV, went to bed."

"Alone?"

"Yes."

Why that made him feel relieved, he'd rather not think about at the moment.

"You're divorced."

"Yes."

"Any kids?"

She lowered her lashes, and he knew he'd struck a nerve. He hadn't meant to, but he could see by her response she had issues attached to that simple question.

"No," she said quietly. "No kids."

He shifted his stance. "You have boarders who live here, right?"

She sighed. "Yes."

"Any of them see you that night?"

"No. We live separate lives."

"Still, maybe they heard you coming in, running the water, banging around in the kitchen."

"I do not bang in the kitchen," she said flatly.

He wasn't about to ask her where she did bang, so he said, "Names of your boarders?"

Throwing her hands up in a gesture of surrender, she said, "The Ichabod sisters, Eden and Flora, and my mother, Victoria Jones." She walked over to the chair she'd sat in earlier and dropped into it. "You can't possibly think I had anything to do with this poor Iris Reynold's murder. You're just yanking my chain."

"Iris Reynaud," he corrected. "Doesn't matter whether I do or not. Only the evidence counts."

She lifted her hands in the air. "I hope Jack Griffin didn't commit that murder. But it doesn't change what I felt and what I saw."

Nate went to the table and pulled out one of the chairs, gesturing to it. "Okay, Ms. March. I say we just see what you saw, or say you saw."

She rolled her eyes. "I'll bet you can't say that again."

"Sit. I'm going to tell you a dream I had last night, and I want you to tell me what you *see*."

Standing, she balled her fists at her sides. "You're going to test me? *Again?*"

"Yes," he drawled, "but no letter grades will be given. It's pass-fail, Ms. March. Unless you want to confess, of course. What's it going to be? We do the séance here or at the station?"

"*Séance?*" She wrinkled her nose and shook her head. "I interpret dreams, not communicate with the dead!"

"Well, whatever you call it, you're going to do it right here, right now—unless, of course, you would prefer we do this downtown?"

Downtown. Tabitha's stomach tightened and she felt queasy. A moment later when the nausea began to pass, the terror set in.

"No downtown," she whispered. What if they

locked her up? How would she survive it? She'd be in a small, dank, crowded space—trapped. She would suffocate. He didn't understand, and he wouldn't, even if she told him.

In silence, she moved to the table where the detective was already waiting.

"Are you going to lie to me again?" she mumbled, as she slid into the chair across the table from him.

"You tell me." He turned his hand over and, without smiling, wiggled his fingers.

Tabitha gazed down at his hand, then took in a deep breath through her nose. Letting it out slowly through her mouth, she employed the relaxation techniques she always used before a session, clearing her mind of her own thoughts so the images she got from the client would be pure, not influenced by whatever was going on inside her own brain.

Reaching out, she clasped Darling's hand.

The erotic tableau she'd seen before did not form. She felt something inside her mind stir, but she blocked it, keeping her focus on *him*, not on *them*.

"Please close your eyes," she instructed. "When you're ready, tell me your dream."

Tabitha let her lids drift down, her shoulders relax, allowing the warmth of his large hand to seep into her body. He had good energy, strong, vital. She worked to go deeper, and deeper, and down . . .

Silence stretched between them. She heard the tick of the grandfather clock in the foyer outside the closed door of her office. High overhead, a jet droned by. In the backyard, Winkin barked . . .

"I dreamed I was on a ship," Darling began. "I don't know where it was bound, but the ship was large and I got lost looking for my cabin. There were lots of people and I—"

"Stop," she said. "Stop right there."

Tabitha opened her eyes to see Darling watching her. "You're making it up."

Behind his glasses, his brown eyes widened innocently. "Am not."

She struggled to pull her hand free of his, but he curled his strong fingers around hers and hung on.

"If you're going to test me," she said as she tugged against his grip, "the least you can do is show me enough respect to be honest. Besides, how will you know I can do this if you don't tell me a *real* dream?"

His cheeks flushed a little, and Tabitha figured it was probably a rare thing. He didn't let go of her, though. And what was worse, she stopped resisting.

They held hands across the small table like lovers at a sidewalk café. Looking into her eyes, he said finally, "I wasn't trying to be dishonest. I, uh, I don't dream."

He looked dejected, like a puppy that had been disciplined for being too playful. Something inside Tabitha's heart gave a little twitch.

"You do have dreams, Inspector," she assured him. "Everyone does, no exceptions. But for some reason, you just don't remember them. I can show you how to keep a diary, and advise some methods you can use to recall your dreams. Dreams are symbolic insights into our minds and our lives and emotions. You should pay more attention to them."

"If you say so."

"When was the last time you had a dream you recall vividly?"

He let go of her hand and rubbed his temples, then adjusted his glasses.

"I was a kid," he said. "About fourteen, I guess."

Some sort of odd sympathy washed through her at a grown man not having any dreams he could remember, enjoy, cherish, for probably twenty years.

"Take my hand," she said quietly, "and tell me about that dream."

He sent her a strange look, as though he were preparing to walk naked onto the stage of the San Francisco Opera House. Reaching across the table, he clasped her hand. One end of his mouth kicked up in a smart-ass grin. "This won't work, you know."

"We'll see. Now close your eyes and begin when you're ready."

Tabitha waited until he'd closed his eyes, then she closed hers. A moment later, he began to speak.

"I . . . I was with my brother and sister. Ethan's older, Andrea's younger." He paused, as though he were debating whether or not to continue. Then, "We were at some movie. The theater was really dark. I didn't like the movie and I wanted to leave, but Ethan and Andrea kept watching it, ignoring me."

Behind Tabitha's closed lids, the picture began to assemble itself. It was dull at first, fuzzy pastels, but as Darling spoke, the images became clearer, stronger, more vivid in detail.

"When the movie was over," he said, "we started walking up the carpeted aisle and somehow got separated. Even though the theater was empty, suddenly it was huge, like an airplane hangar, and I couldn't find them. Finally, I spotted them way over on another aisle going out the door. I tried to follow, but two men stepped in front of me."

Inside Tabitha's head, the image took shape.

Yes, it's dark. The men are big and dressed in blue

suits. They won't let you go with your brother and sister.

"They said they were the police," he continued, his voice lower than before. "They handcuffed me, put me in the back seat of a car. One man sat on either side of me. Then we were driving by a house, the house we'd lived in when I was a little boy. But nobody was there. The curtains were closed. I knew it was empty. I had this . . . longing to go inside. It was all I wanted, all I could think of. But one of the cops looked me in the eye and shook his head. 'You can never go there again,' he said. As we passed, I turned so I could see the house through the back window of the car, and I knew he was right. I never could go there again . . ."

And you wanted to, desperately. You'd lost something very important there, something you've never found since. When you woke up from that dream, you were crying, and you vowed nothing and no one would ever make you cry again.

Tabitha slowly raised her lids to see Inspector Darling looking straight at her. The cockiness she'd seen in his eyes earlier had been replaced by a deep yearning. He was that young boy again, and he was lost.

But he blinked, set his jaw, and it was business as usual once more.

"Would you like something to drink?" she asked gently. "Water? Cof—"

"Just get on with it." He cleared his throat and squared his shoulders. The fingers that had gripped hers so tightly as he'd related his dream went lax, and she slid her hand from his grasp.

Instantly her mind went dark, as though she'd been shut in a closet. A moment later, reality began to come back online, like a computer rebooting, running its start-up routine. Darling's dream faded and she was suddenly out of his head and back in her own.

She took a deep breath, stretched her arms, adjusted her thoughts.

"Okay, um, basically, I should tell you that there are four types of dreams. Prophetic, release, wish, and problem-solving. It would help if you told me what was going on in your life at the time of your dream."

She already knew, at least a little, but he needed to say it.

He eased back in his chair and eyed her with skepticism. "You're the expert. You tell me."

Letting his attitude pass, she said, "I saw you. Your hair was very blond then. Ethan has dark hair, but Andie's is more like yours."

He stiffened. "Andie?"

"Andrea. Isn't that what you call her?"

His gaze sharpened. "Go on."

"I think the movie you were watching was your life at that time. Your parents, perhaps. This wasn't a prophetic dream, and it wasn't problem-solving, either. I don't get the sense you dealt with something and then let it go. So that leaves us with a wish dream."

"What was I wishing for?"

Gently, she said, "You know."

"Maybe I do. But if you guess right—"

"I don't guess," she said flatly. "I *see*. The house could have been you. Houses often represent the dreamer, and each room has a certain significance, but in this case, since it was a particular house, one in which you had lived, I'd say you longed to go back to a time when your family was together, when you were little and taken care of. Food was always on the table, there were trees to climb and puppies to play with. You could be with your brother and just be boys. As a teenager, when you dreamed this dream, you felt pressure to grow up quickly, but you missed your family, and you wanted those sweet simpler times back again."

He was staring at her as though he'd seen an astonishing, mind-boggling circus act.

"How did you know about my parents' divorce? About Ethan and Andrea?"

"From your dream. Your brother and sister went with one parent, you went with the other. You knew those old days would never come again, and your subconscious was trying to deal with that, which is why it gave you the dream."

His brows lowered. "I don't believe you got that from holding my hand."

"That's your right, Inspector."

She knew he wasn't going to accept any of this now, not in his present mood. It happened that way sometimes.

Pushing herself to her feet, Tabitha said, "I think I passed your test, so, if you'll excuse me, I have work to do."

She wanted to hug him. She wanted to hold him. She wanted to tell him it was okay, stroke his brow, ease his pain, but he wasn't that little boy anymore, so instead, she showed him to the door.

"You have my card," he said from the bottom step of the front porch. "When you hear from Griffin again, give me a call."

Tabitha watched him walk away and felt a sinking feeling in the pit of her stomach. He'd think about the session and eventually convince himself she'd simply guessed at everything. Skeptics had a way of talking themselves out of whatever they chose not to believe, even when the evidence rose up and smacked them on the nose. His next conclusion would be that she was a total fraud.

Closing the front door, she leaned against it and wondered just why she cared what Inspector Nathan Darling thought of her. In all likelihood, she'd never see him again, and that was good, both from an official and a personal point of view.

She heard the phone ring twice, but her mother must have picked it up.

"Tabby, honey?" her mom called from the kitchen. "Are you done with your session?"

Tabitha moved away from the door and walked toward the sound of Victoria's voice.

"Coming, Mom." Entering the kitchen, she greeted her mother with a smile. Victoria Jones at fifty-six was a lovely woman. A little on the plump side, but her light gray hair was thick and shiny, and her complexion smooth and rosy. In one hand she held the phone while the other was cupped over the mouthpiece.

"It's for you," she said. "Says he's one of your clients and needs to see you right away."

Tabitha's stomach flipped as she reached for the phone. "Did he give his name?"

Her mom nodded. "Griffin. Jack Griffin."

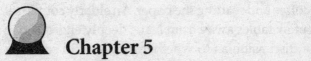

Chapter 5

If a woman dreams of making a bed, she will soon have a new lover.

FOLKLORE

Just a few blocks down from the March house, bright light streamed through the polished windows of the Gold Nugget Coffee Shop, rousting any lingering shadows from the corners of the small diner, but not from Nate's mood. He needed time to let his insides settle down—his head, his gut, and his nerves.

The encounter with the March woman had left him with more questions than answers. His instincts told him she wasn't involved in the Reynaud homicide; his instincts told him a lot of things about Tabitha March.

The aroma of strong coffee permeated the air, while the smokier fragrance of frying bacon teased his nose. His stomach growled in response. He ignored it.

The place was quiet; only a few customers dotted the swivel stools at the counter, most sipping coffee and reading the paper. An elderly couple sat a few tables away from Nate, deeply engrossed in a discussion as to whether they should sell their house and buy a motor home and travel the country, or invest their money in their grandchildren's college funds. They sat on the same side of the table, their chairs scooted close together. The woman's gray head lay on her husband's shoulder as he lazily stirred his coffee. He said something to her and she smiled, chuckling deep in her throat and patting his arm.

> Grow old along with me
> The best is yet to be
> The last of life,
>   for which the first was made . . .

As a kid in school, when Nate had first read Browning's poem, it hadn't meant much to him. Grow old? Hell, who wanted to do that? And how could being older be better than being young?

He smiled at the callow youth he'd been. Like most guys, he'd been young with all of his might. But there was something to be said for being a little older, having some experience under your belt, and instead of a string of girlfriends, investing your time and emotions on just one woman.

Glancing over at the old couple again, he felt a pang of envy for the lifetime of shared experiences they had created together. Could that sort of thing happen for him? Maybe it was too much to wish for, but then again, a man made his own luck in this world . . .

A young waitress in a too-tight pink uniform sauntered up to Nate's table and seemed disappointed when all he asked for was coffee.

The urge to call Ethan crept over him, but he didn't feel in control enough yet to initiate what was certain to be a stressful interaction with his straight-laced, sour-faced older brother.

Even so, he had to contact Ethan sooner or later. Working things out with his brother was one of the reasons Nate had moved back to the Bay Area. The only problem was, his brother didn't seem inclined in the least to reciprocate.

Gripping the cell phone in his left hand, he rubbed his thumb lightly over the autodial, fighting the urge to press it. Not yet, he cautioned himself. He needed another minute or two. One had to be prepared before an encounter with former SFPD Detective Lieutenant Ethan Darling. The man had the tact of a tornado—touching down for a moment, wreaking havoc, then flying off in another direction, a trail of broken bodies strewn on the ground.

Ethan's skills as a detective were legend, inspiring awe and hero worship in everyone. That kind of notoriety made it difficult for mere mortals such as Nate to find common ground with the Great Man.

He gave the waitress a nod as she smiled and placed a steaming mug of coffee in front of him. Judging from her body language and the glint in her eye, it wouldn't take much effort on his part to score a bed partner for tonight, but the fact of the matter was, he wasn't interested in casual sex, especially not tonight.

Grousing at himself for being such a prig, he took a quick sip of the bitter coffee, then thumped the mug down on the plastic veneer tabletop.

Tabitha March sauntered across the back of his mind like she belonged there. She didn't, so he placed both his hands on her ass and shoved her aside. In response to his fantasy, the palms of his hands warmed. Biting down a curse at how he'd let her invade his own personal brain, he squeezed the autodial on his cell phone.

Ready or not, Ethan. Ready or not.

As the connection rang through, Nate sloshed cream into the mug, lightening the coffee until it resembled liquid khaki.

"Yeah?" Ethan said, by way of hello.

"Nice hearing your voice, too, big brother," Nate drawled. "Why so snarly? I didn't accidentally *interruptus* anything, did I?"

"If that had been the case, I wouldn't have answered the damned phone," Ethan scoffed. "I'm a busy man, Nate. What do you want?"

Lifting a dented spoon, Nate stirred his coffee.

"Nothing special," he lied. "I found myself longing for the sound of your voice, so—"

"Bullshit. You wouldn't give me the time of day unless you wanted something. Somebody die? You need money?"

Nate let a wry smile curve his lips. He'd been expecting that one. "Would you give it to me if I did?"

Silence.

"I thought so." Nate laughed. "Same old Ethan. I think it's nice how well we know each other."

"At the cost of repeating myself," Ethan said, "bullshit. I don't know you, and you don't know me. Let's just keep it that way, shall we?"

Nate felt his anger well up all over again. Jesus, Ethan could be a hard-nosed son of a bitch.

"*Goddammit*, Ethan," Nate growled. "Lighten the fuck up. I don't know what I did to piss you off, but you've treated me like garbage for the last twenty years. I moved back home to try and . . . hell, I don't know, reconnect with you or something, but I'm doing all the damn work while you just take verbal potshots at me! What in the hell's your problem?"

There was silence on the other end of the line, then, "You done?"

Nate slapped his palm on the table in front of him. "Always the cool one, eh, Ethan? Always the one in control. No emotions. The ice man, is that it?"

"Listen, Nate, I've spent the last twenty years taking care of Mom and Andie. Working two jobs to make sure there was food on the table and a roof over our heads, while you went off with Dad without a care in the world."

"Is *that* what you think? That I abandoned you just because Dad . . ."

Nate let his voice trail off. Not now. Going there now would only cause more grief, open the wounds he was trying to heal. It was obvious Ethan's hate for their father included Nate—and maybe it always would.

When Ethan didn't respond, Nate blew out a long breath. "Look, I called you for a reason."

Silence for another moment. "Make it quick," Ethan said, his voice slightly less harsh than it had been.

Such a simple question, Nate thought. But so hard to ask.

"Remember the house in San Rafael?" he said. "The one we lived in when Andie was born?"

"Shit, Nate, that was nearly thirty years ago. I was only a kid."

"Yeah, seven. I was five. It was brown with a

big yard in back and a tree house and swings. We had a puppy. Pounce. Mom named her that because she reared up and jumped on everything. Remember?"

Long seconds ticked by while Nate waited for his brother to answer. Finally, "Yeah. I remember."

"Do you, uh, do you ever . . . think about that house?"

For a heartbeat, Ethan said nothing, then murmured, "Not really."

Taking in a full breath, Nate said, "Okay. So, uh, listen, here's the deal. I have this bizarre case, and I've checked out all I can, and thought maybe you might have a few insights."

At the other end of the line, Ethan cleared his throat. Business, Nate thought. Safe turf. "All right. Let's hear it."

Nate explained about the homicide in Golden Gate Park, the red dress with white spots, and the dream interpreter. "So," he said, finishing up. "Possible? Not possible? Ever hear of anything like this when you were working out of Homicide?"

Nate took a gulp of coffee and waited for his brother to accuse him of being a complete idiot for considering the possibility the March woman had actually seen the murder through the mind of her client. What in the hell had possessed him to call Ethan? The guy was even more grounded in facts and evidence than Nate was. There was no way Ethan would ever—

"Yeah," Ethan said. "We had a couple of cases where we used a psychic."

It took Nate a moment to realize what his brother had said, and another to form some kind of cogent response.

"Really. What happened?"

"We only approached psychics as a last resort, unless they came to us with information first, but I'd say they had close to an eighty percent success rate. Never used a dream interpreter, though, but this is California. Something for everyone."

"So, you think she could be on the level?"

Ethan gave a sharp laugh. "What does your gut tell you?"

Just what *did* his gut tell him? That he was attracted to Tabitha March. Sure. But that didn't count. That the details she'd given him matched the homicide. That her guesswork regarding his own boyhood dream had been too close for comfort. "I'm willing to suspend belief long enough to give her a shot, I suppose."

"She could be the killer, or an accessory."

"I know."

"But you don't think she is."

"No."

"You said her name's Tabitha March?" Ethan

asked. "I'll run a background. See what pops."

"Oh, right," Nate drawled. "Paladin Private Investigations has all the best toys."

"Damned straight, little brother," Ethan said. "I can have more information on the lady in five minutes than you can get in a week."

True enough. Ethan's PI firm had state-of-the-art everything, and the manpower to back it up. Paladin was a roaring success, pushing Nate's brother into millionaire territory. The SFPD could never keep up. Nate had some information on Tabitha, but using his brother's connections would garner him a whole lot more in a fraction of the time.

"Thanks," Nate said. "You have my number."

As he was about to disconnect, Ethan spoke again. "Hang on, Nate. My turn. I have a question. Consider it a trade. A thorough background check on the March woman for one straight answer from you. Deal?"

Nate's spine straightened and his instincts went on alert. What in the hell was this about? "Depends on the question."

His gaze settled on the round clock above the counter across the room. Twelve minutes after ten. With military precision, the thin black blade of the second hand twitched across the numeral four. As it slid over the five and dropped toward six, Ethan finally spoke.

"Fair enough."

The second hand ticked on by seven, starting its upward climb. As it passed over eight, Nate said, "So? Ask."

"Why did you really want to know about the house in San Rafael?"

Did the game go on, or did it end here? Nate wondered. The truth, for once, or more charades?

Averting his eyes from the clock, he grabbed his coffee and took a gulp. They were adults now. Men. The time for mind games with his brother was over.

"Remember when we lived in that house, you know, with Mom and Dad and you and me, and then Andie was born? I know it was a long time ago, still . . ."

He tapped his spoon against the side of his cup. "We, uh, we had a clubhouse made out of cardboard, next to the garage where we played poker for Good & Plentys. But not the pink ones because they were for girls. We fed the pink ones to Pounce and then she threw up licorice all over Mom's favorite bathroom rug. Remember?"

"Yeah," Ethan said quietly. "What about it?"

Nate rubbed the bridge of his nose. "I, uh, I was happy in that house. Life was uncomplicated. You and me, we were good back then. We were content or something in a way I haven't been since. You know what I mean?"

When his brother said nothing, Nate growled, "Ethan? Goddammit, Ethan. Did that answer your question?"

"Yeah," Ethan said. "It answers my question. And you're right, Nate. It was a long time ago."

No sooner had Tabitha hung up the phone than the front doorbell chimed.

Grabbing for her purse on the table in the foyer, she dug around until she found Inspector Darling's badly crumpled card, then raced back to the kitchen.

At the sink, Victoria was busy filling a teakettle with cold water, oblivious to her daughter's distress.

"Mom," Tabitha whispered. When her mother glanced over her shoulder, Tabitha said, "Take this card. Call this number. Tell him to come. Now."

With her free hand, Victoria reached for the card. Squinting at it, she said, "Now, honey, you know it's just one big blur without my glasses." She laughed. "Why, I can barely see your hand, let alone such tiny print. Getting old is such a pain in the—"

"I know, I know," Tabitha hurried. "Get your glasses and call this number. It's very important."

The doorbell chimed again.

Victoria turned off the tap and set the kettle on the stove. "Tabby? Is something the matter?"

Tabitha backed out of the kitchen. "No. I mean, I'm not sure. I'll explain later, Mom. Call the number. Tell him Mr. Griffin is here. Tell him to come *now*."

Practically running to the front of the house, she curled her fingers around the doorknob, dread clenching her stomach into a tight knot.

"Mr. Griffin," she said through a strained smile as the door creaked on its hinges.

He stood on the covered porch, facing her, his body tense, fists balled at his sides. Through blue eyes rimmed with red, he watched her. His mouth, a straight line across his face, was nearly lost under the growth of beard stubble.

Buy time, she told herself. *Do everything slowly. Buy time.*

Behind her, Winkin clattered and skidded to a halt on the hardwood floor, barking up a storm.

"Shush, Winks," she scolded, then licked her dry lips. After the dog had satisfied himself it was somebody he recognized, he sneezed and clicked back down the hall to the kitchen.

Jack Griffin appeared anxious and disheveled. Instead of the neat clothing he usually wore, he was in torn jeans and a gray sweatshirt, looking like he'd spent the night curled up inside the corner of the drunk tank. Lowering his gaze, he neither smiled nor acknowledged her existence as he brushed past her to head straight for her office.

Tabitha peered outside, searching the sidewalks, hoping against hope Darling had hung around the neighborhood—but the street was empty and silent.

Her heart thudded heavily as she walked toward her office. Slipping inside, she began to close the door, but left it slightly ajar . . . just in case. Griffin sat at the table, his hand outstretched, his foot tapping in nervous jerks.

"Would you like something to drink?" she offered. He looked up at her, shook his head.

Taking the seat across the table from him, she said, "Are you all right? I couldn't help but notice you seem very anxious."

His back hunched over, his shoulders drooping, he nodded, then wiped his jaw with his hand. His fingers trembled.

"Mr. Griffin, please tell me what's wrong." Her voice was a whisper, and she hoped he hadn't heard the fear in it.

"Dream," he said at last. "Bad. Uh, I, uh—" He swallowed, bit his lower lip. "Can we start, please?"

Tabitha reached for his hand, but her attention was on the street outside. No sirens, no shouts, nothing. Had her mother found her glasses and called Inspector Darling, or was she on her own with this possibly homicidal killer?

She laid her hand palm up on the table, and

Griffin set his into hers. His skin was damp and she wanted to yank her hand away and run.

"Close your eyes," she instructed, doing the same, "and tell me your—"

"I killed someone," he rushed. "Again. I . . . it happened, I mean, the dream happened four nights ago."

Behind her closed lids, Tabitha began to see shapes, vague outlines, pastel silhouettes, but no solid forms.

"Go on." Her voice sounded amazingly calm, considering what was going on inside her stomach at the moment.

"I wrote it down, in the dream log, like you said. The dream had faded a lot by the time I was awake enough to make notes, but the more I wrote, the more I remembered."

He sucked in a raspy breath. "In the dream, I was walking up a steep city street. I don't know which one."

"Okay, I see it," Tabitha whispered. Buildings formed in her head, bay windows protruding. Cars parked bumper-to-bumper, half on the sidewalks on the narrow San Francisco street.

She felt Griffin's hand clench into a ball and she curled her fingers around it to try and ease his trembling.

"An old man appeared from around a corner," he rasped, "and I realized he'd come out of an alley. I was afraid of him for some reason. He asked me for money, but I didn't have any. He . . . he went back into the alley and I followed him. It was dark and I couldn't see anything. Then I heard him make a screaming sound and I looked down and I had this bottle in my hand. I don't know how it got there."

"Mr. Griffin," Tabitha soothed. "Maybe you'd rather not—"

"I hit him!" he cried. "I hit him, and he went down without a sound. He lay there, staring up at me, knowing as he was dying what I'd done, that I'd taken his life. I—I stood there and realized he knew me, knew who I was. He called my name . . . and it was a sad sound." A sob escaped his throat and he choked. "A real sad sound."

The alley assembled itself in Tabitha's head. Dark shapes, two men, one standing, one lying on his back, arms outstretched as though he were floating on a sea of crumpled newspapers. Garbage bags, like glossy black boulders, stood in misshapen heaps along the corridor.

A moan, then a bottle smashed to the pavement, shattering into a thousand pieces.

"What happened after that?" Her own voice trembled as she asked the question.

"I . . . I let the bottle fall from my hand. It broke,

and I stared down at the pieces like they were a beautiful green mosaic, all glittering-like, and fitted together in some crazy design."

He jerked his hand free of hers, holding it cradled against his chest.

"Mr. Griffin," she said quietly. "Perhaps you need to seek the help of a therapist. I can see how your dreams have increasingly distressed you, and while I can help you interpret them, I can't go beyond—"

"But it wasn't a dream!" he shouted, jumping up from his chair. "I mean, it was, but then there was the blood! All the blood!"

Tabitha stood and stepped back from the table, back from Jack Griffin and his wild eyes and shaking hands.

"I didn't see any bl—"

"When I woke up," he choked, his voice thick with panic. "My hands were covered with blood. How did it get there? Am I crazy? I *am*. I'm *crazy*, aren't I?"

"Mr. Griffin . . ."

Where in the hell are you, Darling?

"Why don't you sit down," she suggested. Her heart was running a mile a minute, pounding in her ears. She kept the table between them while she thought of ways to calm him. "I can make you some tea and we can talk about—"

"You know about me, don't you?" he accused. His eyes burned like blue flames in their sockets as he glared at her. "You know what I did."

"I know what you *dreamed*," she reasoned calmly. "That's . . . What are you doing? No. Stay there. No! Mr. Griffin!"

He lunged across the table at her, and she reached behind her for anything she could grab. Her fingers wrapped around a book, but before she could slam it into his face, his fingers were at her throat.

"Listen to me," he begged through clenched teeth. "Please, just *listen* . . ."

She tried to scream, but he'd effectively stifled her lung power. With the table between them, she couldn't knee him in the groin, so she let her body go slack, dropping to the floor, shifting her weight, and throwing him off balance enough to break his hold.

As she went down, her head slammed into the wall, sending a burst of starlight behind her closed lids. Amid the sparkling display, an image formed of the detective who hadn't arrived in time to save her life.

Chapter 6

Before you go to sleep, place a horseshoe, a leaf, or a key under your pillow, and you will dream of a future lover.

FOLKLORE

"I'm 'kay . . . yeah, okay . . . 's all right . . . I'll be okay . . ."

Someone was speaking, but Tabitha couldn't make out who it was. With her eyes half closed, she tried to concentrate on the voice. Then she felt her lips move.

"I'm all right," she whispered slowly, knowing now it was she who spoke. How long had she been muttering away like an overmedicated parrot?

She opened her eyes to stare at a woman standing directly in front of her. The woman appeared vaguely familiar, but her skin was pale and she seemed a little fuzzy around the edges. Tabitha blinked again, and so did the woman.

Like a zombie waking from cryogenic storage,

she gradually became aware of her fingers, and that they were curled over something smooth and cool. She looked down. White porcelain. A sink? Her head lifted and she gazed into her own reflection in the oval mirror.

Two people floated behind her in the reverse bathroom. To her right, a short woman with worried blue eyes held a cloth to the back of Tabitha's head.

"Oh. Hi, Mom," she murmured. "Don't worry. I'm fine."

Her mother nodded, but said nothing.

To her left stood a tall, hot-looking man in a suit. The man had his arm around her waist and seemed to be holding her up. He'd tucked her into his side, and for a moment she gazed at him dreamily and hoped they were together. His eyes were an incredibly soft, sensitive brown, and she wondered if he loved her.

"Hi." She smiled sleepily.

His eyes showed surprise for a moment, then he gently said, "Hi, yourself." He had a great voice. Deep and sexy.

She vaguely remembered being married. Was this her husband? He'd make a great father to her babies . . . they'd be so beautiful . . .

"I'm okay," she said to him, and he grinned down at her as though she'd said something adorable.

Mmm. His mouth. Curves and edges. Kissability quotient high. She smiled at him again and was about to ask him his name, when a dark image pushed its way into her brain. Memories began snapping into place. In her heart, that little flame of hope she'd had about him—and them, and their babies—weakened and died.

She remembered now. It was *him*.

"*You're* not the father of my children," she accused.

His brows arched. "Depends. Where were you the night of—"

"You're that detective person." She waited for him to deny it.

"That's quite a bump you've got back there," he said, his unsympathetic brown eyes hard and callous—now that she knew who he was.

"I'm fine."

"Tabby?" Victoria said, her voice shaky. "Are you really all right? How many fingers am I holding up? What's your favorite color? Who won the 1962 World Series?"

"Geez, Mom, I'm not a Nazi spy," she said, even though her head throbbed where she'd slammed into the wall. "I'm really all right. You're holding up two fingers, and my favorite color is garnet." Aware of Darling's hand against her ribs, just below her breast, she wiggled a little and said, "You can let go of me now, Inspector."

"Sure. When you tell me who won the 1962 World Series."

In the mirror, their eyes met for a moment, then Tabitha glanced away. Inspector Darling was too good-looking and she had learned a long time ago to avoid a man who would never love a woman more than he loved himself—even if he would have given her beautiful babies.

"Did you catch him?" she said to the antique porcelain hot-water knob.

"Griffin? No."

"It's my fault," Victoria rushed, tossing the damp cloth into the sink. "By the time I found my glasses and called the detective—"

"It's okay, Mom." She patted her mother's hand. "Not to worry. Why am I in the bathroom?"

Inspector Darling spoke up. "When I arrived, you were halfway down the hall, muttering over and over that you were okay. Maybe you thought you were going to be sick. Are you?"

"I told you, I'm fine. You can let me go now."

He dipped his head to try to catch her gaze in the mirror. "You probably don't even know who played in the 1962 World Series, let alone who won, do you?"

This time, she did look at him, and scowled. "San Francisco Giants versus the New York Yankees, Candlestick Park. Final score, one–zip . . . Yankees. Damn their hides."

For a moment his eyes went all dreamy, like he'd just heard a band of angels sing the national anthem or something. "You really know your baseball." His eyes hardened again when he continued, "Did Griffin assault you?"

She shook her head. "He grabbed for my throat, but I was on the other side of the table and he couldn't get a good grip. I jerked backward to try and get away, and banged my head against the wall. I don't remember anything after that."

"I heard the commotion," Victoria offered. "But by the time I got there, he was running out the door."

Darling raised his hand to gently move Tabitha's hair out of the way while he examined her throat. Frowning, he touched her skin. His fingers were rough and warm, and she took special care to guard herself against any images.

"Okay, Ms. March," he said. "How about we go sit down. I want to get a complete statement—"

The sound of a siren blasting up the street cut him off.

"Paramedics," he said when she looked up at him. His fingers were still pressed into her ribs.

"I don't need—"

"Is she always this bullheaded and argumentative?" he interrupted, shooting a quick look at Victoria.

Her mom cocked her head as she seemed to

consider the question. She slid her gaze to Tabitha, then to the detective, then slowly back to Tabitha. A gleam sparked from her eyes, as though she'd just gotten the punch line of some subtle joke.

"Mm-hmm," she purred. "But something tells me she may have met her match."

Peter O'Hara closed the bedroom door behind him, and with the palm of his hand flipped the brass deadbolt, letting the staccato *snap* reverberate in his head. His shoulders relaxed.

There. Safe now. Safe at last.

He'd managed to make it to his room without encountering his sister, the housekeeper, his private secretary, or any of the maids. Jesus, what would they think if they saw him? What did he think of himself, for that matter?

The drive across the Golden Gate Bridge to his estate in Marin had been a nightmare, but he'd stayed focused, obeyed all the traffic laws, done nothing to attract attention. Turning onto the long drive leading to the house, the four gardeners, busy trimming and mowing the grounds, had recognized his car, and all smiled and waved. He'd tooted the horn in acknowledgment, glad he'd opted for the tinted windows in the Jag, glad, too, his employees couldn't get a load of his ravaged appearance.

He parked in the eight-car garage next to

Zoey's white Bentley convertible, hoping he could make it to the house without running into anyone. But as he crossed the pavement in front of the first staff bungalow, he spotted Lee draped over the fender of the '68 Shelby Mustang they'd purchased at an L.A. auction a week ago. The mechanic popped his head out from under the hood and lifted his hand in a friendly wave.

If the man wondered what Peter was doing home in the middle of the day dressed like a bum, Lee's pleasantly lined face gave no indication.

Now, with his back against his bedroom door, Peter brought his trembling hands around so he could see them. No blood. He wanted to sob with relief.

Jesus God, had he hurt her? After she'd jerked back and hit her head, he'd wanted to stop and see if she was okay, but someone had called her name, and he'd run. Without thinking, he'd simply run—prey now, not predator.

Was he a predator? He never intended to be, didn't want to be.

Scrubbing his jaw with his knuckles, he wondered how badly she was hurt. What if she was dead? It would be his fault for scaring her and then leaving her like that . . .

He hadn't meant to hurt her, hadn't wanted to make a grab for her. His fingers remembered the warmth of her skin, the tense muscles of her neck as he'd begun to close his grip around her windpipe. He hadn't *wanted* to choke her, but the way she'd looked at him, it was as though she *knew*. He'd only wanted to explain . . ..

But of course she knew, he raged at himself. He'd been the one to tell her! But that was when he thought they were only dreams, only some damn stupid *dreams*!

He slammed his fists into his head, once, twice, again, hard, harder, until the pain penetrated his skull and he let out a sharp sob. Damn, damn, *damn*. If only he could *remember*!

Letting his head fall back against his bedroom door, he felt tears dampening his cheeks. His eyes felt like somebody had poured salt in them. The muscles of his arms and legs were shaky and weak. Maybe he should take Miss March's advice and see a doctor, a psychiatrist, check himself in somewhere. Maybe then he could figure out why this was happening, why he was losing it, why he had turned into some kind of monster. Maybe they'd lock him away and people would be safe again.

Sure, he'd been working hard, but it felt surprisingly good. Since his father's death after a long bout with cancer, the burden of the O'Hara wealth and holdings now rested on Peter's shoulders. Four companies and their subsidiaries, thousands of employees, money and lives at stake. He had to be a success now for *them*, to keep it all going the way his father had wanted, to keep the dream alive and thriving.

He couldn't let it fail, not on his watch.

Over the years, his father had tried to bring Peter into the business, but unlike Zoey, who seemed to crave the role of corporate leader, Peter had balked. After all, there were Boards of Directors, VPs, CEOs, lawyers . . . the family business didn't need *him*.

But he needed *it*. That little epiphany had been stunning . . . then sickening . . . then terrifying, and finally . . . satisfying.

Though he knew his sister was probably far more capable of taking over the reins, Peter had decided to go for broke, learn all he could, do the job his father had entrusted to him. For the past eleven months, he'd worked sixteen-, eighteen-, twenty-hour days. It was all for the business and nothing for himself. Hell, he couldn't even remember the last time he'd gotten laid. Maybe it had all become too much and his mind had snapped.

And then, three months ago, the dreams began. Nightmares. Cutting into his brain and leaving him exhausted.

Letting his hands fall to his sides, Peter closed his eyes. What was the use, anyway? He was cut out to be a rich man's son, not a corporate giant. He'd planned on skating through life, spending money, playing around with his friends, putting an impressive dent in the family fortune. His only ambition had been to bed as many leggy blondes as he could. Hell, let his sister be the one to marry and produce little heirs. Since he couldn't take any of it with him, what did he care what happened to the O'Hara megamillions after he died?

Yet the day he'd suddenly found himself at the helm, that had all changed. He'd changed. He'd asked questions and worked hard and learned, and maybe it was simply killing him.

Or turning him into a killer.

Moving wearily to his bed, he let his body drop onto the coverlet, face down. He was weary, but couldn't rest. No time. He had that two o'clock with the board, then a tour of the Alameda facility, and tonight Zoey's dinner party. His sister would kick his ass all the way to Alcatraz if he begged off another of her charity functions.

He rolled over onto his back, catching a glimpse of the notebook sitting on the bedside table. His dream log. Sitting up, he reached for it, opened it. His own handwriting on the pages. Innocent, mostly illegible words, scribbled when he'd been half asleep. Phrases to make him recall the dreams so he could tell Miss March and she could help him solve the riddle. Most of the dreams were unremarkable. Images, sounds, colors, silly events that made no sense and were even laughable.

Most. But not all.

Tossing the book onto the bed, he rubbed his eyes. Rest. He needed rest. Maybe he'd ask Zoey if she had anything he could take. Hell, his sister's bathroom cabinet looked like a mini-pharmacy, she must have something in there that would let him get a little shut-eye. Maybe then he would sleep the way he used to, before his father died, before his world shifted and the nightmares came, leaving his hands and his face and his clothes covered with blood.

"I don't care what you say, Inspector, I'm not going to press charges."

Tabitha gazed into Darling's eyes, put her hands on her hips, and set her jaw. The detective stared back, his hands on his own hips, his stance wide, aggressive. He was doing that *Oh, yeah?* man thing, where they make themselves big to fool and intimidate their enemies.

She had to give him credit—his stance and stare were intimidating and intense, or would have been, if he'd been trying it on anyone but her.

"I was wrong about Mr. Griffin," she explained. "I'm not going to compound the problem by pressing charges."

She waited for the detective to explode, but all he did was . . . smile. His despicable magnetism wrapped around her like a coy snake. Against her will, it drew her in.

"Whether you press charges or not," he said softly, "I'm going to dust in here."

"Great," she drawled. "When you're finished in here, you can start on the bookcase in the den."

"I mean dust for prints, and you know it," he said. "You're just being obstinate again." His brown eyes glittered. "You watch TV?"

"Selectively." She cocked her head. "Are those crime scene shows realistic?"

"No." He chuckled. Adjusting his glasses, he gave her a long look. "I'll bet you're an *Animal Planet* fan."

"Winkin and Blinkin watch it. I just change the channels for them. No opposable thumbs and all that." She wiggled the thumbs in question.

Tabitha watched as he dropped his gaze to her thumbs, lifted it to her mouth, then made eye contact.

After a moment he said, "Griffin touch anything in here—besides your neck, I mean?"

He let his attention settle on the neck in question, and she felt herself warm all over. Didn't the SFPD have any old, wrinkly detectives?

After the paramedics had pronounced her okay, Darling had escorted her back to her office—the scene of the attack. Even though she was fine, she must still look a little woozy because he seemed poised for action, as though she were a football and he needed to be ready to catch her as she dropped into the end zone.

Tabitha's fingers felt for her throat as she remembered Griffin's hand there, tightening until she could barely breathe. While the encounter had been terrifying at the time, she'd been thinking it over since then, and had reached certain conclusions.

"Mr. Griffin did not come here to hurt me. I'm sure of it. He was confused, desperate, but murder wasn't on his mind."

As her hand lay against her throat where Griffin's fingers had been, she caught a flash, an image, an emotion, and something else . . .

"I was wrong about him, Inspector. He's not a murderer." She rubbed her neck gently and looked away.

"What was his nightmare about this time?"

Tabitha lowered her hand and shrugged. "He said that a few nights ago he dreamed he killed a homeless man in an alley. He was highly agitated and his clothing was a mess. I got the impression he hadn't slept since then."

Darling walked to the front window, pulling the curtain aside as though checking the street for cars. "Dreaming of murder isn't a crime, Ms.

March. But assault is." He let the curtain fall back into place and turned to her. "If I find—"

"No matter what you find, he didn't intend to hurt me, and I'm not pressing charges. I think his actions shocked him as much as they did me. If I hadn't lurched away from him, I wouldn't have hit my head."

In what was becoming a familiar gesture, Darling jammed his hands into his pockets and scowled at her. "Pardon me, ma'am, but that's the stupidest thing I've ever heard. Griffin had his fingers wrapped around your throat and you reacted. His was an act of aggression, also known as assault. You have absolutely no way of knowing what his intentions—"

"I do so," she snapped. "When he grabbed me, I saw inside his mind for a moment. He doesn't know what's happening to him. He's terrified—"

"*Inside his mind?*" Darling barked. His eyes narrowed on her. "You saw inside his *mind*? Great! Did you happen to catch his real name and address while you were in there?"

Tabitha felt hot fury surge through her body.

"I'm not an idiot, Inspector. If I thought I was in danger, I'd press charges. But I don't get that from him at all. I was afraid, but then . . . but then, when he grabbed me, I got an image . . . the dreams he told me about . . . something's wrong. Off-kilter.

I—I don't understand it, but I don't fear him. Not anymore." Crossing her arms over her stomach, she said, "He needs help. He needs friends—"

"Hey, with victims like you, who needs friends?"

Darling raised his hands in obvious frustration.

"Fine," he sighed. "*Don't* press charges. I can't make you. But if you'll recall, *you* came to *me* to discuss whether this man was a killer. And now he's attacked you. Whether or not he had anything to do with Iris Reynaud's death, he's violent and may have something to hide. I'm very, *very* interested in talking to him."

Ignoring his outburst, Tabitha said, "How will you even know the prints you get are Griffin's? Lots of people come and go in the house all the time."

"I won't know. The fact is," he continued, bending to retrieve a black case sitting next to the sofa, "at many crime scenes no fingerprints are found at all, and even when they are, they're often not clear enough to use. But if I luck out and snag one of Griffin's prints, and if he has priors and is in the AFIS database, I'll get an ID."

"That's a lot of ifs."

Opening the case, Darling rummaged around inside and brought out a square plastic container. "Maybe he didn't touch anything today, but he's been here several times before."

Tabitha nodded.

"And he sat at the table with you. Put his hands on it, right?"

She glanced over at the table and nodded again.

"Unless you scooted him in, he must have touched the chair." He let the words hang in the air while he stared down at her.

There they were again, standing toe to toe, glaring into each other's eyes. She knew he was only trying to do his job, and he was right—she had been the one to contact the police. But that was before she'd realized that, despite his nightmares, Jack Griffin was no killer.

Suddenly the air filled with music. Inspector Darling's cell phone had come to life, playing "Can You Feel the Love Tonight," and Tabitha realized the handsome detective probably had a girlfriend.

Oh, well, fine. Of course he did. Most people were in relationships. Why would he be any different? Maybe he was even engaged.

She took a small breath and let go of the emotions that welled up at that thought.

He yanked the phone from his pocket and flipped it open. "Yeah?"

That certainly didn't sound like a man in love.

Glancing at Tabitha, he looked away. "Yeah, I'll be there." He snapped the phone closed and let it drop in his pocket.

Maybe they'd had a fight.

Before she could stop herself, she said, "Girlfriend?"

Shoving his glasses back up on his nose, he said, "My brother."

She snorted a sardonic laugh. "Your brother? 'Can You Feel the Love Tonight'?"

"You'd have to know my brother."

Refocusing, she said, "Okay, look. I have a client in an hour. How long will it take you to dust for the prints?"

Darling's shoulders relaxed a little. "Give me fifty-nine minutes, then I'll be out of your hair." Meaningful pause. "Hopefully for good."

The cable car bumped along, the ride smooth but noisy. In the middle of the front of the car, where Tabitha sat, the burly gripman wore a beaming smile as he worked the grip lever with his hands, pulling back hard like a gondolier surging an oar through thick water.

The conductor appeared to be Asian and was half the gripman's size. He moved through the car collecting fares, including Tabitha's, finishing up in the back, where he took hold of the rear grip.

Under the belly of the brightly painted maroon and yellow car, the cable, buried beneath the street, whirred along at its standard nine and one-half miles per hour. Next to Tabitha, the gripman sounded one bell, signaling the conductor to apply the rear brake.

"California Street!" the gripman sang out as the car bumped to a halt. People hopped off, others clambered on. All grinned, found space on the polished oak benches to sit, and eagerly turned their faces forward toward the next hill.

Two bells clanged, telling the conductor the way ahead was clear. The car eased forward and began to rise like a boat riding the crest of a gigantic wave. As the car climbed, the giggling passengers slid back, smooshed together like the last sardines in a can.

At the summit of the hill, the car glided over it, then headed down, metal and wood and bones and muscles creaking, down, and down, and down Powell Street. The tourists in front of Tabitha squealed and chattered away in German with as much delight as if this were a theme park joyride.

Tabitha smiled to herself, remembering her first cable car experience, and how she, too, had squealed while her mother had held her tightly in her lap as the car tilted over the rim of a high hill, then lurched forward to descend almost straight down.

They bumped across Post and Bush and Sutter, and into Union Square.

The bell clanged again. "Geary Street!" the

gripman yelled as the car ground to a silent halt.

Tabitha stepped onto the pavement and walked to the curb. Traffic had come to a stop—all hail the conquering cable car, its right-of-way ensured by its inability to meander or swerve or yield.

She watched as it slid on down Powell Street, its happy passengers grinning still, anticipating the next hill, the next valley.

The sun ruled today, and the water of the bay gleamed like a carpet of rough-cut sapphires. The omnipresent fog had cooperated by rolling back to the far horizon so the elegant red lines of the Golden Gate Bridge stood in bright contrast to the blue of the sky.

Everywhere there was bustling, an orchestration of movement and melody that was the city. The downtown, the wharf, the shops. The city smelled good, too. Of sweet air, chocolate, bread, saltwater, and flowers.

And suddenly she was thinking of Inspector Nate Darling. His face, boyishly handsome, the gleaming brown of his eyes that were at once humorous and serious, that wide, sensuous mouth, the timbre of his deep voice. It had been a long time since she'd found herself daydreaming about a man, but he was a lot of man, and she had a lot of dreams to catch up on.

The light at the corner of O'Farrell and Powell changed to red, and she realized she'd been so absorbed in her thoughts of the sexy detective, she hadn't been paying attention and had stood rooted to the spot for a whole light cycle.

When the light flashed green, cars began to move in front of her. A returning Powell cable car neared the intersection and began grinding to a halt, but as it drew close, Tabitha's senses heightened, and she became aware of the crowd around her, shifting, subtly shoving her forward nearer the curb.

Then she felt a hand splayed against the small of her back. An image burst inside her brain, but she didn't have time to analyze it as she felt herself being pushed hard into the middle of the street, shoved directly into the path of the oncoming cable car.

Chapter 7

Tabitha lifted her lids, and stared into her rescu-
er's face. He was sort of blurry, and he faded in
and out a little, but there was no mistaking those
glittering brown eyes, even though he'd lost his
specs somewhere during the tackle.

She blinked up at him, not quite sure what had
happened. One moment she'd been on her knees
in front of an oncoming cable car, the next she'd
found herself rolling across the pavement with a
man on top of her.

Swallowing, she whispered, "Where did you
come from?"

His eyes serious, he said, "Well, when two people love each other very much—"

"Not that kind of come from," she growled. "I

got that speech from my mom in the fifth grade. Were you *following* me?"

"Sort of. Unofficially. Accidentally. Yes."

"I'm outraged," she choked. "Thank you."

"You're welcome."

"Did you see who pushed me?"

His eyes went dark, his focus sharpened. "What are you talking about? When I saw you dart out in front of that cable car, I thought you were just a klutz with a death wish."

Tabitha blinked again, suddenly aware of a crowd of people around them chattering to each other about her and her well-being.

" . . . call an ambulance . . . see what happened? . . . quite the hero . . . should have looked before she . . . totally cute sandals . . ."

Inspector Darling eased himself off of her. "You're trembling. Do you think you can stand?"

Nodding, she let him take her hands and gently pull her to her feet. She could feel the strength in him, in his muscular body, as he easily brought her up. He slipped his arm around her waist to steady her, and she realized she liked the feeling a lot.

For one outrageous moment, she wanted him to put his arms around her and hold her close. Reassure her she was okay. Maybe pamper her a little. She glanced longingly at his shoulder and thought it would be comforting to lay her head there, sink into him, absorb his warmth, his strength. He was the kind of man who made a woman feel safe, and though she wanted nothing else from him, for some reason, at that very moment, she wanted that.

He retrieved his glasses from the pavement and put them back on, making him look more adorable and approachable than ever. She started to say something, but before the words would form, the gripman was beside them, his gray eyes worried, his fiery red hair tangled as though he'd been running his fingers through the long strands.

"You okay, miss? Jesus, you scared the shit out of me, er, the crap, er, the stuffin', I mean. You ought to know better than to come running out in the street like that—"

"I didn't," she interrupted. "I was pushed."

He drew in his chin and gave her a questioning look. "Naw. You must be mistaken."

"I'm not."

Inspector Darling flashed his badge. "I'll need your statement, Mr.—"

"Greevey," the gripman said. "Mick Greevey."

"I'll need a statement from you, Mr. Greevey, and the passengers on the car as well."

Mr. Greevey gave Tabitha an anxious look. "Somebody really pushed you? You okay?"

As she thanked the gripman for his concern and

assured him it wasn't his fault, two police cars pulled up from opposite directions, their sirens cutting off in midblare. She felt Nate squeeze her arm for a moment, then let her go while he went to talk to the uniformed officers who had begun making their way through the crowd. When he presented his badge, all four of them snapped to attention, flicked glances at her, then at the on-lookers, nodded, and moved to begin working a little crowd control and talking to some of the witnesses.

When the detective returned to her side, he gently took her by the elbow and escorted her to one of the police cars. "You'll be more comfort-able sitting down while I get your statement."

It only took a few minutes to relay what had happened, after which he spoke to Mr. Greevey, while the uniformed officers talked to passengers on the cable car and the bystanders on the side-walk.

When all was said and done, nobody had seen anybody push Tabitha in front of the cable car, although those who noticed anything at all won-dered why she seemed to leap from the sidewalk right into its path.

Tabitha rubbed her arms. An hour had passed since the incident, and every muscle and bone in her body had stiffened. Her skirt was torn, her knees bruised, and her hands scraped raw from the hot asphalt, making the prospect of waiting for a bus or cable car home seriously daunting.

As though reading her thoughts, Darling said, "I'm taking you home."

She smiled and hoped the gratitude showed in her eyes.

"My car's this way." He gestured with his left hand at the parking garage just up the street.

She stared at his fingers. No ring. She hadn't noticed that before, but then, she hadn't looked before. Not that it mattered. Either he wasn't married or he was the kind who didn't wear a wedding band. Either way, it made no difference to her. Well, maybe a little difference.

A small trill of something buzzed up her spine at the sight of his empty ring finger and the possibilities it presented, not that she was interested in possibilities with Nate Darling. Yet every time she saw him, she seemed to find herself drawn in a little more.

"Why were you following me?" she asked, brushing dirt off the sleeve of her blouse.

"I didn't really mean to." He escorted her through the crowd of pedestrians all hurrying about their business. "I was just coming out of the garage when I happened to see you at the intersection. Serendipity."

They walked in silence for the few minutes it took to reach his car, a late-model metallic charcoal Honda sedan. One hand still on her arm, he opened the passenger door with the other. Before she got in, Tabitha turned to face him.

"You saw me on the corner, but you didn't see who pushed me?"

"Sorry. I wasn't looking right at you at that moment, uh, exactly."

"Where were you looking?"

His eyes flicked away. "Let's just say I'm your typical disgusting male and leave it at that."

She made a *tsk* sound with her mouth. "You were ogling my chest."

His cheeks flushed and he looked a little sheepish. "Uh, no, ma'am. Actually, there was this girl standing next to you on the curb, and she was wearing these shorts and this crop top thing, and, well, I—"

Tabitha's eyes widened and her jaw dropped. "You were ogling the chest of the girl standing *next* to me?"

"Isn't that better than ogling your chest?"

She wasn't sure. True, nobody'd ever called her busty, but nobody'd ever called her flat, either.

"You're right," she sighed. "You are disgusting. If you hadn't been lusting after some bimbo, you *might* have seen who pushed me."

Lowering his head, he gave her a bashful smile and blinked innocently. He looked like a little boy about to confess he'd hacked the Pentagon's computer system just to see if he could. He was absolutely adorable.

Tabitha felt her resistance begin to puddle.

"God knows I've tried to overcome it," he said, obviously not sorry at all. "But how was I to know what was going to happen? *I'm* not psychic."

They eyed each other as she slid into the black leather seat and fastened her safety restraints. With a slight twist to his mouth, he continued, "By the way, if you're so psychic, how come you didn't know you were in danger before it happened?"

She watched as he closed her door and walked to the driver's side, a cocky look on his face. So smug.

Over the years, she'd dealt with others in law enforcement who'd treated her abilities with the same casual disrespect, so she wasn't surprised at Inspector Darling's attitude. Not surprised, but a little disappointed. Something inside her wanted him to be better than that.

When he settled in next to her, she drawled, "Listen, Inspector Gadget—"

"Wow, so original. You're just mad because I wasn't ogling *your* bosom."

"There's nothing wrong with my bosom."

"No kidding," he said under his breath while not looking at her or the bosom in question. "It's just that hers was exhibited in such a way that made ogling a mandate."

A *mandate*? Testosterone-driven idiot.

Ignoring her rising irritation, she said, "My psychic abilities are somewhat . . . mitigated. I'm tactile and don't get much unless I touch a person or object. You might try keeping an open mind."

"I've had some experience with psychics before," he said, glancing over at her. "Which is why I can say with some authority that it's a bunch of baloney."

Flattening her mouth, she said, "Okay, actually, I did get something as I was being pushed, but it flashed so fast, there was no time for it to register in my brain before I was out in the street."

Darling cranked the ignition and headed out of the parking garage.

"What do you mean, you *got* something?"

"An image, an . . . *impression*, for want of a better word. But then I felt the hand shoving me, and the next thing I knew, the cable car was bearing down."

He slid her a skeptical look. "If you say so, but it sounds like a crock to me."

Finally losing patience, she took a deep breath and reined in her burgeoning anger. "This is *California*, Inspector Darling. *San Francisco*, California, to be exact. Renowned the world over for its extraordinary, stupendous, first-rate, A-one, peerless, matchless, five-star, off-the-charts left-of-center views of . . . everything, including the extrasensory. Like, have you been living under a rock or something?"

"No." He shifted gears and took a corner. "I've been living in Olympia." Flicking a glance at her, he said, "That's in Washington."

She widened her eyes. "Really? Like, next to the White House and Congress and stuff?" she trilled like the airhead he obviously thought she was. When he shot her a look she said, "I know where Olympia is. I even know it's the state capitol." She stuck out her lower lip. "Such a grumpy, growly detective. Sounds like somebody needs a Starbucks."

Pulling up in front of her house, he put the car in neutral and set the brake. But instead of looking over at her, he kept his eyes focused on the distant horizon.

"I was born in San Francisco, but left when I was thirteen. For twenty years in the Northwest, I lived among normal, sane people, so returning to my roots has been like a marriage between Martha Stewart and Richard Simmons."

"Oh? Which one are you?"

His mouth flattened as he got out of the car and moved around to her side to open the door. As he helped her out, his gaze ran over her body.

"You're sure you're okay?"

"You keep asking me that. I'm fine."

Abruptly, the twangy notes of Johnny Cash's

"Folsom Prison Blues" began playing in Nate's jacket pocket. "My lieutenant," he said, reaching for the cell phone. After a brief conversation, he slipped the cell back into his pocket.

"Tabby?" Tabitha turned to see her mother standing on the porch, an odd smile curving her lips, a calculating look in her eye. "Would you like to invite the detective in for coffee?"

Inspector Darling raised his hand in greeting. "Thank you, ma'am, but I've got to respond to another call."

Victoria nodded and went back into the house, leaving the front door ajar.

Tabitha watched her mother go, then turned to Darling. "Will you let me know if you find out anything about today?"

"Yes, ma'am," he said as he went around to the driver's side. Before he got in, he stopped and casually placed his open hands on the roof of the car. "What kind of plans do you have for the week? Nothing strenuous, I hope."

"No," she said, wondering where he was going with this. "I teach an adult ed class once a week, but I don't think that'll put any kind of strain on my scraped knees."

He gave her one of "those" looks again. "Adult ed? When?"

What did he care? Why was he so interested in what she was going to be doing, anyway?

"Thursdays at Merced High," she said. "Dream interpretation. The details are on my website in case you decide you want to take a walk on the wild side and set your staid, inflexible, myopic, rigid, skeptical standards aside."

He grunted. "I'll keep that in mind. If you hear from Griffin again, let me know."

"Yes, Inspector."

"Stay safe."

"Yes, Inspector."

"Don't do anything foolish."

"No, Inspector."

He slid in behind the wheel, put the car in gear, and took off down the street. She watched him go, and realized she felt both exhilarated and let down at the same time.

Sure, he was handsome and intriguing, but way too high-maintenance for her—even if he was interested, which she doubted. And since she wasn't interested, either, he might make for some sexy fantasy fodder, but that was about it.

Victoria hadn't been wearing her glasses and probably hadn't noticed that anything was awry, so Tabitha took the opportunity to sneak upstairs, shower, and change her torn skirt and dirty blouse.

About a half an hour later, she found her mom sitting cross-legged on the kitchen floor, cleaning out the cupboard next to the stove, while Winkin and Blinkin lay curled up together under the table.

"Inspector Darling is very attractive," Victoria said as she rearranged stacks of soup cans.

"Mmm, is he?" Tabitha said absently, hunting in the cupboard over the counter for a water glass.

"Tabitha—"

"Okay," she sighed. "I guess it would be silly and contrived to say I hadn't noticed. When do Eden and Flora get back from Maine?"

"Tomorrow," her mother said. "And don't change the subject. I think he likes you." Victoria emerged from the cavernous pantry cupboard. She'd put her glasses on, and they sat akimbo on her nose. With her thumb and index finger, she straightened them. Her plump cheeks were flushed, her eyes bright, her familiar smile tipped in a gentle grin. "He's the first man you've shown any interest in since Cal."

What? "What!" Tabitha abandoned her hunt for a water glass to stare openmouthed at her mother. "What are you talking about? I haven't shown any interest in Inspector Darling at all. I barely know him. It's been strictly official. How can you sit there and accuse me of . . . well, he's incredibly arrogant, not to mention he's a nonbeliever. I could never become involved with a man who doesn't understand . . . well, that's the dumbest . . ."

She let her words trickle off as her mother's smile widened and Tabitha realized she was protesting way too much.

Victoria sent her a skeptical look. "All I know is you left here on the bus, but *he* brought you home. Did you have some kind of secret rendezvous, or did you just sort of bump into each other on the street?"

"Um, yes," Tabitha said. "Bumped, um, on the street. You got it."

Like a freight train into a rag doll. She could still feel his arms around her, the weight of his body on hers, not to mention the look in his eyes when he asked her if she was all right.

There went that feeling again, that warm, melty feeling she'd begun to get whenever she thought of Nate Darling.

As for the "bumping into" thing, there was no way Tabitha was going to tell her mother what had happened. It would only upset her, and what with the menopause, the repairs the house needed, and still grieving for her faithless husband, Victoria really didn't need one more calamity to deal with. Griffin's attack had been bad enough, but if her mom knew somebody had pushed her in front of a cable car, there was no telling how she'd react. Besides, it had been a near miss. Scraped knees and hands, sore muscles and bones, no big deal.

"I have some work to do now," Tabitha explained. "Transcribing for Dewey, Cheatum and Howe."

Victoria burst out laughing. "You made that up!"

"Yes, Mom," Tabitha said sarcastically. "I made it up. It's actually Dooley, Chissom and Hall, but I just can't resist."

As she reached the kitchen doorway, she stopped and turned to her mother, now on her knees in front of the open cupboard. "You have plans tonight, Mom? You want to take in a movie or play Scrabble or something?"

Victoria eased herself to the floor to sit on the old patterned linoleum, a cleaning cloth crumpled in her fingers. She gave her daughter a nervous grin. "Actually, I'm going to be online tonight."

"A chat room?"

"No," she said evasively. "Not a room, just a chat."

"*Mom.*"

"Now, Tabitha," Victoria said, her voice shaking a little. "I've told you before, it's perfectly safe. It's anonymous and there's no way any of the men could ever figure out who I am or where I live. Marlene Gregory—you remember her, she used to sell Tupperware in the neighborhood— well, *she* met a nice man on the Internet, and I have a friend down at the pier who's been dating a guy she met through RomanticNotions.com and it's getting very serious."

Victoria's soft blue eyes begged Tabitha not to make an issue out of this, but to Tabitha, it was an issue.

"How much did it cost you to join?"

Her mother brightened. "Oh, it was very affordable. The one-year plan saved me the most money, so I signed up—"

"A *year*, Mom? Do you really think you can meet a man and fall in love online, and—"

"Why not?" Victoria said, her eyes wide with naïveté. "The only problem is, I don't scuba dive, or ski, or rock climb, and I don't know a thing about cliff diving off Cabo."

"What are you talking about?"

"Well, it seems every single man out there my age is in great shape, and hikes and skis and ice skates and bike rides and climbs mountains and does yoga, and they're all looking for a woman who can do all those things with them. Don't men stay at *home* anymore? Now, I do walk a lot, but I haven't skied since I was a teenager, and besides, the arthritis in my knees is so painful. As far as scuba diving, well—"

"Mom," Tabitha interrupted. "Do you really think every fifty-something-year-old man on RomanticNotions.com is an athletic doctor with the sexual prowess of a seventeen-year-old who's looking for a woman *over* the age of twenty-five to share his gigantic retirement fund with? Don't you think maybe some of them are lying?"

Victoria blinked and widened her eyes. "But what would be the point in that?"

"I'm sorry to break this to you, but those guys aren't looking for true love, or a soul mate, or any of that crap. They're looking for an easy lay, or at the very least a woman with a steady job whose bank account they can tap into."

"You're bitter."

"No shit, Mom. That doesn't make what I'm saying any the less true." Tabitha leaned against the doorjamb. Softening her tone, she said, "I love you. I don't want to see you get hurt or taken advantage of, not in person, and not online, either. Cyberspace is filled to overflowing with losers and lotharios who prey on lonely women and have no intention of becoming involved in a real and honest relationship."

Victoria set the cleaning cloth on the floor next to her knee. "I know you're very resentful about what happened with Cal, and I don't blame you. I was, too, after what your father did to me. But I'm moving on, or trying to, and you need to as well."

Tabitha rubbed her nose with her knuckle. "I'm glad for you, Mom, even if it is through some fly-by-night online dating service, as long as you're careful. I just don't think there's a perfect man out there for me."

"Perfect?" Victoria cocked her head and smiled. Her shoulders relaxed a bit. Sitting there on the floor, she was surrounded by the coffee mugs she'd been rearranging in the cupboard. Some were old, some were left over from sets, some were new. There were tall mugs and short ones, patterned ones and plain, but the most common quality to the array seemed to be that they were all different.

"See these mugs?" Victoria said, waving her hand over them like Vanna turning a new letter.

"Of course I see the mugs, Mom."

"I've been working in the kitchen all day, cleaning shelves, rearranging the plates and cups and saucers, getting rid of the old, making way for the new. These are all the coffee mugs we own. I've had some of them from before you were born."

"Okay."

"Since they're all sort of individuals," Victoria said casually, her voice light, "I tried to match them anyway, find two that were perfect for each other. I tried by size, color, pattern. I tried by type of clay, porcelain, or stoneware. I tried by number of ounces each would hold or the shape of the handle. Nothing worked." She lifted her eyes to meet Tabitha's. "I never found two that matched.

Then I decided my approach was all wrong. I gave up on finding two that matched, and decided to look for two with similar flaws."

After a moment of silence, Tabitha said, "You're very clever, Mom. And very perceptive."

Victoria nodded. "Nobody's perfect, sweetie. Nobody and no thing. Cal hurt you, deeply, and you've never been one to forgive a hurt too quickly. But for your own sake, you need to find a way out of your isolation. You're sweet and beautiful and smart. Any man would be very lucky to win your heart."

For some ungodly reason, an image of Nate Darling pressed itself into her head, and even though she blinked several times to flutter it into oblivion, it stayed.

"I'll, uh, I'll think about what you said, Mom."

Victoria smiled and tilted her head a little. "That's all I ask."

Chapter 8

Nate sat at the café table, letting his nerves uncoil while he listened to the music. People who'd never lived in a big city, maybe never even visited one, didn't understand about the music. Every city played a different tune, rolled along to a rhythm all its own. Some jumped erratically, their notes all over the scale, like a jingle, like L.A. Seattle was a ballad, a slow, easy love song of gray skies and lullabies. Others pulsed to a frenetic beat constantly moving never stopping never slowing never sleeping; New York.

And San Francisco, well, San Francisco hummed. It was seductive, a melodic undercurrent that tugged at you, grabbing hold and not letting go. Cool and damp and enticing. It sounded to the ear the way fog felt against your skin.

He glanced around. Next to his table, pink jasmine climbed a white trellis, then tumbled across the wooden awning, lending the air a sweet, sultry scent he could almost taste. He closed his eyes, and he was naked, adrift on a cloud of perfume, ready to greet his lover in languid anticipation.

Which brought *her* to mind.

Nate let his attention fall to the file beneath his hand. Running his index finger over it, he rounded the stiff edges, slipped his thumb under the cover, and contemplated what he'd just read.

Ethan had been thorough, and Nate would pay a high price because of it. His brother had never been one to do something for nothing, and he knew Ethan would call in the favor when it was least convenient. Fair enough, he supposed, because Nate now knew everything there was to know about Tabitha March—more than she probably knew herself.

But it wasn't enough.

Today was Thursday . . .

He checked his watch. Picking up the file, he tossed a couple of bills on the table and headed for his car.

The Merced High School parking lot was nearly full by the time he arrived. He wasn't sure what room she was in, but he figured he could just follow all the vacant-eyed nutcases and they'd lead him right to her.

Pushing the double glass doors open, he stepped into the hallway and spotted a huddle of five or six women chattering among themselves like a gaggle of brightly feathered geese. Though the women were of assorted ages and ethnic backgrounds, three sported granny glasses, four had their hair in braids, none wore makeup, all wore baggy clothes, socks, and Birkenstocks.

Ah, he thought. This must be the place.

The women turned in unison and began scuffling down the corridor to enter the last room on the left. Setting off in their direction, when he got to the open classroom door he peeked around the threshold.

He couldn't have said why his heart gave a lurch when he saw her—or maybe he could, and that was part of the problem. Tabitha March was a contentious, adverse, disrespectful, smart-mouthed latter-day flower child . . .

And she was hot. He knew he'd be wise to stay away from her, but for the life of him, he couldn't. Now that he knew all about her, he wanted to know more.

She stood in profile to him, engaged in conversation with an elderly man wearing an oversized gray jogging suit and blindingly white athletic shoes.

Nate let his gaze take Tabitha in, head to toe. Her glorious mass of hair had been tamed into a sexy knot at the nape of her neck. He didn't know about other men, but for him, the nape of a woman's neck was one of the places on the female body that made his blood simmer.

The blue outfit she wore looked more like a form-fitted Victorian nightgown than a dress, scooped kind of low with a little white lace to accentuate her cleavage. With her hair the way it was, she was pretty, alluring, and tempting as hell.

He knew the moment she became aware of him. Her speech stalled, and she *ummm'd* and *uhhh'd* a lot. Finally, she turned in his direction as though she were preparing herself to face a firing squad.

Their gazes locked. Her blue eyes widened, then narrowed. *What in the hell do you want?* they said.

He cocked his head and gave her his best smile. Her cheeks flushed and she said something to the elderly man, who nodded and returned to his seat.

"Do you have an admittance slip?" she said to Nate, her mouth in a tight, succulent rosebud. God, that mouth.

"Gosh, Miss March. Do I need a hall pass, too?"

"What are you doing here?" Her voice was husky and just a tone away from being a growl. He liked it.

"Research," he said, and left it at that.

Around them the classroom mutters and murmurs quieted as all eyes turned to watch their teacher greet her new student. Nate could tell by her expression that Tabitha had noticed as well—and didn't like it.

Plastering a phony smile on her face, she said too loudly, "Of course you can monitor the session before you decide whether or not to join the class. Please take a seat, *Nate*."

So she didn't want anybody to know he was a detective. And she obviously didn't want to call him Darling. His name had caused confusion on more than one occasion and had led to several fistfights throughout his school years—fights he generally won.

But, damn. His name on her lips did something to the region just below his navel he really didn't want to think about—even if she had said it with a little more bite than was warranted.

He grinned and nodded, sorry that he hadn't had time to change his clothes. Showing up for a class in psychic woo-haa-hoo dream interpretation called for jeans and a T-shirt, not a gray pinstriped suit and .38.

Sliding into one of the seats near the front, he decided this hadn't been a half-bad idea after all. She was the teacher, he the student. That gave him free rein to stare at her for two hours—legs, hips, and . . . well, the rest. Not to mention her pretty face, and hair that made his fingers tickle to touch.

By the time the clock above the door read seven straight up, nearly all the seats in the classroom were filled. Glancing around, he noted the women outnumbered the men two-to-one, and the young outnumbered the old. All of them eyed him and his suit like he was a gangland hit man.

Since his weapon was secured at his shoulder, he couldn't shrug out of his jacket, so he kept it on, but loosened his tie and unbuttoned the collar of his shirt. Adjusting his glasses, he stretched his long legs out in front of him and turned his full attention on the best-looking teacher he'd ever had.

He watched as Tabitha ran her gaze over the length of his body, then reached for the tumbler of water on her desk. Taking a few gulps, she set the glass down, cut him a stern glance, and finally turned her attention to the rest of the class, apparently determined to ignore him.

He considered it a personal victory that she felt she needed to try.

"Welcome to class, everyone," she announced. "This is our fifth session and I hope you've all had a chance to practice what we've discussed so far. To get things going tonight, does anyone have a dream they'd like to share?"

Several hands went up. Gesturing to a thirty-something woman with short black hair, Tabitha said, "How about we start with you, Kismet?"

The woman named Kismet smiled and left her seat to stand at the front of the class. She was a somewhat plump, attractive woman with expressive brown eyes and a generous smile.

"Well, a few nights ago," she said, concentrating on her fingers, "I had the most bizarre dream. I was in a sort of a prison. I've had prison dreams before, lots of times, but that's beside the point, I suppose." She made a nervous giggle in the back of her throat. "Anyway, I was in this prison and there was a big courtyard and I watched as the guards wheeled in a flatbed cart kind of thing, and on this cart was a gigantic baked potato. I mean, it was the size of a Toyota!"

She glanced over at Tabitha, then lowered her head again. "Well, see, the potato had been cut open and fluffed, you know like they do in restaurants? But it didn't have any toppings. Just fluffy potato!"

Giggling again, she shrugged. "Anyway, this other prisoner—actually, it was Russell Crowe, if you can believe that . . ."

Everyone in class laughed, and Kismet's cheeks flushed.

"Um, Russell Crowe and I agreed it would be a good idea to climb, like, inside the potato? So when the guards wheeled it away, we could escape. We did that, and we got out of the prison. I can't imagine what it means!"

Kismet grinned sheepishly as the class nodded and scribbled notes. Tabitha stepped forward and asked Kismet to return to her seat.

To the class she said, "In order for Kismet to understand what her dream is trying to tell her, she needs to think about what's going on in her life right now. A prison escape and a giant potato, and even a famous actor, are going to mean something different to each of us. Those dream interpretation books you can buy generally don't help much because different symbols mean different things to different people."

Nate watched as Tabitha crossed the room and scooted her butt onto her desk to face the class. Crossing her ankles, she smiled at Kismet.

"Having said that, a prison can usually be interpreted as confinement, either emotional or physical. And a potato certainly represents food to one degree or another. And Russell Crowe . . . Kismet envisioned him, while you or I would have dreamed up a different person entirely, depending on what he symbolizes to us."

Shifting gears a little, she said, "Was Kismet's dream prophetic, release, wish, or problem-solving?"

The classroom bubbled with lively conversation and musings as the students debated with each other as to what kind of dream Kismet had experienced.

"Nate?" Tabitha said, looking squarely at him. "Which do *you* think it was?" Conversation trickled off and the room grew quiet.

He squirmed a little in his seat. "Wish?"

"Very good," she said, her eyes alight with mischief. "I agree. What is Kismet wishing for?"

He squirmed again. "She, uh, she wants to go out to dinner with Russell Crowe?"

Behind him, several women tittered, a man laughed, and Kismet choked.

"I doubt that's it," Tabitha said, amusement warming her voice. He felt his body respond to her in spite of himself. "That doesn't explain the prison aspect of the dream, Nate."

Returning her attention to the class, she said, "Anybody else have—"

"Wait!" Kismet rose from her seat. Her fingers clutched a tissue as tears slid down her plump cheeks. "I . . . I think I know. I want to tell you—"

"It's not necessary, Kismet," Tabitha interrupted, her voice calm and soothing. "I think I understand now, but you don't have to talk about this in class." Her eyes were soft and sympathetic, filled with compassion, and some kind of pain Nate didn't understand.

Kismet shook her head. "I want to . . . my husb-husband," she stammered, her voice thick with tears. "We don't have a good marriage. He's so controlling, you see. Harsh. Physically, if you know what I mean? I eat. It's what I do, to escape, to be kind to myself. Even though I realize it, I can't seem to stop." She wiped her eyes. "I think the prison represents my m-marriage, the potato was the food I use to cope, to escape. It's probably obvious just by looking at me." She sobbed again. "Russell Crowe was, well, maybe he represents my an-an-anger." She was crying full-out now.

"Take a break, everyone," Tabitha said quietly. "Please."

Quickly crossing the room, she pulled the weeping woman into her arms. "It's okay," she murmured. "You're safe here."

The other students stood and began filing out of the room, throwing looks of sympathy Kismet's way. Nate went to the door, but didn't leave.

So Kismet's SOB husband hit her. He felt his stomach tighten and his palms get damp. Bastard. There should be a special place in hell for men who abused women.

Tabitha lifted her head and looked across the room at him. Their eyes locked, and there was no mistaking the plea in her gaze.

As he walked toward the two women, Tabitha

placed her hands on her student's shoulders. "Nate is a police officer, Kismet. Maybe he can help you."

"Ma'am?" he said.

Kismet raised her tear-stained face to him and brought the tissue to her nose, but said nothing.

"I *can* help you," he continued, "but you have to file charges against your husband. Are you willing to do that?"

Taking a card from his pocket, he held it out to her.

"It's a shelter, downtown," he said. "It's safe. Call them."

She gazed down at the card, sniffed, then took it. "Thank you," she mumbled. "I'll think about it. I have kids, and—"

"Then do it for them, if not for yourself. Okay?"

Kismet nodded again, then turned to Tabitha. "I'll think about it. I'm going to go now. I've never told anybody about this before. I can't believe I said anything. I'm so sorry."

"Kismet," Tabitha said, her voice soft. "You have absolutely nothing to apologize for. A person can only take so much for so long. You wanted it to finally come out, and your dream was telling you it's time. Please take the detective's advice and let the police help you."

Kismet nodded, then went and gathered up her purse and notebook. Silently, she walked to the door. At the threshold, she paused, turned to Tabitha, and smiled. Then she was gone.

"She won't call, will she." Her words were not a question.

"No."

"Is there anything we can do?"

Nate blew out a long sigh. "No."

"She's a nice woman."

He nodded and muttered, "Yeah. They usually are."

As the students returned to the room, Nate took his seat, and for the next ninety minutes he watched Tabitha conduct class.

She sure seemed to know her stuff. It was mostly woo-woo bullshit, of course, but that was beside the point.

Her hands were expressive and she moved them as she spoke. He got to study her mouth, too, as it formed all kinds of words—smart words, kind words, sweet and even sentimental words. With each word she spoke, she became more beautiful to him, and more desirable.

After class, a few students lingered to ask questions. He bided his time, waiting until they had all gone and he was alone with her.

Tossing a stack of papers into her briefcase, she said, "Do you have a question, Inspector?"

"I liked it better when you called me Nate, Tabby."

She snapped the lid closed. "I liked it better when you called me Ms. March." Grabbing the handle of the briefcase, she said, "Well, if there's nothing else, I'll be—"

"I like how you care about your students, Tabby. I thought you handled Kismet's situation really well."

"Oh, um, thank you. I hadn't realized until tonight how much she's hurting. I just wish there was something more I could do."

He lifted a shoulder. "She knows she can come to you. She knows there are people who care about her. Maybe that'll give her the strength to leave that prick."

Tabitha gazed down at her hand on the briefcase. "You seem to have very strong feelings about domestic violence."

He nodded, remembering many encounters he'd rather forget. "When I was in uniform," he said, "we got calls all the time. It made me sick to see how badly some of those women had been beaten. I never could understand it. I'd cut off my own arm before I'd hit a woman. The card I gave Kismet is for a shelter I volunteer at one day a week."

Her head lifted and she looked him in the eye. "You volunteer at a shelter? That's wonderful."

Shrugging again, he said, "It's damned sad, actually. Some of the women are afraid of me when they first meet me; some of the kids are, too. I'm a big guy and I know I can intimidate, so I just try to be nice, quiet, keep them from feeling threatened. Let them know that not all men are bullies."

She looked up at him as though he'd just donned a suit of armor. He liked it.

"Hungry?" he blurted without thinking. He hadn't intended to say it, but now that he had, he decided to run with it. "Want to grab a bite to eat?"

She blinked and looked taken aback for a moment. "Now that you mention it, I am sort of hungry."

"Good. What's your pleasure? Chinese? Italian? Tofu burgers with yogurt hollandaise?"

She hesitated a moment, then eyed him with suspicion. "You mean, like, go eat, and talk about the Griffin case? Not like a, uh, a date kind of a thing."

"Exactly like a date kind of thing. I'm not officially on the Reynaud homicide, and Griffin's involvement is sort of a gray area right now anyway, so I'm pretty much free to ask you out. I came to your class. Come to my date." He adjusted his glasses and gave her the smile he knew would do the trick.

Averting her eyes, she said, "No."

His best smile crumpled on one end. Damn, the woman was a tough nut to crack.

"I'll tell you what," he cajoled. "Maybe I'll let you hold my hand again and you can interpret another dream. I had a really good one last night."

"You said you hadn't dreamt since you were fourteen."

"Not until last night. Go figure. Anyway, it was about a ventriloquist."

"A ventriloquist?" she said, her lips curving into a suspicious smile. "That's not so—"

"Did I mention that the ventriloquist was a ten-foot-tall pineapple with an eye patch and a lisp?"

She laughed at that. "Sounds more like *The Muppet Show* than a dream," she said dryly, "but, well, all right. It's not a date, though."

He took the briefcase from her hand. "You are an unattached woman, I am an unattached man. We are attracted to each other. Don't deny it. I'm escorting you in my car to a restaurant where we will eat and drink and engage in conversation, after which I will pay the bill. In my book, that's a date."

She wrangled her briefcase from him. "A date is not defined so much by what happens during the course of the evening as by what generally occurs at its culmination. That is to say, sex, or at the minimum, a good-night kiss."

Snaring the briefcase from her grip, he held it behind his back. "And you'll be so worried about fending off my unwelcome advances, you won't be able to relax and enjoy our date."

"But if it's *not* a date, there won't be any advances, unwelcome or otherwise, thereby allowing both of us to enjoy the meal without any pressure or expectations. That's why I think—"

"You think too much," he muttered, setting her briefcase on the desk. "Let's just make this issue moot, okay?"

Sliding his hand around to the nape of her neck, he tugged Tabitha toward him. She gasped in shock, but before she could pull away, he bent his head and kissed her.

Chapter 9

It is bad luck to divulge the nature of a dream before breakfast.

FOLKLORE

Don't stop him—stop him—don't enjoy it—enjoy it—don't kiss him back—kiss him back . . .

Oh, yes . . . by all means, kiss him back . . .

Tabitha's brain fought a losing battle with her desires as she let herself go limp against Nate's wonderfully warm, hard body. While his torso felt like tempered steel, his mouth was soft, his lips coaxing, parting over hers.

How had her hands found their way to his chest? She gripped the lapels of his jacket as though letting go meant she'd blow away in the wind. How had her breasts come so snugly up against him? If he moved, she'd crumple to the floor. When had her tongue touched his? Had he made the first move? Had she?

The kiss seemed to go on and on, too long, and

not nearly long enough. He pulled back slowly, licking her bottom lip, suckling it, finally breaking contact.

She sighed as though she were a cat being petted in long, languid strokes. Staring up into Nate's eyes, she muttered, "I . . . um, well, that was, um . . . hmm."

The detective only gazed down at her, and she wondered if it was because he'd been rendered speechless as well. Behind his glasses, his brown eyes looked sleepy, and very, very warm—like mocha cake right out of the oven.

Stepping away from Tabitha, he picked up her briefcase with one hand and cupped her elbow with the other.

"I'm hungry," he mumbled under his breath, and she couldn't help but wonder whether he was talking about food. "What's your favorite restaurant?"

She uttered the name of the first place that came into her head, a new restaurant she'd read about in the *Chronicle* last Sunday. Nate Darling's kiss was so potent, she could barely recall what planet she was on, let alone the names of eating establishments.

Panicking, she tried to think of something to say, but nothing came to mind—nothing except Nate kissing her again, everywhere. Every naked where.

It had been so long since she'd had sex. Maybe too long. Maybe that's all it was. Maybe she really didn't like him so much as want him, since a mere kiss had opened the door to her neatly-stored-away sex drive—which had been *in absentia* since she'd divorced Cal.

As it turned out, she'd blathered out the name Chez François—which was actually a second story eatery in Ghiardelli Square that overlooked the bay. If Inspector Darling thought her choosing a French restaurant for a casual dinner was a bit over the top, he didn't say so.

The dining room was airy and spacious, elegance evident in every neat little table, every bouquet of fresh flowers, the straight line of every waiter's spine.

From where they were seated, Tabitha could look out the window and see Alcatraz Island, the "Rock" and its forlorn buildings illuminated by amber lights. Choppy waves broke the reflection on the dark water, making the island appear to be floating on a sea of iridescent blue gems.

As soon as Tabitha and Nate had settled in, a gray-haired waiter wearing a black coat and white bow tie appeared and offered them menus.

"*Monsieur, mademoiselle*," he announced, his French accent thick. "*Bon soir*, and welcome to *Chez François*. I am Maurice. This evening, our sole in butter and garlic sauce is especially *délicieux*."

Across the table, the detective looked down at the menu, then up at the waiter. "*Est-ce que je peux obtenir un bifteck?*"

Tabitha stared, impressed more than she would have imagined. Nate Darling spoke French? "You speak French?"

His lips quirked. "*Oui. Mais mal, le plus souvent.*" Then he grinned at her, and she felt her cheeks heat.

Addressing the waiter once more, Nate asked a series of questions in French.

The waiter paled, slid his gaze around the room like a rabbit on the lookout for marauding dogs. Lowering his voice, he said, "Listen, pal. I'm just trying to make a livin' here. You want a steak, I can get you a steak, but stop tryin' to impress the lady and cut to the chase, okay?" Diverting his attention to Tabitha, he resumed his French accent, saying loudly, "And what will the lady have?"

"I, um, I think I'd like to start with the free-range escargot."

"An excellent choice, *mademoiselle*."

Across the table, Nate choked. "What the . . . *free-range* escargot?" He looked down at the menu, then back up at Tabitha, his eyes glittering with mischief, or was that malice?

"*Free-range* escargot?" Shaking his head, he said, "They must be a bitch to round up, being so fast and all. Nothing slipperier than a rampaging herd of wild escargot making a dash for freedom. I guess they need special escargot wranglers with itty-bitty little lassos, and—"

"You are being so juvenile," Tabitha stated.

Resting his elbow on the table, he let his chin fall into his palm. With an amused glint in his eye, he said, "Free-range escargot. Only in California."

Tabitha felt heat warm her blood at the insult to her native state.

After Maurice finished taking their order and strode away muttering something about testosterone overload, Tabitha leaned forward a little, making sure to display some cleavage. When she was sure she had Nate's attention—and judging from the flushed cheeks and glazed eyes, she did—she whispered seductively, "*Un asno es más elegante que usted.*"

Blinking shyly, as though she had just complimented him instead of calling him a stupid ass in Spanish, Nate pushed his glasses up on his nose. The male ego, she mused. What a piece of work it was.

"I don't speak French," she explained sweetly. "I speak Spanish, *usted ganso tonto.*"

"Why, thanks," he said with a wide grin. He relaxed back in his chair and took a sip of wine. "How did you know I like farm animals?"

He couldn't possibly know she'd called him an

ass *and* a silly goose. "What do you mean?"

His eyes glittered. "Yes, I love all sort of critters, especially, oh, say, donkeys." With a tilt of his mouth, he said, "Throwing in the thing about the goose was a nice touch."

Tabitha felt her smile turn upside down. "You speak Spanish, too."

"*Sí.*"

"You could have warned me."

"So?"

"You know what I should do?"

"Sue?" He winked.

Tabitha felt her lips twitch. "No, but if you keep this up, I might just—"

"Sigh?"

As the waiter set salad plates in front of them, then departed, Tabitha locked gazes with Nate and once more felt the crackle of attraction course between them. Despite her best efforts, she felt herself returning his smile.

"That was clever," she said. "I probably shouldn't say this, but you have a killer smile, which I'm sure you're very well aware of, and use without compunction to your advantage."

His grin broadened. "So if you like me, why'd you call me an ass?"

"Because you're cocky and stubborn and you insulted my home state."

"I have the right. It's my home state, too, remember. Why don't you relax a little? You've been acting pissed off ever since I kissed you, even though I know for a fact you liked it."

She licked her lips. "I have my reasons."

He stared into her eyes for a long time, then casually turned his attention to the food.

As they worked their way through the meal, a tense silence filled the narrow gap across the linen-covered table. Covertly, she watched Nate's hands as he cut his steak.

He had lovely hands, square and masculine. She wanted those hands on her again. She remembered how his rough palm had warmed her skin when she'd done his reading. And how his strong fingers had felt curving around her ribs, just under her breast, as he'd held her against him after Griffin's attack.

Looking over at him, she said, "So. What else would you like to know?"

His head raised. "I haven't even asked you anything yet."

"Oh, come on, Inspector. Surely you did a background check on me. All cops do it. Everybody knows that." She took a bite of bread. "Did I pass muster, or did those outstanding warrants for armed robbery catch up with me?"

"I don't know what you're talking about."

She shook her head. "That's a very innocent look you've cultivated, but I'm not buying it."

He seemed a little peeved, but nodded. "Okay, yeah. I checked you out a little."

"A *little*? I'll just bet, Sherlock."

Though she kept her wry smile in place, Tabitha's chest began to tighten uncomfortably, and her appetite vanished. She should have known better than to have dinner with him. So he really had checked into her background. How much did he know? Did she care what he found out? He would judge her now and, being a skeptic, would find her lacking.

With a sick feeling in her stomach, she realized she did care what he thought. Dammit, how in the hell could she have let that happen?

Nate slowly eased his empty plate away. How much should he tell her? She probably wouldn't be happy about some of the things her file had disclosed, but then again, how was he going to learn more if he avoided the very topics he wanted to know more about?

She was nervous. She hadn't been before he'd admitted to doing a background check, but now her mouth had tightened and she kept her eyes on her half-empty plate. Very unlike the confrontational, feisty, take-no-prisoners attitude she'd displayed ever since they met. He would have to tread carefully.

"Honestly," he ventured, "I think it's only fair

that I know *something* about you, since you know so much about me."

She leveled her blue gaze on him. "What are you talking about?"

"I shared my dream with you about Ethan and Andie. I'm sure there are things you supposedly 'saw' or guessed about that you're keeping to yourself. So I figure it's only right I know a bit of secret information about you, too."

"That's stupid."

"All's fair to share, I swear, but beware, I, dare, uh, say."

She blinked, then blinked again. "What in the hell was that?"

Squirming in his chair, he muttered, "Poetry."

Across from him, Tabitha pressed her lips together and blinked at him once more. "Poetry. You do . . . poetry."

"Yeah, well, I was on this case in Washington, about a year ago. Undercover, posing as a famed yet reclusive poet. Sort of got me interested in, uh, poetry."

He let his eyes meet hers, and realized she was laughing at him.

"Well, it isn't easy, you know," he growled defensively. "Apparently not all poems begin with *There once was a man from Nantucket . . .*"

She made a sound very close to a giggle. "I suppose not." Assessing him closely, she said, "But you're trying to get me off track, Inspector. Let's get back to what you think you know about me."

"Okay, despite your earlier remark," he said, "you have no outstanding warrants. Your main source of income is legal transcribing, which you do from home. You began the dream interpretation sideline two years ago, to modest success." He took a sip of wine, then set the glass down. "Your bills are paid on time, and you live within your means. No credit card debt. You have a checking account, but not much in the way of savings. Your mother lives with you in the house you inherited five years ago from your paternal grandmother. Your father divorced your mother two years ago to marry another woman. You divorced your husband a year ago when you discovered he was being unfaithful. Since then, you have not been seriously involved with anyone."

There was more, but he thought he should keep it as high-level as possible. Taking it deeper might freak her out, maybe even hurt her, and judging from the panicked look in her eyes, she was wary of exactly how much he knew.

Tossing her napkin on the table, she said, "My, my. Aren't we thorough."

"Look, Tabby, I—"

"Not a problem," she huffed. Pushing herself

away from the table, she grabbed her purse from the chair next to her and stood. "Thanks for the eats, Inspector. I'll see myself home."

Nate shot to his feet and made a grab for her arm. Wrapping his fingers around her wrist, he said, "I'll see you home. Give me a sec to pay the bill, and I'll—"

She shook him off. "I'll pay my own bill and see myself home, thanks. Yes, I interpreted your dream, but I didn't violate your privacy, Nate. Checking me out like that was very, very low."

"I don't think I said anything—"

"It's what you *didn't* say. The other things. You know about those, too, don't you?"

He nodded. "I'm sorry for what you've been through. I had no idea. I'm sorry."

Clutching her purse to her breasts, she said, "You don't know the half of it, Inspector. It wasn't for you to find out. It was for me to share with a man I've grown to trust, a man who cares about me, a man who has a right to know. Not a smug, smart-assed detective whose only goal was to see whether I was good enough to take out to dinner. You are a *jerk*."

Around them, the other diners raised their heads in curious interest. Across the room, Maurice frowned and began moving toward their table.

"Okay, yeah, I admit it," Nate rushed. "I'm a jerk. But let me take you home, Tabby. Please."

Maurice arrived and glared down his nose at Nate, but addressed Tabitha. "Iz zere a problem, *mademoiselle*?"

Without taking her eyes from Nate's, she said, "Maurice, would you please call me a taxi?"

The waiter gave her a quick nod. "You got it, sister," he growled. "Come with me. You can wait in the ladies' lounge."

Well, Nate thought as he tossed some bills on the table, as first dates went, this one sure sucked, and not in the way he'd hoped. He should follow her home, for her own safety and his peace of mind, but she'd probably have him arrested for stalking her. Just when he decided to do it anyway, his cell phone began to chime "I Walk the Line." It was his partner.

"What's up?" he said, watching Tabby follow the waiter across the dining room.

"Hate to disrupt your evening," Bob said solemnly. "But we got one."

"Location?"

Bob gave him the address. "Looks like it's a transient, maybe. In an alley. ME says the carotid was sliced and the guy bled out. Pretty messy."

"On my way."

Nate shoved the phone into his pocket and headed for Tabby. Walking through the open door of the ladies' lounge, he spotted her sitting on a plush sofa, digging through her purse.

"Hey," he said, and she looked up, astonish-
ment widening her eyes. Reaching for her arm, he
tugged her to her feet. "I got a call for a possible
homicide in your neighborhood. I'll drop you at
your car at the school, then follow you home. And
don't argue," he said, when he saw her mouth
form a protest.

He quickly escorted her out of the lounge and
toward the front door of the restaurant. When
Maurice stepped in front of them to block their
exit, Nate flashed his badge and the waiter instantly shrank back, his surprised gaze flicking
between the two of them.

"Well, that's one restaurant I can never eat at
again," she muttered, as he pulled her toward his
car and opened the door for her.

As he slid behind the wheel, he said, "The
day Griffin attacked you, you told me he'd had a
dream about killing a guy in an alley."

"Y-yes," she said, her voice uncertain. "Why
. . . what—"

Pulling into traffic, he said, "Tell me about it
again. And don't leave anything out."

Chapter 10

The crime scene was cold. From the look of things, the vic had lain for some time unnoticed among the debris choking the small alley behind the Acacia Palms Apartments.

That he'd been overlooked was no surprise, Nate thought. Garbage pickup day wasn't until tomorrow and the Dumpster was filled to overflowing with white plastic bags, black garbage bags, green waste bags, paper bags, rag bags, newspapers, magazines, bottles, and cans. When the elderly resident of Apartment 3C shuffled out to dispose of her trash, she'd noticed a stench emanating from behind the crammed Dumpster and called the police.

Garbage was one thing, Nate thought grimly as he approached the old lady. But the odor of death was foul—overpowering and unmistakable, even by someone who'd never smelled it before.

"Mrs. Sanchez," he said, addressing the tiny woman whose milky brown bespectacled eyes were wide with obvious apprehension. "I just want to ask you a couple of questions. Okay?"

Her lips didn't quite curve all the way into a smile, but she nodded. "*Sí*, yes, okay."

Nate led the woman to a short brick wall that served as a planter at the corner of the ground-floor apartment and the alley. Mrs. Sanchez brushed aside some tendrils of ivy and settled on the narrow ledge, curling her bony fingers around the throat of her cotton print housecoat.

"Mrs. Sanchez, your apartment overlooks the alley, is that correct?"

She nodded. "*Sí*, yes. It is small, but the rent, it is good. And the *padre* is just there. Not so far for these old bones to go." She gestured to the Catholic church across the street. "My granddaughter, she comes on the Sundays to take me to pray." Her voice, like her papery brown skin, was frail and thin and dry.

"So if there was any commotion down in the alley, you might hear it?"

She shrugged her narrow shoulders. "Sometimes. Maybe." Averting her eyes, she focused her attention on the faded pink puffs of slippers she wore.

"Mrs. Sanchez," Nate said quietly. "There is nothing to be afraid of. I just need to know if you saw or heard noises in the alley recently. Voices, yelling, perhaps a fight?"

Pressing her lips together, she gave a quick nod. "I think it is maybe the drugs, yes? I don't want to get caught in the middle of nothing."

"You won't," he assured her. "What did you hear?"

She swallowed, glanced into the dark alley, now crazy with beams of light and activity. "There is yelling. A man. He is crying, too, a little, I think."

"When was this?"

"Eh, four nights ago. I was watching the tellie vision. And then, outside the window, the noises start. A man. He screams, 'No!' and I am hearing the footsteps, ehm, running. Another voice I hear then. *Mucho más suave*, softer, see? I don't hear the words."

"What did you do?"

"I look around a little, but it is too dark."

Nate glanced up at the third-floor window belonging to Apartment 3C. While the window was tiny, it did command a view of the entire alley all the way out to the street.

"Tell me what you saw."

"Very dark," she said, her thin voice cracking. "I think at first there is just a shadow on the sidewalk, but it moves." She lifted her chin, indicating the spot where the aid unit stood now, its blue and red lights swirling against the high walls of the buildings that created the alley. "*Un momento*, he is not moving, and then, poof!" She raised her hands in a gesture of bewilderment.

"*He?* Are you sure it was a man?"

She made a sound in her throat. "Could be man, could be woman. Very dark."

"What happened then?"

"He goes down the hill, that way. It is very steep, this hill. Easier to go down."

Nate handed her his card. "*Gracias. Usted ha sido muy provechoso, Señora Sanchez.* If you think of anything else, I want you to call me, okay?"

Taking the card, she glanced at it, then gave him a nearly toothless smile. "You look to me like a man in need of a woman to take care of him, *Detective del Señor*. My granddaughter, so beautiful—"

"Sorry, *Señora*," he interrupted gently. Patting her cool hand, he said, "It's against the rules."

A uniformed officer escorted Mrs. Sanchez back to her apartment, while Nate sought out his partner. He found Inspector Stocker popping a couple of antacids, a scowl on his rugged face. His short gray hair was mussed like he'd been running his fingers through it in frustration, or agony.

"You ought to get a wife, Stocker," Nate snorted, "before your own cooking kills you."

Bob curled his lip and snarled good-naturedly, "Had a wife. Couldn't keep her."

"Put her in a pumpkin shell?"

"And there I kept her very well," he drawled, "'till Jack Sprat came along. It's been fifteen years, Darling. Like I'd ever be dumb enough to get married again, but I'll tell you what. You go get your own ass married and if *you* live happily ever after, we'll talk."

Nate unzipped the body bag and looked at the victim's face. "I might just do that," he mumbled, studying the gaping wound on the dead man's neck. "ME says maybe a broken bottle did this? Anybody find it?"

Bob glanced around the alley. "In all this crap? Lots of broken glass, but nothing we picked up had blood on it. Rat shit, bugs, the usual. Hard to get anything good."

Zipping the bag closed, Nate began meandering around. In the area where the body had been discovered and outlined with tape, he crouched and pulled a small flashlight from his pocket. A sticky black stain pooled at the spot where the old guy had fallen and bled out.

Newspapers littered the asphalt, some saturated with blood, some not. Nate nudged the papers out of the way and shone the light on the broken green glass underneath. Most of the pieces were too small to get any kind of prints from, but he kept hunting around, finally revealing part of an intact bottle neck.

"Hey, Bob," he yelled over his shoulder. "Hand me an evidence bag, will you?"

"What'd you find?" Tossing him the bag, Bob peered over Nate's shoulder. "There's tons of broken glass in this alley. What makes that piece special?"

Nate used his handkerchief to slide the shard into the plastic bag and seal it. "Because it's the only green glass near the body."

"So?"

"So, maybe nothing," he said, staring at the shard. "But most beer bottles are brown and fairly small. Not big enough to knock a man down, even an old man. Liquor bottles are bigger, but are usually made of clear glass, which is generally thin. I'm guessing the vic was slammed with an empty bottle, which would have made it even lighter, which means it would have to be a heavy bottle to begin with."

"Like a wine bottle."

Nate nodded. "Like a wine bottle, most of which are green. He has a contusion on his temple. If he was struck and the bottle broke on impact, the killer might have taken another swing at the guy with the broken piece, slicing open the carotid."

Bob cocked his head. "Okay, so our perp hits

this guy with an empty wine bottle. It breaks. The old guy's got to be stunned, probably down. Why take another swipe? Why kill him?"

Nate labeled the evidence bag. "What did you find in his pockets?"

"Not much," Bob said. "Five bucks and change, so unless the perp got scared and ran off before he could rob the old guy, there must have been another motive."

"Another motive," Nate repeated softly as he stood and switched off his flashlight. "That worries me, Bobby. That worries me a lot."

"Mom?" Tabitha closed and locked the front door, then turned out the porch light. As she walked through the foyer, Winkin and Blinkin came tearing out of Victoria's open bedroom door on the second floor and down the stairs, making enough noise to rattle the walls. They sniffed her and slid their fluffy bodies around her legs. Winkin flung himself onto his back in the hopes of a protracted tummy rub.

After cooing and complying for a few moments, Tabitha stood. "Enough for now, you two," she said, and climbed the stairs to her mom's room.

Reaching the threshold, she peeked in and said, "Hey, Mom. Have the Ichabod sisters come back . . . Mom? Oh, God, what's wrong?"

Victoria sat in her nightgown and robe on the

edge of the disheveled bed, tears dampening her flushed cheeks. In her fists, she gripped enough tissues to lead cheers at the next 49ers game.

"I'b fide," she choked, though it was obvious she was anything but fine.

Tabitha hurried to her mother's side and sat next to her on the rumpled white spread. Scooting closer, she urged, "First blow your nose, then tell me what's wrong."

Victoria nodded, buried her face in a fistful of tissues, and blew. And blew. And *blew*. Tossing the used tissues into the little straw wastebasket next to the maple nightstand, she grabbed another handful from the dispenser and blew again.

"Mom, *stop*. You're moving into brain cell territory."

Victoria laughed into a handful of fresh tissues, but it was a choky, watery sound. "I'b glad you're hobe, honey. How did your class go?"

"Screw my class, what's *wrong*?"

With a labored sigh, her mother tossed everything into the wastebasket, then folded her hands in her lap. "It's silly, really. I'm silly. Silly . . . and old."

"That's not true, Mom," she whispered, sliding her arm around her mother's shoulders. "You're not silly, but you are wonderful and beautiful, and the best mom anybody could ever have."

Victoria's head bobbed up and down. "You're

my daughter. You're biased. Not everybody in the world sees me the way you do."

"Such as . . . men?"

Big sigh. "Such as men."

"Men are jerks, Mom. We know this to be true."

"Then God is very cruel, because there is only one alternative and I'm just not into that." Swallowing, she lifted her red-rimmed gaze to Tabitha. "If I tell you, you'll only laugh. I might even laugh, it's so stupid."

"Tell me anyway," Tabitha urged softly.

Victoria's smile was shaky, but it transformed her face into the lovely woman she was. "I guess I felt a little down today. Eleven men rejected me this week on the match site. I'd heard that while women read the descriptions and consider what the men say about themselves, men only look at the pictures." She averted her eyes as if to say, *And they didn't like what they saw.*

Tabitha blew out a harsh breath. "Like I said, men are idiots."

Her mother shrugged. "I posted my best photo, but the truth is, I'm fifty-six, not twenty-six. No spring chicken."

"Mom, you're letting a bunch of creeps you don't even know make you feel bad about yourself. *You're* the prize here. *You.* If those men rejected you, for whatever reason, you're better off without them!"

"I've never had a lot of self-confidence, honey. Your father dumping me was quite a blow. We were together for over thirty-five years. He was not only my husband, he was my best friend. Sometimes I, well, I feel such a loss, I hardly know what to do."

"Is that why you're crying?"

"Not exactly. I was tired, so I went to bed early. Just before you came home, I . . . I had this dream."

"Tell me about it," Tabitha coaxed.

Reaching for the nightstand, Victoria picked up a glass of water and took a few sips.

"I dreamed I was playing a card game," she began, setting the glass back on the nightstand. "It was a tournament, and I was a champion."

"What kind of card game?"

She licked her lips. "It was Hearts. I was playing against this man, and I just *knew* I had a winning hand. I'd been dealt great cards and I was playing flawlessly. I was going to win. I *knew* I was going to win."

"What happened?"

Her mother shook her head. "We started out playing in this one place, somebody's house, and I was clutching my cards, when an official came in and said we had to move to another house. I held on tightly to my cards, because I was going to win, you see, and didn't want to lose them. So

suddenly I'm in this *other* house, and we're playing, and then we're told we have to move *again*. So
we did, and when I looked down, my cards had
changed. They were all different, but they were
good ones, and I knew I still held a winning hand.
But the officials weren't letting me play. I couldn't
win if I couldn't finish the game, and with all this
moving around, they were keeping me from finishing the game.

"Just as I looked down at my cards again, I
began to worry somebody was going to trick me
and I'd somehow lose. But I had *such* a good hand.
I woke up then, and felt a tremendous sense of
frustration and loss. It was . . . I was . . . I never
got to finish the game, you see? I never got to *win*.
And I so wanted to win . . ."

Tabitha's throat closed and her eyes burned
with tears. She tightened her arm around her
mother's trembling shoulders. "Do you, um, want
to know what I think it means, Mom?"

Victoria smiled. "Oh, I don't suppose I need a
psychic dream interpreter, or even Freud, to figure this one out." Her pretty blue eyes filled with
more tears. "Hearts," she whispered. "I wanted to
win at *Hearts*. I guess you can't get more symbolic
than that, can you, Tabby? I'm a very nice woman,
and I was a good wife, but your father didn't let
me finish the game. Instead of being the man he
should have been, instead of working on our rela-

tionship, it was easier to dump me and move on. He changed the rules so I couldn't possibly win."

"Like I said, Mom, men are . . ."

The image of Nate Darling pushed its way into her head. "Some men," she amended quietly. "Some men are jerks, like Dad and Cal. But just when you least expect it, you'll meet somebody nice, Mom. I believe that."

Victoria giggled in a congested sort of way. "Men my age don't want women my age. Younger men don't want women my age. Hell, even those really old farts out there don't want women my age. They all want twenty-five-year-olds, and they all think they can *get* them!" She snorted. "I'm angry because I really wanted to finish the game, to win, you know, at *love*. To have somebody at the end of my life to share with me whatever those years hold. I have what it takes, but I'm being *denied*. I have to tell you," she said with a huge sigh, "that really . . . hurts."

"I know, Mom," Tabitha whispered. "I understand completely."

Victoria sent her a wryly tilted smile. "Thank you for letting me have a pity party all over you. Now that I've gotten that pathetic little mess out of my head, I feel much better." Adjusting her cream chenille robe, she said, "Let's talk about you. Did you go out with some students after class?"

Tabitha slid her arm from around her mother's shoulder, then stood. "No, I, uh, actually, I had dinner with Nate Darling. He sat in on the class tonight."

Victoria's eyes widened and her face split into an enthusiastic grin. "*Really?* Is he interested in you? I mean, he must be or he wouldn't have . . . oh, Tabitha! He's so smart and good-looking and—"

"Mom," Tabitha interjected. "Before you reserve the chapel and order flowers, you should know that it was just dinner. Nothing more. I probably won't be seeing him again."

"Oh, I'm certain you will."

"What makes you so sure?"

"Because that's what woke me up. The phone."

Just then the doorbell rang and Winkin and Blinkin scampered out from under the bed to scurry down the stairs toward the front door.

Tabitha narrowed one eye on her mom. "Who was on the phone?"

"Your Inspector Darling. He told me to tell you he was coming by to talk to you."

The doorbell rang again. With a watery smile, she said, "I'll bet that's him now."

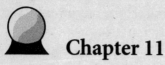

Chapter 11

To dream of large hands means you will soon enjoy sexual satisfaction.

FOLKLORE

"Good evening, Ms. March. I'm Inspector Stocker. I think you know my partner, Inspector Darling."

Tabitha stared up at the tall, distinguished gray-haired man at her front door, then shot a quick glance at Nate, standing a few paces behind, his gaze locked on her, his hands in his pockets.

"I'll explain in a moment, ma'am," Stocker said, offering her a disarming smile. "May we come in?"

Thoroughly confused at Nate's tense silence, Tabitha opened the door to allow the men entry, then showed them into the main parlor.

While the office was Tabitha's domain, the parlor was her mother's special world. Decorated in bashful peach tones and mossy greens, the room was cozy and inviting, reflecting Victoria's own warmth. Her mother had strived to keep the original ambience of the era in which the house had been built by decorating with antique mahogany tables and cherrywood bookcases. Family photographs dating back to the Civil War were displayed in a variety of frames on the far wall, while Tiffany lamps and milk-glass vases added to the tasteful atmosphere.

Indicating that the two men sit on the gold and cream brocade sofa, Tabitha took the chair in front of the fireplace. More photographs and an assortment of cream, pink, and green candles lined the mantel.

"My mother's not feeling well," she said before either of the detectives could speak. "This isn't a good time, so if you could be brief . . ."

"We won't keep you, ma'am," Inspector Stocker assured her. Next to him, Nate seemed to have his jaw wired shut. "Inspector Darling is with me in an advisory capacity only tonight and will simply observe our conversation without contributing to it. He's excused himself from the case because of his personal affiliation with you."

Nate raised an eyebrow.

"We don't *have* a personal affiliation," Tabitha said, frowning at Nate. "That dream you asked me about. What happened? Did you find . . ." She let her voice trail off, hoping one of the men would say it had all been a mistake, that no old man had been killed in an alley.

Stocker leaned forward, placing his elbows on his knees, tenting his fingers. "We've just come from the scene of a homicide which closely resembles in detail the, uh, dream you told Inspector Darling about."

"Oh, God, no. W-who?" she stammered. "Who was it?"

"A John Doe," Nate said. "An old guy, in an alley."

Their eyes remained locked for a moment until finally she couldn't handle the intensity of his gaze and she lowered her lashes. "Like in the dream. Griffin's dream."

She stood and walked to the fireplace, focusing on a small photograph her grandmother had taken of her family as it had been nearly three decades ago. A much younger Victoria March stood behind Tabitha, pushing her on the backyard swing, while her father smiled and looked on, a soft bundle held tightly in his arms. They had been innocent times, for Tabitha hadn't yet suffered the trauma that had opened the door to her psychic gift.

Gift. Sometimes. Sometimes not.

Nate came up to stand behind her. When he spoke, she felt the waft of his warm breath on the back of her neck. Stupidly, she wanted to sink back into him, feel his arms come around her, hear him telling her everything would be all right. But she knew it wouldn't happen.

"An old man in an alley, Tabby. A broken wine bottle was used to slice the artery in his neck."

She turned to face him. He looked down at her, his brown eyes clouded with bewilderment.

"I'm so sorry," she whispered, but before she could say anything else, she felt his strong fingers on her shoulders.

"How did you know?" he ground out between clenched teeth. "How in the hell did you know, and don't give me any more of that dream bullshit. I want to know who Griffin is and I want to know where he is, and if you don't tell me, I'm taking you in as an accessory."

Tabitha felt her mouth flatten as she blinked up at him. "Arrest me, if that will make you feel any better, but I've told you everything I know."

He stood only inches from her, close enough for her to curl her arms around his neck and pull him down for a kiss. Close enough to lay her head on his shoulder. Close enough to feel the heat pulsing from his body, smell the spicy scent of him, hear the breath leave his body as he spoke.

Close enough to knee him in the groin, the idiot.

"You can't think I had anything to do with that man's death." Her voice was soft, but she stared hard and deep into his eyes. "If I knew who Jack Griffin was, do you think I'd keep it from you? Two people have died. What can you possibly think of me, if you think I would do such a thing?"

He looked at her for a long time, just looked. His expression never changed, but before he could speak, Stocker said, "Sit the hell down, Nate. You're not part of this now, remember?"

Nate's gaze dropped to her mouth and lingered there, then slowly lifted to her eyes. Without another word, he let go of her shoulders and stepped away.

"I'll wait for you in the car," he mumbled as he passed the other detective.

After he'd gone, Stocker offered her his card.

"If you can think of anything else, would you please give me a call?"

As she took the card, she heard her mother's voice coming from the open doorway behind the detective.

"Tabitha? Is everything all right?"

Stocker turned to face Victoria, and Tabitha watched her mother's eyes light up. "Oh."

Inwardly, Tabitha scoffed. Sure, the man was nice-enough-looking, but he had to be pushing sixty . . .

Oh!

"Um. Inspector Stocker, this is my mother, Victoria Jones."

The detective walked toward the doorway in which Victoria stood. As he neared, her cheeks flushed, her eyes widened, and she reached up and fiddled with a lock of her hair.

Uh-oh.

"Nice to meet you, ma'am," he said with a cordial smile. "Sorry to have disturbed you. I'll see myself out."

Victoria grinned and turned another shade or two brighter. Tabitha watched in amused silence as Stocker brushed past her mom, who lowered her lashes and looked away as females do when trying to hide their attraction to a male.

After he'd gone, Victoria sighed and let her body slump against the doorjamb. "I don't know what crime you committed, honey, but would you mind doing it again?"

Tabitha went to the window and pulled aside the curtain in time to see Stocker slide into the car where Nate sat waiting. When the door closed, the interior light dimmed to nothing, making it too dark to see the men any longer, but as the sedan rolled away, she had the distinct impression Nate's accusing eyes were on her.

In one of the little chambers of her heart, the tiny door she'd only recently had the courage to open quietly swung closed.

Getting to sleep was a bitch. Nothing Tabitha did to get comfortable worked. Her head hurt from lack of sleep, and her eyes felt like they each had at least a tablespoon of sand in them. Oh, how she wanted them to stay closed, and oh, how they refused. She was about to head downstairs to warm some milk when she remembered the taste of warm milk was disgusting. It formed that skin on the top as it cooled. Warm milk always seemed to work in the movies, but in real life, it was just gross.

Giving her innocent pillow a hearty punch, she tried to maneuver it into the size and shape that would allow her weary head to rest. But as soon as she did and her eyes fluttered closed, the images that popped up behind her lids kept her tossing and churning and kicking and cussing.

A good cry, that's what she needed. Let those emotions spill out, let those tears go, turn on the waterworks and sob like a banshee until she was empty. Then, when she was exhausted, her muscles spent, she might be able to sleep.

Sex would work, too, if she only had a partner . . . extra points if he was Darling.

Frustrated, Tabitha bolted upright and switched on her light. Where in the hell had she put that, eh-hem, catalog?

As she opened the top drawer of her nightstand, her phone rang, the line she used for business. Picking it up, she glanced at the clock. Eleven forty-nine. She checked the phone's display: *unknown caller*. "Hello?"

"Miss March?"

Eerie music slithered into Tabitha's head, like a

violin bow gliding across an endless sour chord. She forced air into her lungs.

"Mr. Griffin?"

"Uh, yes. I'm sorry to call so late," he rushed, "but I need to talk to you. I'm ... I'm so sorry about the other day. It's trite to say it, but I don't know what came over me. Are you all right? I didn't hurt you, did I?"

"No," she said carefully. "But you *could* have hurt me, and you risk hurting others in the future if you don't get help." He seemed to still be listening, so she pressed onward. "I can give you some referrals, Mr. Griffin."

"I don't want referrals," he protested. "I only want you. You seem to understand. No one knows about . . . I mean, I can't talk to anybody about the dreams. Just you. You're kind and sweet, and you don't judge me."

What to do? She didn't want to say anything that would make him hang up, maybe forever, not when the police wanted to talk to him.

"Mr. Griffin, it would help a lot if you would share your name with me. Jack Griffin isn't your real name, is it?"

When he started to balk, she hurried, "Okay, maybe just your first name. That's all. I—I could help you better if I knew your first name."

There was silence for a moment. She knew he was still on the line because she could hear the rumble of passing cars, the blare of a horn, distant conversation.

"You're right," he said, and Tabitha's heart gave a mini-leap. "Jack Griffin isn't my real name. I'm a big H. G. Wells fan. Did you ever read *The Invisible Man*? Jack Griffin is the character's name."

"And sometimes you feel invisible?" she whispered.

"Yeah. Sometimes I do."

"Thank you for trusting me enough to share that with me. So, um, what is your real name?"

"I'll tell you, but in return, you have to do something for me."

The possibilities tumbled through Tabitha's head. What would he want her to do? She wasn't getting a thing from him psychically. He was all shut down and the only way she could get him to open up was to assure him he had her trust.

"All right," she said. "You tell me your first name, and I'll do something for you in return. In all fairness, though, I need to know what I'm agreeing to before I decide."

"No. If I'm going to trust you enough to tell you my name, you're going to have to trust me, too."

Tabitha let all the breath out of her lungs and closed her eyes. Envisioning a protective pink light shimmering around her body, she opened herself up to whatever thoughts or feelings she could get from him. She simply breathed . . . in and out, in and out . . . until she felt her muscles relax. A sense of quiet came over her, a sense of peace. It would be okay. Whatever he wanted, it would be okay.

Opening her eyes, she said, "I agree to your terms. Tell me your name."

There was the briefest silence on the other end of the line, then he said, "My name is Peter."

"Peter," she repeated, and knew he was telling the truth. "It's a nice name."

"Thanks," he said quickly. "Now, Tabitha, here's what I want you to do."

Chapter 12

If you have a dream on a Friday night, and discuss it with others on Saturday, it will come true.

FOLKLORE

"Okay, you're not gonna like this, but he wants me to meet him . . ."

The impact of Tabitha's words slammed into Nate's skull like a fist to the temple, and he nearly dropped his cell phone. Cursing under his breath, he punched the voice mail button to start her message again.

"Hi. It's Tabitha. Um, listen, Jack Griffin called me a few minutes ago. I know you're probably off somewhere ogling some bimbo's bosom or practicing your Spanish or something, but just in case you're not . . ."

Her voice was the epitome of confident self-assurance, and Nate might have bought it—if not for that subtle quaver he detected in the *in case you're not* part.

"*I made a deal with him . . . well, he made a deal with me. Anyway, we made this deal, and I think it's really okay. I do have a few instincts of my own, Inspector.*"

The instinct for survival apparently not being one of them, Nate thought.

"*He promised to tell me his first name if I'd do something for him in return. That would help your case, wouldn't it? To get his name? Okay, you're not gonna like this, but he wants me to meet him, and I said I would . . .*"

Nate's heart seized. "Shit," he hissed. "Wrong answer, cupcake."

"*Don't think I didn't hear that, Inspector.*"

Yeah? Well, she was going to hear a lot more than that when he got his hands on her.

He checked the time. Twelve-fifteen. She'd left the message at a couple of minutes after twelve, and if he hadn't been in the goddamn shower, he'd have heard the cell's ring.

"*I'm meeting him at twelve-thirty at the Powell cable car turntable. You know, down by the waterfront. There are always lots of people around, even this late, so, you know, I, uh, I figured it would be safe. There's no way he can corner me or, you know, um, anything.*"

Nate closed his eyes. *Not unless he pulls out a gun and shoots you from across the fucking street!*

"I know you're going to think I'm really stupid for doing this—"

Nate clamped his jaw tightly shut. If that son of a bitch touched one hair on her head . . .

"—but I think this is the only way to draw him out. I don't have a cell phone . . . I guess I really should get one . . ."

Nate jerked the damp towel from around his hips, tossed the phone down on the bed, and yanked on a pair of soft denims and an old sweater—no time to stop for jocks or socks; Tabby could already be in trouble.

As soon as he'd tied the Nikes on his bare wet feet, he grabbed his weapon, picked up the cell, and ran for the door, punching the voice mail button again to get the rest of her message.

"He just wants to talk about his dream log and even said he might bring it. That would be helpful, wouldn't it?"

Flinging the car door open, he bolted behind the wheel and jammed the key into the ignition.

" . . . and because I wasn't born yesterday, I already called Inspector Stocker. We're rendezvousing on the grassy area just west of the turnaround. I called him because I'm still mad at you, but if you get this message in time, you can come, too. Oh, and, um, Nate? Jack Griffin's real first name is Peter."

By the time Nate turned the key and shifted into first, he was on the phone to Stocker.

"She's the only one who can identify this guy," Bob said, "and she refused to stay out of it. She said she was confident the San Francisco Police Department would keep her safe."

"Damn."

"Yeah. I've already requested backup. Once she and Griffin make contact, we'll move in. I haven't seen her yet, but it's foggier than pea soup. Get your ass down here, partner."

"Copy," Nate said, rounding a tight corner.

Dropping his cell into his pocket, he roared down Powell, dodging cars and late-night pedestrians. He checked his watch: twelve thirty-seven. *Shit*. Another red light forced him to slow, but as soon as the intersection cleared, he edged through it hoping to hell he wouldn't get T-boned. He was still five blocks away and didn't dare use his siren for fear of scaring Griffin away, or making him hurt Tabby.

As he approached the intersection of Powell and Bay, the light turned red. Cranking the wheel, he shot the Accord into a loading zone, jumped out, slammed the door, and began running like hell the final two blocks.

His heart thundered in his chest as he approached Beach Street, where the cable car line ended and the gripmen had to manually turn the cable cars around to head back up the hill into the city.

Staying on the far side of Beach, Nate scanned

the area—what he could see of it. In typical springtime fashion, San Francisco had shrouded herself with a dense, damp fog that obliterated any objects more than twenty yards off. Despite the weather and the hour, people milled around, tourist types walking through the small park adjacent to the empty cable car platform, reading the engraved brass markers that told about the cable car's history. Couples strolled along the sidewalk, their arms entwined, enjoying the cold night air and each other. Taxis hugged the curb, claiming the few vacant parking spots on the car-crammed boulevard. But while there were people around, none of them appeared to be a lamebrained strawberry blonde biting off more than she could chew.

This far from the water, the fog thinned somewhat, and he caught sight of two units parked up the street a half a block from the corner, lights off, the uniforms nowhere in sight. Where in the hell was Bob?

He called dispatch, who put him in touch with one of the uniforms.

"We've been on scene about ten minutes, Inspector. We're on the perimeter, just been keeping an eye out, like Inspector Stocker asked. So far, no suspicious-looking men approaching any lone women. The fog's making it tough, though."

Just then he spotted Tabitha emerging from the

mist, sauntering up the path from Pier 41 to the park. She was wearing jeans and a denim jacket, but it was her hair that snared him. There couldn't be another woman on the planet who had hair like that.

"I've made visual," he said into his cell. "Stay put for now. I'm going to approach."

"Copy."

Dodging cars, he crossed the street against the light and headed in her direction. Still no sign of his partner, but then, in this kind of fog that wasn't a surprise.

Nearer the water now, he felt the bite of salt water in his nose. Every breath he took bathed his lungs in icy dampness. The silent mist created a sphere of gray, like the inside of a snow globe, shutting the bright world out, creating a miniature realm of wet grass, dull lights, and soft edges. Tabitha looked like an angel moving out of a cloud, coming toward him, coming to carry him to heaven. And he'd go.

She hadn't ID'd him yet. Head up, arms at her sides, she walked along like she owned the place. Her eyes were alert, her demeanor assured. He didn't know for sure, but it looked like she'd had some training in self-defense, or at the very least, how to march along like you're not a victim waiting to happen.

He smiled to himself. Damn if she wasn't something.

When she slowed down for a moment to get her bearings, he moved toward her.

"Miss?" he said loudly in a pseudo-Southern drawl.

She looked at him as recognition dawned. He wasn't sure, but was that a hint of relief he saw in the deeps of those blue eyes?

"Miss, I'm sort of lost. Maybe you could point me in the right direction?"

She licked her lips as she flicked quick glances around the area.

"Where is it you want to go?" She looked into his eyes, and he could see she was nervous. Not afraid, but maybe getting there.

"I'm lookin' for Pier 41, ma'am," he said. "Supposed to meet up with some friends."

"It's back that way." She raised an arm and gestured to her right. "I'm meeting someone myself, but he hasn't shown up yet."

A couple holding hands came up behind Tabitha, wove their way around her and past Nate, then kept walking, huddled together, sharing an intimate conversation.

Nate nodded, scanned the area in an interested tourist kind of way. "This fog's a mite thick. I can stay with you until your friend comes, if you like, ma'am. A pretty woman such as yourself, wandering around alone in the dark, ain't exactly safe. In fact"—he lowered his voice to a growl—"some would say it was downright asinine."

Narrowing one eye on him, she said, "No need. I can take care of myself, cowboy. But thanks for your concern. You can just mosey on along now like a good little wrangler and go brand something."

"Tabitha?" A man's voice emerged from the fog a split second before he did.

From the corner of his eye, Nate had seen a vague figure approaching through the mist, but Tabitha jumped at the sound of his voice.

"P-Peter?"

He stepped forward, coming within a few feet of her. He wore a heavy parka and a knit cap pulled low over his forehead. His jaw was unshaven, and in the dim light Nate couldn't quite make out his features.

Speaking to Tabitha, he gestured to Nate and said, "Is this man bothering you, Miss March?"

Nate fought down his sense of irritation and focused instead on the small book the man clutched in his left hand.

"Peter?" Tabitha said, shifting toward him, her eyes wide. "Are you okay? You look . . . awful."

Griffin never took his eyes off Nate. "You're intruding, pal. Take a hike."

"This guy a friend of yours, miss?" Nate drawled. "Don't seem very friendly."

Did he have a weapon?

In his peripheral vision, he saw Bob cautiously making his way toward them, the uniforms undoubtedly behind him in the fog. Now that Nate had made contact, to ensure Tabitha's safety nobody would do anything until he gave the signal.

Griffin was standing too close to her. Nate needed to get between them, then take the guy down nice and quiet. No need for violence. After all, he only wanted to talk to him.

Just then a group of people emerged from the fog, chattering and filling the path with in-the-way bodies, temporarily obscuring Nate's view of both Tabby and Griffin.

As the crowd cleared, he saw Griffin make a grab for her, snaring her wrist in his grip.

"Peter, don't!" she choked, her eyes wide with alarm.

That changed everything.

Nate rushed forward, thrusting his free arm around Griffin's neck, putting him in a lock.

"Police officer," he growled as Bob and three uniformed officers, weapons drawn, materialized out of the fog. "You're under arrest for assault—"

"What in the hell?" Griffin choked. "Let me go! I didn't do anything!"

He began to struggle, reaching forward, clawing at the mist with his fingers, making a grab for Tabitha. But she stepped back, tears in her eyes, both hands covering her mouth.

"Peter," she sobbed. "I'm sorry. I didn't know what else to do—"

"You set me up?" he rasped as Nate kept him in a hold. "You fucking set me up? I trusted you! You were the only one I trus— Goddamn you! Let me go!"

"Settle down, pal," Nate warned. "Don't make this—"

Behind them, a woman screamed and one of the uniformed officers turned in her direction. Griffin lashed out with his foot, kicking the officer in the side of the head, sending him sprawling onto the wet grass. The woman screamed again.

A crowd gathered, and one of the other officers shouted for them to stay back. Griffin took advantage of the distraction to elbow Nate in the gut. Not a hard blow, but enough to knock him off balance.

Griffin was as big as Nate, and quick. His fist came back, smashing Nate in the nose, nearly blinding him with pain. As the two men grappled for domination, Griffin broke free of Nate's hold.

Like a shot, he was on the run, Nate right on his heels.

"Hold your fire!" he yelled to the uniforms as he drew his own weapon.

All of a sudden there were too many people in the way, blocking Nate's view of Griffin, slowing his pursuit. A man stood frozen in the confusion, two women ran for cover, another man shouted and pointed, a dog barked and pulled at its owner's leash.

Cussing, panting, his nose bleeding like a son of a bitch, Nate peered into the fog trying to tell which way Griffin had gone.

"Fuck!" He ran his fingers through his hair. The fog closed in, welcoming the fleeing suspect into its embrace, but shutting Nate out.

For an hour they combed the entire area, but it was too late. Griffin had vanished.

Tabitha watched in horror as Nate and his partner and two of the cops took off after Peter. The third stayed with her, the one Peter had kicked in the head. The officer positioned himself between her and the small crowd that had gathered.

"Stay behind me, ma'am," he ordered. "I don't think the suspect will come back, but just in case."

"I understand." She took in the blood on the side of his head. "Are you all right, Officer?"

Clutching a white handkerchief in his fist, he put it to his temple and grinned. "I've gotten worse just roughhousing with my kids."

Dear God, she hadn't meant for any of this to happen. What had she done? Maybe she should have met Peter alone after all . . .

No, that would have been really stupid.

She glanced around. What if Nate's pursuit of Peter got one of them hurt? She'd never forgive herself if anything happened to either of them . . .

But especially to Nate.

Shut up, she told her conscience. She had enough to worry about besides whether she was letting herself fall for some cynical cop.

As the hour grew later, the crowd, with little exciting left to see, dissipated. Tabitha narrowed her eyes and tried to peer through the fog, but nothing moved out there now.

She pulled the collar of her jacket more tightly around her throat. Damn, it was cold tonight.

As the officer continued to keep tabs on the situation via his radio, Tabitha paced. Why didn't Nate come back? How long would he pursue Peter before either catching him or giving up?

Dammit, why had Peter grabbed her like that? That had given Nate the excuse he needed to use force rather than reason. *Men.* Total and complete idiots.

A police helicopter hovered overhead, the rhythmic beating of its rotors obliterating all other sounds. As its searchlight illuminated the mist around her, she thought she saw something in the grass a few feet away. As she walked toward it, the bright beam brushed it again, and she bent to pick it up. Nate's glasses, lost in the struggle. And three feet away . . .

Moisture from the wet grass seeped through the fabric of her jeans, chilling her knees and shins as she knelt down to take a closer look. She reached forward to pick up the dream log, when a voice stopped her.

"That's evidence. No touchy."

Tabitha yanked her hand back as she raised her head to see Nate emerge from the mist. His sweater was torn, his face smeared with blood. He had a bruise just below his left eye, and a cut lip.

He looked glorious, like a medieval warrior just returned from battle. She wanted to peel his clothing away and bathe him, tend to his wounds, feed him a bowl of hot gruel and a mug of mead . . .

"You look like hell," she whispered, while some insane joy quickened the beat of her heart at the realization that he was okay. "You should see a doctor."

"Are you all right?" he said quietly.

"Yes."

Crouching down next to her, he took his glasses from her shaking fingers. "Thanks." He put them on and leveled his gaze on her. "You sure you're okay?"

She nodded, suddenly unable to speak. How sick was it that with his hair mussed, his slightly stubbled jaw bruised, and wearing those glasses, he looked hotter than ever?

Instead of telling him that, she said, "Does this kind of thing happen to you all the time?"

Pulling a plastic bag from his back pocket, he said, "Not so much anymore. Your friend got away." Using the edge of his sweater, he eased the dream log into the bag and sealed it. "Where'd you park?"

When she gestured toward the waterfront, he rose, and with a touch to her elbow, brought her up with him. "Let's go."

"Why are you angry?"

His mouth flattened. "You shouldn't have agreed to meet him without consulting us first. We could have used a policewoman as a decoy and had more control over the situation. *And* kept you out of harm's way."

"But there was no time—"

"Wait right here," he ordered, and turned away to talk with the other cops for a moment.

When they were done, with a nod of his head in her direction, Inspector Stocker and the uniformed officers left. As they walked away, Nate took her by the arm.

"Here's the plan, little Miss Sherlock. We're

going to your car, which we will use to go to my car, which I hope to hell hasn't been towed away by now. Then we will proceed in an orderly fashion to my apartment, where I will obtain clean clothing, after which, we will proceed to your house, where I will park my carcass on your couch, unless you have a spare room."

"Wh-wha . . . why?"

"For the simple reason that it's nearly three in the morning, I'm dead on my feet and need some shut-eye before I take this diary in to have it analyzed, dusted for prints, and a copy made that I can read. In the meantime," he growled as he soldiered her along the path to her car, "Jack Griffin or Peter Whose-its may take it in his head to get even with you for setting him up. If he does, I want mine to be the first face he sees when he comes knocking on your door."

Tabitha stopped in her tracks, halting Nate's forced march. "I know he was surprised and . . . and . . . angry, but after he cools down, I mean, you don't really think he'd try to hurt me—"

"Yes, O Magnificent But Daffy Swami, I *do*."

"And here I'd wanted to *nurture* you!" she sputtered, pulling her car keys from her pocket. "I have news for you, Inspector, I can change *nurture* to *neuter* with a little imagination and a sharp knife!"

As they reached her white Civic, with a quick motion, he turned her, backing her up until her butt was pressed against the passenger door. His hands came down on the roof on either side of her body, trapping her.

"I don't think you want to do that, Tabby," he murmured, leaning closer. His eyes held a glint that could have been menace—or lust. "I don't think you want to do that at all."

Chapter 13

Pin your socks in the shape of a cross at the foot of your bed, to keep bad dreams away.

FOLKLORE

He'd lost the book! In the struggle with that cop, he'd dropped the goddamned dream log!

Peter fought to calm himself and think.

Maybe the cops wouldn't find it. The night had been dark and foggy. Some kid could come across it tomorrow and toss it in the trash. Nobody knew what it was, just a bunch of scribbling that wouldn't mean anything to anybody who didn't *know*. Even if the cops did find the thing, it was just one of those blank-page journals his sister had bought and never used. He'd never put his name in it; it would be quite a stretch to connect it to him.

Fingerprints. Damn, yeah, fingerprints. But he'd never been printed, so even if they lifted some, there was nothing to match it to.

But Tabitha . . . she'd seen it and could identify it as belonging to him.

Peter's stomach squeezed hard, and he thought he might puke.

Well, nothing he could do about the diary now, he thought. Damn. The only thing he could hope for was that it had been overlooked in the fog. He sure as hell wasn't going to go back there to look for it.

Dawn played with the horizon, lightening it a shade or two, teasing the sun to rise and give California another perfect day.

He slid the Jag into the garage and turned off the ignition. Finally able to relax, he let his tired body slump behind the wheel as anger and depression hollowed out his insides.

She'd set him up. The woman he'd trusted with his innermost thoughts, with his worst fears and literally his most horrific nightmares, had set him up. She'd been his last hope; now he had none. There was nowhere to turn.

His heart in shreds, his brain a tangled mass of emotions, he walked from the garage toward the private entrance that led upstairs to the bedrooms.

His eyes burned in their sockets as he quickly took the flight of back stairs at the opposite end of the upper hallway from the grand staircase. At the landing, he stopped and listened before head-

ing for his room. The only sound came from the
ancient grandfather clock that stood in the mar-
bled foyer below, its deep and steady ticking like
the beat of an innocent heart.

Peter rubbed his eyes. Sleep, rest, a total and
complete zone-out, that's what he needed. He'd
sort all this out tomorrow. Somehow, some way.
He wasn't a killer, he just *couldn't* be. But the
dreams . . . so real . . . so violent . . .

"Peter?"

He jerked around to see his sister standing a
few feet away in the open doorway of her room.
Her hair was pulled back in a ponytail, and she
wore her gold and black running outfit.

"Z-Zoey," he stammered. "Kind of early to be
going for a run."

His sister was three years older than he and
nearly as tall. She looked as beautiful as she had
when they'd crowned her homecoming queen
twenty years ago. A well-disciplined exercise fa-
natic, she was toned and trim and her clear complexion glowed with health. Her eyes were blue,
like his, like their father's, and at the moment
were bright with alarm.

"Are you hurt?" she said, taking him in, rumpled hair to soggy shoes. "What's happened? Is
that *blood* on your shirt?"

"I'm okay," he rushed. "It's okay. I just need
to get cleaned up, get some sleep. It's . . . it's not

what it looks like. Just a little accident."

Her delicate chin lifted and she looked deeply into his eyes. He hadn't fooled her at all. She knew him better than anyone, better than he liked. When she spoke, her tone was almost parental.

"Something's been going on, Peter, and I want to know what it is. You come and go at all hours of the day and night, and you just look like hell. I think it's time we talked."

He swallowed past a painful lump in his throat. Taking in a breath, he blew it out slowly, letting his shoulders drop, letting his heart quiet, letting it all go.

"Yeah, Zoey," he said quietly. "Let's talk."

"So he spent the night at your house?" Rajani Jaspreet's dark eyes widened, gleaming with mischief. She tucked a lock of shiny hair over her ear and leaned across the small café table. "In your bed? Did you have sex? *Tell* me you had sex with this guy. *Tell* me the earth moved."

Tabitha assessed her best friend over the rim of the paper Starbucks cup she held in her hand. "He slept on the couch in my office. By the time I got up he was gone, but he'd folded the blankets, made coffee, rinsed out his mug, and put it away."

"He folded . . . rinsed . . . put . . ." A dreamy look crossed Jani's face. "God, if he was that considerate with a coffee mug, imagine how he'd be in bed."

"Not going there." Tabitha sipped the decaf orange nonfat no-whip iced mocha through her straw. The glop of crushed ice rattled as the volume of liquid in the dome-lidded container dwindled. "What time do you have to pick up the girls?"

Checking her watch, Jani said, "Not until three. We still have a half an hour, and don't change the subject. His name is actually *Darling*? How perfect is *that*? Tabitha . . . Darling . . ."

"Stop it!" Tabitha tried to suppress her smile, but it didn't work very well. "Grown-up women do not play that game."

Jani snorted. "Right."

The two had been best friends since college. They'd each married about the same time, but while Tabitha and Cal had problems right from the start, Jani and Jay's marriage had flourished. After Jay finished med school, they'd gone ahead and begun their family, which consisted of Anjali and Meera, who, at the ages of two and five were probably the prettiest, smartest, most angelic creatures on the planet . . . when they were asleep. Awake, they were black-eyed, raven-haired, giggling she-devils, into everything and impossible not to adore.

"Jani," Tabitha said with a halfhearted scowl.

"Nate Darling is totally wrong for me. First off, he's a cop. Second, he's arrogant. Third, he's dictatorial. Fourth, skeptical—"

"Apparently he's also a hunk and a half with a sexy case of myopia, and you haven't had a good roll in the hay since Cal left." She drained the rest of her jasmine iced tea and set the empty container on the table. "Seduce him. You're beautiful. He won't resist. He'll thank you for it. You'll thank yourself for it. Hell, *I'll* thank you for it because you'll stop being so snippety and edgy all the time."

"Wha— I'm never snippety and edgy!"

Jani arched a brow.

Tabitha sighed. "Point taken. And I'm not beautiful, but thank you for saying so." She rolled her straw between her fingers. "He investigated me, behind my back."

Understanding softened Jani's eyes. "Well, he *is* a detective, and you *do* have a suspicious client. I wouldn't beat him up too badly over that, Tabs."

Tabitha considered her friend's words. "Yeah, you're right. I only got upset because it was *him*, and now he knows stuff about me. If I only thought of him as *just* a detective, that would be one thing, but I, uh, I don't."

"What do you think of him as?"

"I obviously find him attractive, and I don't just

mean physically. I think he's somebody I could *be* with."

She sat back in her chair and tilted her head. "He's very smart, and has this sort of off-the-wall sense of humor . . . just the kind I like. And he's got a social conscience. He volunteers on his own time at a women's shelter. And then there's this look he gets in his eyes sometimes, like there's something deep down inside his soul that he's a little bit sad about. A yearning for something he's lost."

"Oh, dear," Jani said with a sympathetic smile. "Nothing is more attractive to a woman than a man who needs her. You're falling, aren't you?"

"I feel like I am, but it's so confusing." Furrowing her brow, she said, "At what point does love begin, anyway? First you find someone physically attractive according to your own criteria of what's appealing. Then you interact with him for a while and he either continues reinforcing that attraction until you realize you're in love, or his words and actions have the opposite effect, and you eliminate him as a possibility."

"That's how women do it, anyway," Jani said. "Most men seem to fall in love with a face and body, and if she's not a total bitch—and sometimes even if she is—that's love to them. Over time, they may develop a stronger attachment, because, let's face it, men need women more than women need men—"

"That's a pretty cynical point of view, coming from a happily married woman," Tabitha laughed.

"Happily married," Jani countered, "but not deaf, dumb, and blind. And definitely not stupid. Jay's wonderful, and I know he loves me, but underneath it all he's a *man*, first and foremost."

Tabitha shrugged. "I don't know how to fall in love like a man does it. I only know how to fall in love like I do it, but I'm not sure I want to. After what Cal did to me, I swore off men."

Jani smiled. "Well, swear them back on again. This Nate's good-looking, built, smart, funny, interesting, has a steady income, and he likes you. He's caring and compassionate and sweet. Stop overanalyzing the situation and go for it. See what happens."

Tabitha pressed her lips together. Avoiding Jani's full-frontal challenge, she said, "I don't want to get hurt."

Lowering her palms to the table, Jani whispered, "You, and about a bazillion other women on this planet. It's only sex, hon, not a life sentence. You need to get back in the saddle, and this guy sounds like the man to do the job. Like, ride 'em, cowboy. And if that doesn't work, think of it as therapy." She grinned. "If you need to show him a note from your doctor, I can get Jay to write one for you."

Tabitha crossed her arms over her stomach. Shifting her attention away from the dilemma at hand, she looked beyond Jani's shoulder at the Golden Gate Bridge in the distance, its elegant towers, dipping cables, and rigid trusses turned crimson in the afternoon sun.

"You know, the Golden Gate Bridge isn't really red," she mused aloud. "It's international orange."

"I care."

Tabitha stabbed her friend with a fake look of shock. "Well, you should. As a San Franciscan—"

"Tabs," Jani said softly. "What are you going to do about your sexy detective?"

Tabitha tossed her empty coffee container in the trash behind their table. "I don't know. The next move is up to him, if there is a next move to this . . . situation. He was very upset with me for going to meet Peter. I've tried talking to him about my abilities, but Nate just doesn't believe in them. He isn't even willing to entertain the possibility that the paranormal can coexist alongside what he considers normal, and that some of us can live in both those worlds."

"Is he coming to your house again tonight?"

"No, but he called me earlier with a list of dos

and don'ts—do not go here, do not go there, don't
do this, don't do that." She snorted. "For a list of
dos and don'ts, it was pretty skimpy on the dos.
He says these rules are for my safety. He says he's
being cautious because he says Peter may be bent
on revenge."

"*He* says. What do you say?"

Tabitha closed her eyes for a moment, trying to
sort out what she knew, from what she thought,
from what she sensed. Opening her eyes, she said,
"On the one hand, we have Peter, who has dreams
of killing people who actually turn up dead."

"That would sure freak me out," Jani said.

"Agreed. Then he came to my house and tried
to choke me."

"Not exactly the actions of an innocent man."

"Maybe. Maybe not. When he realized I'd set
him up, he became furious."

"Tabs," Jani said, her dark eyes clouded with
worry. "This does not sound good. I mean, this
Peter guy could be a homicidal maniac, and now
he's pissed at you. Like, get a gun or a big dog or
something."

Tabitha nodded. "I know it looks bad. It really
does. But I also trust my instincts. I always have,
and they've never steered me wrong."

"What about Cal?"

"Okay, they were briefly blinded by love and
crashed into a wall. But with Peter, I don't know

how to explain it except to say that, even though there's all kinds of evidence he could be a killer, I'm remaining hopeful that there's another explanation."

Jani's mouth flattened and she looked skeptical. "Maybe your subconscious simply cannot accept you could know a man who could commit murder."

"Yeah. Maybe. Damn. I just . . . I feel terribly helpless, stuck in the middle of all this, and I don't even know what *this* is. I feel like I want to do something, take some kind of action. And on top of all that, I can't get the police to work with me. If Nate would just acknowledge my psychic abilities and take advantage of them, I might be able to help."

Jani nodded a few times and relaxed back into her chair. "You need an edge here. Some kind of attention-getter. This guy played football, right?"

"Yeah, he has that *I literally eat cheerleaders for breakfast* quarterback look about him."

Tabitha tried not to imagine Nate after a game, all sweaty, muscles ripped, hair tousled, heading for the showers with only a towel wrapped around his hips. When that didn't work, she tried not to groan out loud.

With a Cheshire cat smile on her lips, Jani said, "You need to bring this man around, show him what you want, on your terms. Find a way to make him listen to you and take you seriously."

"And while I'm at it, I'll cure world hunger, plug the hole in the ozone, and keep Paris Hilton out of the tabloids."

Picking up her purse, Jani stood. "It's not as impossible as you might think. I'm taking you to the sporting goods store. They'll have just what you need. We can pick up Anji and Meera on the way."

Tabitha slipped the strap of her handbag over her shoulder. "The sporting goods store? What I need for what?"

"It's a little something I've been using on Jay. Works like a charm. C'mon. We have some shopping to do. Hut-one, hut-two . . ."

"Goddammit."

Nate flopped down in his chair at the precinct, a carefully made copy of the dream log in his hand, the acid of disgust etching his insides. His nose hurt like hell, his muscles ached from last night's tussle with Peter, his self-esteem sucked, and the latents the lab had gotten off the diary had careened him into a dead end.

To top it all off, he'd awakened that morning on Tabitha's couch with a killer erection, making it impossible to pee for nearly half an hour. To pass the time and take his mind off sex, he'd folded the blankets, made some coffee, and finally found a mug that didn't have kittens or "World's Best Mom" on it. By the time he'd cleaned up his mess, his body had begun to cooperate.

Bob Stocker appeared beside Nate's desk and slid into the extra chair. Popping his gum, the older detective chided, "Looks like somebody needs a hug."

Tossing the packet of copies onto the mass of paperwork cluttering his desk, Nate said, "The lab picked up lots of prints on the front and back covers of the dream log. Problem is, from the time it was manufactured to the time it was purchased, any number of people had their paws on it. Bottom line, the covers are a mess."

Bob slid his glasses on, then scratched his chin with his knuckles. "What about inside, on the pages?"

"A good idea, except the paper is that real artsy-fartsy grainy stuff. Which leads me to think the book was a gift, or borrowed from a wife, daughter, girlfriend. A man probably wouldn't buy something that cutesy for himself."

"Maybe a gay friend gave it to him?"

"*Queer Eye for the Straight Homicidal Maniac?*" Nate snorted. "Anything's possible."

He relaxed back into his chair, stretched out his long legs, and crossed them at the ankles. "Most of the prints the lab was able to lift from the pages were either incomplete or too vague to read. They scored a couple, though. Ran those through the database. There were no hits, but . . ."

Bob snapped his gum and folded his hands over his flat belly. "That *but* sounds promising."

Leaning toward his partner, Nate said, "One of the prints matched a partial we found on that broken glass in the alley."

"The shard of green wine-bottle glass?"

"Yeah. However, the other print from the diary didn't match anything at all. The cashier, maybe, or a customer thumbing through it in the store. The prints I snagged from Tabby's office came up zero for a match against anything."

If his partner picked up the fact Nate had referred to Ms. March by her first name, he didn't react. Instead, he said, "Well, the good news is, you placed the owner of the dream log at the scene of the alley murder. Good work, Inspector."

Not so much, Nate thought. If Tabby hadn't told him about the green bottle in Griffin's dream, he wouldn't have gone looking for one.

Since the implications of what that meant were too much to handle for his metaphysical resistors, and challenged every belief he'd ever had, he let it go for now.

Bob's gaze flicked over Nate's face. "You doing okay? That was quite a smack you took last night."

He shrugged. "I'm fine. My revenge will come

when I put this guy away. Well, when *you* put this guy away. I keep forgetting I'm not on this case." Handing a copy of the journal to Bob, he said, "I'm keeping a copy. It's a mess, real hard to read, so it's going to take some time to decipher. Guy must have written it down with his eyes closed and his arm in a sling." Glancing at his watch, he said, "It's almost five and the ball game starts at seven. Just enough time to clean up, pick up my date, and get down to the stadium."

Bob sat straight up and his jaw dropped. "No shit? You got tickets to the game tonight? The Giants versus the Seattle Mariners? Who'd you sleep with, the baseball commissioner?"

"A gentleman never tells."

"You're so full of it, Darling. That's just one of the reasons I love ya." Bob frowned. "Damn. They only face off once a season. Guess I know who you'll be rooting for."

"Guess so."

"Who's the lucky lady? And I hope she's a baseball fan, because if she ain't, I suggest you dump her and take me instead."

Nate stood and shoved the copy of Peter's dream log into his briefcase. "Tabitha March."

Bob's brow furrowed and he rapped his knuckles on his knee. "Really. She doesn't strike me as a baseball fan—"

"Bob," Nate interrupted. In a low, solemn voice,

he said, "She knows who won the 1962 World Series. And the teams who played. *And* the final score."

His partner's eyes glazed over and he looked away, staring into space as though mesmerized by the very air. Softly, he mouthed, "Wow."

"Yeah."

Blowing out a big breath, Bob narrowed one eye on Nate. "You think she's on the level? That she really can see people's dreams?"

"No." Nate rubbed his jaw, then shook his head. Shoving his glasses back up on his nose, he said, "Not really. But she believes it, and . . . ah, hell. I don't know what to think anymore. She's intelligent, well educated, grounded in reality for the most part. I don't get how she can believe that she 'sees' her clients' dreams."

"What do you think it is?"

He shrugged. "Guesswork? Finely tuned intuition? The ability to read people really well? Lies? Shit, I don't know. She's licensed, and as long as people willingly give her money and are happy with their results, there's nothing the law can do about it. All I know is, it'll be a cold day in Fresno before I buy into ESP and all that other hocus-pocus crap."

He snapped the lock on his briefcase. Not only was Tabitha the key to the investigation, but she'd affected him as well. She intrigued him in a way no woman ever had. And as pushy and bossy as she was, he liked her, liked being with her, liked the sound of her husky voice, the sparkle in her eye.

When he'd talked with her mom an hour ago, Victoria had assured him that Tabby was home for the evening and had no plans.

Well, he thought as he headed for the door, maybe she didn't have any plans, but he sure as hell did.

Chapter 14

> No mirrors in your bedroom! It is bad luck to
> sleep with any part of your body reflected in a
> mirror.
>
> FOLKLORE

"Ms. March? I'm Lucy Anderson. We spoke on the phone?"

Tabitha smiled at the tall woman standing on her porch.

The San Francisco fog had crawled in once more, pressing against the city streets, chilling the air, and apparently justifying the angora tam, fur-trimmed jacket, and white leather gloves her visitor wore. Even bundled up as the Anderson woman was, it was impossible not to notice her fine bone structure, intelligent eyes, clear complexion, and spa-toned body.

Closing the front door, she escorted Lucy into her office. When they were both settled on the couch, Tabitha said, "You mentioned on the phone that you had some important information concerning one of my clients, but you didn't say which one."

"I thought it best to wait," Lucy replied, her voice pitched lower than Tabitha's, her tone one of restrained authority. "I didn't want to discuss it on the phone. This is very . . . difficult for me."

Lucy's hair had been tucked entirely under the tam, making it impossible to tell its color, style, or length. Even so, she had that look about her, that money look, and Tabitha figured her for frequent visits to the salon and a hairstyle that was simple and yet expensive to maintain.

The money was there, too, in the way she held herself, chin slightly raised, blue eyes gazing at Tabitha steady on, then flicking away to peruse the room as though taking some kind of inventory.

"Difficult," Tabitha said. "In what way?"

Lucy flicked her tongue over her perfectly lip-lined mouth, a quick motion, efficient. "It's an acquaintance of mine. Someone I'm rather fond of. He told me he's been coming to see you. He's been behaving very strangely for the last few months, and when I asked him about it . . ."

Tabitha's stomach cramped, and she felt a lump form deep down in her throat. Swallowing, she nearly choked on her next words. "Who is your friend?"

Lucy gave Tabitha a very odd smile. "Peter."

Ten thousand thoughts clashed inside her brain. She waited a moment while her heartbeat returned to normal, then said, "In what way has he been behaving strangely?"

Lucy settled back into the cushions, crossing her long legs. Her beige slacks were wool and exquisitely tailored. Tabitha didn't know squat about designer shoes—except for the fact she would never be able to afford them—but she'd bet her meager bank balance that Lucy Anderson's shoes were Guccis or Pravdas, or at the very least, Manuelo Blablinks, or whatever in the hell they were called.

"I'd prefer not to go into detail," Lucy insisted. "At any rate, Peter and I had a lengthy discussion wherein he explained he'd run somewhat afoul of the law."

"It's true. Did he tell you the police want him for questioning?"

"Yes. That's why I'm here." She paused for a moment and appeared to gather her thoughts. Then, on a deep breath, she said slowly, "Peter is not capable of murder. Believe me when I say he simply is not. He told me about the dreams, and how he was so troubled over them that he sought your help." She arched an impeccably plucked brow. "He *should* have come to me, but that's neither here nor there at this point."

Lucy straightened a bit and narrowed her eyes on Tabitha. "Are you on the level, Ms. March? Can you really do what you claim?"

"Yes."

Pinning Tabitha with a cold stare, she said, "You haven't helped him."

"I urged him to see a therapist, but he refused. There's only so much I can do." She hated that it sounded like an excuse, but the fact was, unless Peter came forward, there really *wasn't* anything she could do.

With her gloved fingers, Lucy tugged at her tam, then abruptly pushed herself to her feet. "I want you to tell the police they've got the wrong man, Ms. March."

Rising, Tabitha said, "I think you should be the one to talk to the police about this. There's nothing—"

"I don't want to become involved."

"But if Peter's talked to you, you *are* involved."

"Peter is a very powerful man. He has much to lose if he becomes entangled in accusations of murder. There's been enough turmoil since his father died last year as it is. Tell the police to leave him alone."

Tugging her jacket more closely around her body, she said, "I've got a long drive north and I have to get going if I'm going to miss rush-hour traffic over the bridge. Thank you for your time."

Without another word, she left the office and walked to the front door, Tabitha right behind her.

"Please, Ms. Anderson," she begged to the woman's retreating back. "Talk to the police. If Peter is innocent, then he can clear his name. You *do* think he's innocent, don't you?"

When the woman reached the bottom step of the porch, she stopped and turned to face Tabitha.

"Ms. March, I assure you, the only thing Peter is guilty of is writing down some nightmares. That is not a crime. If those dreams resemble actual homicides, it's purely coincidental."

Walking down the short red brick pathway, she opened the wooden gate. Tabitha followed her out to the sidewalk.

"Ms. Anderson, Peter attacked me, *and* he resisted arrest. He accosted two officers. If he has nothing to hide, why doesn't he turn himself in, talk to the police, get this all over with?"

But Lucy Anderson was already on her way to her car. Over her shoulder, she called, "Thank you for your time. Good-bye."

To ward off the chill, Tabitha slid her hands into her jeans pockets and hunched over a little. The thin blouse she wore wasn't nearly enough to stave off the bite of breeze coming up off the bay.

A few cars down from Tabitha's house, just in

front of a red Ford truck, Lucy opened the door and slid behind the wheel of a pristine white, very expensive-looking convertible.

Tabitha hurried to get closer. As Lucy cranked the wheel and rolled slowly away, Tabitha leaned around the truck, focused hard on the California plates gracing the rear bumper, and committed what she saw to memory.

Nate took Tabitha's call while he was in his car, on his way to her house—not that she was aware of that, of course.

"You got her plate numbers?" he said. "This could be just the lead we've been looking for. Great work, Tabby."

Lately, the graph of Nate's success with this case had been a study in peaks and valleys. At the sound of Tabby's voice, and at hearing she'd met a woman who claimed to know Peter, the arrow began heading north once more.

"Give me the numbers so I can run them."

At the other end of the connection, Tabitha seemed to stall. Then, "Um, okay, but I should probably mention that she was parked kind of far away."

"Okay."

"And," she muttered, "she was driving into the fog."

"Yeah. Okay. And . . ."

"And I was trying to stay hidden so she wouldn't see me—"

. "The. Numbers. If. You. Don't. Mind."

"Well, you don't have to get all pissy about it, Inspector."

"Pissy is my middle name, babe." Especially lately, ever since he'd met one very frustrating strawberry blonde. "The *numbers*?"

"Okay, okay," she huffed. "They're 4-N-Q-E-7–5–0. I think. Maybe the *N* was an *H*, and the *Q* may have been a zero. And it's possible the 4 was an *H*, too, and the last zero could have been a *Q*. And, uh, the *E* was maybe a *B*."

Silence.

When he said nothing, she snapped, "Well, at least you have *something* to go on now. Can't you just rearrange them and put them into a computer or whatever?"

His patience went right out the car window.

"I doubt even frigging NASA has a computer powerful enough to calculate the number of possible permutations based on all the variations of that one frigging license plate!"

"You said frigging twice."

"I frigging didn't say frigging nearly enough frigging times!"

Silence again.

"I did my best, Inspector." She sounded wounded, which made his conscience flinch.

"The woman was driving away. I wasn't properly prepared. It was all very spur-of-the-moment. I'm sorry."

He blew out a long breath, calming himself before he spoke again. "I know you did your best. I'm sorry I yelled."

This case was really getting to him. Two people were dead, maybe more. And everything was so elusive; even things that should have been solid—such as a simple license plate number—seemed to slip through his fingers. It still irked him that the suspect himself had gotten clean away. Not Tabby's fault, but his. He had no right to take his frustrations out on her.

"Listen," he said, his tone softer. "Is there anything you can tell me about this woman that I can use? What did she look like? What kind of car did she drive?"

"White."

"The woman or the car?"

"Both."

Was that *all* women knew about cars? he wondered. What color they were? "I mean the *make* of car, Tabby. Or the model."

"I know what you mean," she huffed again, "but I don't know anything about cars. It was expensive, white, a convertible."

"Top down, or up?"

"Up. Although you'd have thought she'd had

the top down, considering how she was dressed."

"Which was . . ."

She described the woman's clothing, finishing with, "I mean, it was chilly today, but she looked like she was on her way to the North Pole by way of Neiman Marcus."

"What did she say, exactly?" He shifted gears and guided the Accord up the hill.

"She said her name was Lucy Anderson, but I think she was lying. She claimed to be a close friend of Peter's, and that he's innocent and she wanted me to tell you, the police, to leave him alone."

Nate took the next corner and began looking for a parking space somewhere in the same time zone as Tabby's house. This time of evening, it could take a while.

"Okay, write everything down that you remember," he said, "and bring it with you."

"Bring it with me, when?"

"I'm circling the block. If I can't find a place to park, I'll just pull up in front and you can hop in."

She made an exasperated sound in her throat. "What are you talking about, Inspector Darling?"

"I'm off duty," he said, pulling beside the line of cars parked along the street in front of her house. "So it's Nate. You'll be screaming it later."

"In your dreams, pal."

"And dress warm. I'm taking you out, as in outside."

"Oh. Really. What if I have plans, Nate?" Again with the sharp *T*.

He smiled, knowing he'd won.

"I have two tickets, second level, first row at the railing behind home plate, to see the Seattle Mariners kick the Giants' asses."

The sound she made this time was more like a gasping squeal, and he had a tough time keeping his mind out of the sack, since it sounded exactly like the throaty sigh he was sure she'd make when he made her come.

Through his windshield, he watched as the curtain over her bedroom window fluttered, and there she stood, glaring out at him, phone in one hand, crumpled lace curtain in the other. Her eyes widened, then pinched, making her adorable nose crinkle.

"You're here!" she accused. "You *could* have given me a little notice."

He smiled up at her. "Sure, but I'm a spontaneous kind of guy." Which was a big fat lie. As soon as he'd found out she liked baseball, he'd moved heaven and earth and paid a premium price for those tickets, but after their date-that-wasn't-a-date, he'd been hesitant to ask her in advance. Now, with him double-parked in front of her house, the lure of two prime seats in his hot hands, she couldn't refuse.

"Unfortunately," she drawled, "the Giants will prevail and your sorry-assed Mariners, who have *never* won a pennant, by the way, will head home in disgrace with their tails between their legs."

He gazed up at her. "Care to place a small wager on that?"

She slid her index finger along the inside of the window glass, and he could almost feel her touch along his belly.

"I'd be ten kinds of fool to bet with you, Inspector, since I have a suspicion a victory on your part would involve some sort of sexual escapades."

He grinned. "You'd be right. But if you're so sure the Giants are going to win, then you have nothing to lose."

"Don't let this fluffy hair and these big blue eyes fool you, Inspector. I only make wagers on sure things, and there's just enough of an outside chance the Mariners could squeak by to make me into a chump for taking your bet."

She disappeared from view, and the curtain fluttered back into place. "I'll be down in ten," she said. "Keep your motor running." The connection went dead.

Oh, his motor was running, all right. Ten minutes. Ten long minutes for him to imagine her tearing off her clothes to put on something appropriate for a chilly evening's baseball game. If she was like most women, she'd change her underwear. A thong would be hot. He let his imagination go with that one for a moment. And no bra. *All the better to get my hands on you.* The hands in question began to dampen. Jeans that hugged her curves would be good, too. Maybe a tight sweater. . .

He ordered his groin to behave as he flicked another glance at her bedroom window, just as the yellow square turned dark.

It didn't really matter what she wore tonight, or how much care she took to get herself all frilled up, because as soon as the game was over, he was getting her out of those clothes—one way or another.

Chapter 15

*To dream of sports is a favorable omen; to dream
of baseball indicates you will have a happy home
life.*

FOLKLORE

Tabitha huddled in her seat, watching the fog
blow in from the bay, softening the ballpark's
bright lights to bursts of gray fuzz.

Curling her hands into fists in her jacket pockets, she hunkered down a little more, waiting for
Nate to return with the drinks and stadium dogs,
hoping he remembered to slather hers with mustard.

The game wasn't going well—not from Nate's
perspective anyway. She grinned. Poor baby. The
Giants were trouncing the Mariners—just as she'd
known they would. He was trying to be stoic
about it, but every time a San Francisco player
had a good at-bat, Nate would grunt. Whenever

a Seattle player struck out, he would remain silent and sullen through the crowd's cheers. At the top of the seventh, San Francisco led ten-to-one. A victory at this point for the Mariners was highly doubtful, much to Tabitha's not-so-secret delight.

She took in a deep breath and caught a whiff of damp, briny air; peanuts and salt from the kid two seats down. The rowdy college guys behind her were drinking beer and she could smell the mellow hops. She caught a pinch of somebody's spicy aftershave, and the beefy scent of boiled hot dogs and relish. Down on the pitcher's mound, the Giants' young relief pitcher wound up and blasted one over plate. His hard-thrown ball smacked into the catcher's mitt like knuckles to the jaw.

"Strike two!" the umpire barked. Swiveling his body, he thrust out his right arm, two fingers extended.

The next pitch brought the knock of a Louisville slugger as it connected with the cowhide ball, sending it high into a pop fly. Easy pickings for the shortstop, ending the Mariners' at-bat. Tabitha smiled with satisfaction and settled back into her seat while the teams changed places on the field.

Watching the game was good, but being with Nate was fantastic.

Sitting next to him, so close she could feel the

electricity charge through his strong, healthy body, she felt a connection with him she hadn't felt with a man for a very long time—maybe ever.

"For you," he'd said as she'd slid into the passenger seat of his car. In his grip, he held a bouquet of pink, blue, and white sweet peas, which he thrust into her hands after she'd buckled her restraints. When she looked surprised, he shrugged and mumbled shyly, "When I talked to your mom she said they're your favorite flowers. My neighbor lady grows them and told me these are the first of the season. They, uh, they smell good."

Tabitha had buried her nose in the bouquet, taking in the spicy sweet perfume. When she raised her head and looked at him, she smiled. "I love sweet peas. Thank you."

Little fluttery things began flapping around in her heart when he smiled back. She felt light and happy and couldn't stop grinning. Jani's words came back to her—*You're falling, aren't you . . .*

No, not really. Not on purpose, anyway. Okay, maybe. A little. Okay, maybe a lot.

When they'd taken their seats at the stadium, he put his arm around her to keep her warm—he claimed—and she'd tucked into him, letting her defenses go for an hour or so, all in the name of warding off the chill, of course. And because being close to him felt so good.

She raised her head to remark on the Giants' extraordinary bullpen, but he'd stopped her words with a kiss. Not a ballpark peck, not a what-a-fun-date smooch, not a teaser. A bedroom kiss. One of those long, deep, wet kisses involving tangled tongues, mingled breaths. Her eyes drifted closed and she envisioned being wrapped in his arms like this night after night after night . . .

Tabitha could almost see the triumphant look in Jani's eyes. *You* are *falling, aren't you . . .*

Yes, yes, yes, oh, yes . . .

When he pulled back from the kiss, she rasped, "If you don't feed me, I'm going to pass out."

"I got it covered," he grinned, then pushed to his feet. "How do you like your dogs?"

"With a cold beer and lots of mustard."

He leaned down then, raised her face with his knuckle, and kissed her again until she could barely breathe. The guys in the row behind them snorted and snickered and elbowed each other. Apparently, Nate didn't care. Against her mouth, he whispered, "Keep *your* motor running."

She watched him make his way through the crowd, and couldn't help but admire his muscular body and the effortless way he moved. He was sweet and charming and fun, and she couldn't help but let herself fall just a little—

"Bith! Bith? Like, hello?"

Tabitha shook her head, abruptly ending her

reverie. Lifting her gaze, she realized there was a man standing at the railing in front of her.

Cal? "Cal?"

Well, if that just didn't put a damper on the evening. She felt her smile head south and the effervescent tingle in her body turn to an uncomfortable electric shock. "What are you doing here?"

He snorted a laugh. "Same as you, I guess. Watching the ball game."

Cal didn't like baseball. "You don't like baseball."

Running long fingers through his perfectly styled brown hair, he said casually, "Tastes change. Besides, my new girlfriend's uncle has season tickets. You really need to lighten up, Bith—"

"Don't call me that," she snapped. "I hated it when we were married, and I hate it now. It comes out sounding like you're just too drunk to say bitch."

"Now, Bith. Would I ever thay that to you?" He fake hiccupped, then laughed, showing the white teeth and deep dimples that had so captivated her back when she was terminally young and hormonally stupid.

Sliding under the railing, he plopped into Nate's vacant seat and curled his arm around her. She tried to squirm away, but he gripped her shoulder, holding her in place.

"I'm going to win, you know," he said lightly

as his fingers dug into her shoulder. "Like I said, my girlfriend's uncle is this crack attorney—"

"And here I thought you were just a weed sort of guy."

"Not that kind of crack. Crack as in, I'm going to get the house, *Bith*. Count on it."

She squirmed harder, then showed him her doubled fists. "Move your arm, or I'm going to hurt you."

From behind them, one of the college kids kicked the back of Cal's seat.

"Dude. Like maybe you should do like the lady says."

"Fuck off," Cal said, then grinned. "Besides, this is no lady, this is my wife."

Before World War III could break out, Tabitha turned to the boys and gave them a reassuring smile. Raising her palm, she said, "Thanks. It's okay. Really. Thanks."

All five guys glared at Cal, and the kid who'd kicked the seat said, "Yeah, okay. But, like, you just say the word."

She nodded, then turned back to Cal.

"Leave before you cause a riot."

"I'll go when I'm ready," he said, letting go of her but not leaving. "How much you figure that old relic is worth? Two million? Three?"

She glared into his calculating gray eyes. "Regardless of its worth, my grandmother left that house to me—"

"She left it to *us*, sweetheart," he corrected. "I want the house or half its value in cash, or I'll keep you tied up in court for so long it'll bankrupt you and you'll be forced to sell it. Either way, I get what's coming to me."

She only wished.

"I *live* in that house, Cal. My mother lives in that house. I have two boarders because the taxes and upkeep are so high, there's no way I can afford to stay there otherwise. It's never been renovated, the plumbing's bad, the wood's rotting in places, the kitchen needs a complete makeover. It would cost thousands and thousands of dollars to bring it up to speed. That's money I don't have, and I'm not plunging into a debt I can't possibly repay by borrowing against the house."

"My heart's breaking for you, sweetheart."

"Please, Cal. Even you can't be that cruel. It's not like I'm using the house as an investment—it costs me money, and it keeps four people, including two elderly ladies, from having to find reasonable housing in a very expensive city. If I do ever decide to sell it, I'll give you your half then, but for now—"

Tapping her nose with his forefinger, he said, "Not . . . good . . . enough."

She jerked away from him, tears of anger sting-ing her eyes. "Cal, even you can't be so mean-spirited—"

"Is there a problem here?"

Tabitha nearly jumped out of her seat.

Nate flicked a glance into her eyes, and what-ever he saw there made his mouth flatten and his jaw tighten. Without a word, he slowly directed that hard gaze at Cal.

In unison, all five guys behind them snickered, then chortled, "Dude."

Cal shot a quick glance from Nate to Tabitha, then back again. "No trouble, pal," he said lightly. "Just saying hello to an old friend."

"Try saying good-bye, *pal*."

Cal stood and dipped under the railing to stand next to Nate. With a small salute at Tabitha, he drawled, "Buh-bye, *Bith*. Remember what I said." One quick glance at Nate, and Cal swiveled on his heel and sauntered away.

Slipping under the railing, Nate took his seat. "Who was that asshole?"

Taking the food, she grumbled, "You read my file. Surely you can guess."

"Your ex."

She sipped the beer and took a bite of dog. Mmm. Mustard, and plenty of it. "Thank you."

"What did he want?"

"Money." She focused on her meal and tried not to think about how much it was going to cost to hire an attorney to fight her ex-husband. When it looked like Nate wanted to pursue the topic, she said, "I don't want to talk about Cal right now. He's a blight on my brain."

Nate gazed into her eyes for a long time, then nodded.

On the field, somebody apparently did something spectacular. The crowd jumped to its feet and cheers went up all around the stadium. In their excitement, one of the guys behind them spilled his beer, and Tabitha lifted her feet to let it trickle its sticky, smelly way down the concrete bleachers.

Nate took a big bite of his hot dog and looked over at her. The glint of humor had returned to his eyes. "Either the Giants did something really good," he said past the bulge in his cheek, "or the Mariners did something really bad."

She smiled, forcing herself to return her attention to the game. Across the field, the scoreboard now read twelve-to-two.

"Will you look at that," she sighed, forcing Cal's dumb-ass threats out of her head. "With only two innings to go, there is *no way* the Mariners can win."

Nate swallowed a gulp of beer. Wiping the foam

from his mouth, he said, "You'd be surprised. We've come from farther behind than this."

"Not this time."

"Bet?"

She looked at the scoreboard again. Two innings? Ten runs to catch up, eleven to win? Candy from a baby.

"Bet."

He switched his beer to his left hand and offered her his right. She took it, sealing the wager.

"If I win . . ." she drawled, then corrected herself. "I mean, *when* I win, we go back to that French restaurant and you order the escargot, and eat . . . every . . . bite."

He thought about it for a moment, then swallowed another gulp of beer.

"Okay," he said. "Fair enough. And if I win . . ."

"Which you won't," she assured him, then smiled sweetly, batting her eyelashes for good measure.

He pursed his lips and seemed to assess her for a moment.

At the base of her spine, a sort of trill, fizz, tickle sensation began making its way through her body to the parts that hadn't trilled, fizzed, or tickled for quite some time.

Leaning toward her, he moved her hair aside

and softly nuzzled her neck just below her ear. He suckled her earlobe, then bit it. "Did I mention I have one of those old-fashioned wrought-iron beds?"

Tabitha's eyes drifted closed and she caught her breath. Every muscle in her body wimped out on her.

"If I win . . ." he whispered slowly, his breath sending frissons of excitement all across her flesh. "*When* I win . . . you . . . naked . . . on that bed . . . stretched out . . . arms above your head, holding on tight . . . while I fuck you every which way from Sunday."

There is no joy in Mudville . . .

Tabitha let the words trickle through her brain like alphabet sludge. The crowd's moans and groans still pealed inside her head like a death knell as she and Nate made their way with the surge of dejected fans out to the parking lot.

No escargot. No every bite. Not tonight.

She swallowed. How had they done it? How in the *hell* had they done it?

When the Mariners tied the Giants' twelve runs at the top of the ninth, Tabitha had an unexpected urge to leap to her feet and shout, *Go Mariners!* But she had refrained. Why give Nate more sexual ammunition than he was already carrying?

Two innings later, Seattle finally brought home the winning run.

Unable to think past the erotic mental image Nate had created in her head, she walked along next to him, her hand captured in his. Every time she blinked, she could see herself stretched out on that bed, see him bending over her, feel him inside her.

If she let go of his hand, she'd certainly sink to the asphalt in a weak-kneed heap.

When they reached his car, he gently pushed her against it while he took her mouth. With her body arched backward, he curled over her, capturing her, completely enveloping her with his powerful sexual energy. Against her lower belly, she felt his erection. He shifted, rolling his hips into hers, and she made a high-pitched keening sound.

"I'm not going to hold you to it," he breathed against her ear. "I want to, but I'm not going to."

If she could have formed some kind of coherent sentence, she would have, but as it was, she was too paralyzed with pleasure to utter a single word.

"The bet," he murmured. "It was mostly a joke. We don't have to . . . I mean, I'm not going to hold you to it." He kissed her again, and her body went limp.

"That's very sweet," she panted against his

open mouth. "Gentlemanly. Considerate. Fair. I appreciate it."

He backed away and opened her door. With one final kiss, he said softly, "Get in. I'll take you home."

Sliding her arms around his neck, she pulled herself close, and when he bent his head to kiss her again, she whispered, "Hold me to it. Please."

He froze, searching her eyes. "You sure? Because if you're not sure—"

She stopped him with a kiss that told him in no uncertain terms just how sure she was.

Somehow, they got into the car. Fastened seat belts. Cranked the ignition ... moved through intersections, by stop signs, people walking ... green light, yellow light, red light. It all became a slow blur to her. *Can't this damn Accord move any faster?*

Every nerve ending she had was on edge. Her body ached with anticipation. Her nipples felt sensitive under her clothing and she couldn't get past what it would feel like when he finally sucked on them.

Finally, he parked in front of a house. She heard a car door slam.

Then he was there, opening her door, helping her out, helping her into his arms.

His mouth was warm, open, on hers. His hands moved inside her jacket, under her sweater. First his thumbs found her taut bare nipples, then his mouth, then his tongue, and she nearly collapsed from the pleasure.

The Seattle Mariners. She sighed. Oh, God, what a great baseball team . . .

Nate pulled away a fraction, swiping her nipple with his rough tongue. "Listen," he panted, running his hand down her belly to her crotch. "I'm only going to offer one more time. It was a silly bet. I'll stop. We don't have to—"

"Yeswedo." The words came out on a rushed exhale. When his finger slid between her legs, she caught her breath. "Don't stop," she softly squeaked. "God, don't stop . . ."

Somehow, they reached his second-floor apartment. Somehow, they got inside. Inside. Deep inside her body, she pulsed with exquisite need.

In the darkness of his apartment, he guided her to the bedroom. He pulled at her clothes, and they were gone. She felt his hands on her naked skin, touching her, not gently, not roughly, but everywhere, and she wanted to scream.

Slowly, he lowered her to the bed, pushing her legs wide, licking her . . . long strokes, wet and hot. A sigh formed in her throat, but before it could escape, he licked her again, and she arched her back, so filled with pleasure she couldn't make a sound.

"Nate . . ." His name was a prayer on her lips, softly imploring as she begged for release.

He moved up, kneading her breasts with his strong, warm fingers, exciting her nipples into peaks. His mouth covered one, and he suckled her, teasing the tight berry with his tongue, then his teeth, until she moaned.

She was totally naked, while he was still clothed. Why that made her feel sexier, she couldn't have said, but her palms began to dampen in anticipation of touching his skin.

Her fingers tugged at his clothing and in moments he was naked and cradled between her thighs. She ran her hands over his muscular body, his smooth, supple skin. Against her belly, she felt the ridges of his abs, the tease of hair around his navel, and lower.

Gliding her hands along the flat plane of his torso, she found the silky, damp tip of his penis, slid her hand down the shaft, curled her fingers around it . . . so long, so hard, so slick.

She positioned him against her swollen flesh. Warm pools of sensation flooded her body and she became restless.

"Put it in me," she breathed, tilting her hips, giving him pleasure, giving pleasure to herself. "I want to feel it, feel you. Hurry . . ."

He slapped at the nightstand. A water glass

crashed to the floor. A magazine went flying. A moment later, sheathed, he pushed into her and she closed tightly around him.

Ohgod-ohgod-ohgod . . .

At first, he did nothing. His breathing was labored, as though he were holding himself in rigid control. She felt the movement of his muscles and bones against her body, and she ached for him to move inside her.

Then he did, torturing her further, pleasuring the swollen nub with his rubbing, urging. She thrust and rolled her hips, and he groaned.

Nuzzling and kissing her neck, he breathed, "Tabby . . . God, you're so beautiful . . ."

She wanted to weep at the depth of emotion she heard in those words. Raising her arm, she cupped his skull in her hand, holding him to her while she closed her eyes and did nothing but feel the two of them together, treasuring the closeness she hadn't felt for so awfully long.

Turning her brain off, she focused on the slide of him, in and out, bringing her closer, and closer still.

He urged her legs wider, placing kisses down her neck, across her collarbone, between her breasts. Capturing a nipple in his mouth, he suckled it, bit it until the pleasure was too much and she began to buck. Her own anguished cries mixed with his harsh pants. She tilted her hips . . . there. Ah, there.

Reaching above her head, she stretched out her naked body, arching her back, and grasping the iron rails of the headboard.

Fuck me, she chanted inside her head. *Fuck me every which way from Sunday . . .*

He slammed into her again, the sound of his breathing harsh and rasping. Pulling back, he thrust in, this time more slowly, so slowly she felt every inch, staying her orgasm, keeping it out of her reach until she wanted to cry in frustration.

Tears filled her eyes—tears of elation, tears of passion, of excruciating anticipation.

Suddenly it was too much, and her body burst with sweet delight, the rush of pleasure flooding her, easing her taut muscles, bathing her flesh in a sensual froth as she clenched around him, and clenched again.

He grunted a satisfied sound, then shifted position, grasping the globes of her bottom in his large hands, and pulled her hard into him. His mouth open over hers, his tongue thrust deeply inside, he came, and she felt it, hot and thick inside the thin sheath.

Tabitha wrapped her arms around him and hung on, never wanting to let go, never wanting this to end, this connection, this closeness that she had never felt with another human being on the planet—not psychically, not physically, not emotionally.

Their bodies pressed close, their hearts slammed against each other's, their stomachs moved in and out, together in time, their sweat intermingled. Sex was messy. Sex was glorious.

For a while, neither of them spoke, but only breathed, and recovered, and savored.

The bones of his hips rubbed the inside of her thigh as she wrapped her legs around his calves. He collapsed against her, still trying to catch his breath.

She kissed his damp brow, ran her fingers lightly through his soft hair. He reached his hand up and slid his thumb along her jaw. They grinned into each other's eyes.

They laughed then, too sated to speak, amazed by what happened between them, its power, its glory.

He kissed her again, tenderly, and she tasted salt on his mouth, and she felt the curve of his smile against her lips.

There should be words to define this elusive and staggering moment, she thought. Words like love and forever and you and me, and she wanted to say them. For the first time in memory, she wanted to say them so badly, holding them back hurt her throat.

Abruptly, he lifted his head and his brow

creased. Seeing the little tear that escaped to trickle along her cheek, he searched her eyes. Tears could be good; tears could be bad. Not asking which, he simply kissed it away, his exquisite tenderness making her want to cry all over again.

Breaking the kiss, he said, "What's that noise?"

Me, beating on your heart with my doubled fists, begging to be let in . . .

Pushing himself up on his elbows, he snarled, "*Shit*. It's the front door."

On the table next to the bed, his cell phone chimed "Can You Feel the Love Tonight."

"Sorry," he said to her, and she could see in his eyes that he meant it. Making a grab for the cell, he thumbed the button. "I can't talk now, Ethan. Somebody's at the d—"

The banging on the front door ceased.

"All right," he growled. "Give me a minute."

Slamming the cell down on the nightstand, he pushed off of her and swiveled into a sitting position, glorious in his nakedness. Reaching for the blanket that had fallen to the floor, he covered her with it, then leaned down and gave her a kiss.

As he pulled away, Tabitha's sensual world closed in around her and collapsed. The heat cooled, the colors dulled, the words she had wanted so desperately to say faded like invisible ink on a page.

"What is it?" she asked, as reality slowly re-claimed her and began gnawing its way into her head. She could breathe now, and with each breath, common sense returned.

"Wait here until I see what's going on," Nate said as he stood and pulled on his crumpled jeans. "It's my brother. He's standing outside my front door, and God only knows why, but I have to let him in."

Chapter 16

For a man to dream of his brother, means trouble ahead.

FOLKLORE

Flinging the front door open, Nate confronted Ethan.

"I gave at the office."

Ethan returned his cell phone to the holster on his belt and pushed past Nate into the living room. "This couldn't wait," he said, casting glances at the furniture and décor, most of which had come from flea markets and garage sales. "I see the SFPD still doesn't pay its detectives a living wage. Why don't you get a real job, little brother?"

"Careful, or you'll hurt my decorator's feelings."

Spying the instrument case standing in the corner by the TV, Ethan said, "You still torture the trumpet?"

"When the spirit moves me and the neighbors

are on vacation. What about you? Still bringing tears to people's eyes with your—"

"Nope. Gave it up years ago."

Closing the door, Nate yanked the chain on the lamp next to the crammed bookcase, illuminating his brother's ever-present scowl. "It's one in the morning, Ethan." And his blood still hummed from sex with Tabitha. Somewhere between the bed and the front door, his body had recovered, and he was ready for round two. More than ready. Why in the hell had Ethan chosen *now* to—

"Mom's okay, right? And Andie? Nothing's happened—"

"They're fine." Ethan turned to face him. "I read Griffin's diary."

Nate's brows shot up. "How in the fuck did *you* get a copy—"

"Her mother said she was with you," Ethan interrupted. "I want to talk to her."

Before he could stop himself, Nate cast a quick glance at the closed bedroom door.

Ethan's gaze followed, then he turned and walked to the bay window that faced the street. "Get her."

Nate's blood heated a few degrees. "You can talk to her tomorrow, during normal business hours. Now get the hell out of here."

Over his shoulder, Ethan said, "If you don't go get her, I will."

Nate made a move toward Ethan at the same time the bedroom door opened. Both men swiveled to face Tabitha.

"No need to resort to fisticuffs, gentlemen. Ethan, is it? How can I help you?"

Nate moved quickly to put himself between her and his brother. She'd gotten dressed and smoothed her hair, but there was no mistaking the soft gleam in her eye, the flush of her skin, her plump lips. She'd just had satisfying sex, and it showed. Not that he wasn't proud that he'd been the man to do the job, but he hadn't planned on exposing her so blatantly to another man's scrutiny immediately afterward.

He suddenly felt like he needed to defend her honor, hide and protect her, make it clear she wasn't just some casual lay he'd brought home. But before he could say anything, Ethan spoke up.

"I'm Nate's brother."

"So I understand." Glancing quickly from one brother to the other, her brow furrowed. "You two don't look at all alike."

"Thank God," Nate mumbled under his breath.

"Prick," Ethan responded.

"Dickhead," Nate muttered. "Now that we've dispatched with the pleasantries, why are you here, and what in the hell do you want?"

*   *   *

Ethan Darling was absolutely gorgeous, in a dark and menacing and complex sort of way. If there was a woman in his life, Tabitha thought, she was either very strong or very weak.

"You wanted to talk to me?" She lifted her chin and looked directly into Ethan's sharp hazel eyes. He narrowed his gaze on her until she felt like she was being scanned by twin laser beams.

"There was a murder in Marin a month ago," he said. "The details match almost exactly one of the dreams in the journal."

Nate's response was immediate and furious. "Tell me how in the hell you got a copy of that diary."

Ethan only flicked a glance at his brother. "Connections."

It was obvious to Tabitha that Ethan was used to being in charge. She couldn't help but feel he was holding himself in check, keeping his emotions, his words, maybe even his thoughts under rigid control. There was anger in him, possibly rage. Here was a man who was all work and no play. To him, the world was a very serious place.

Past a lump in her throat, she whispered, "Which dream?"

"Why do you care, Ethan?" Nate said as he pulled a cream-colored cable-knit sweater over his head. "Was the victim rich and famous? Why isn't the Marin County Sheriff's Department handling it?"

Ethan's stark eyes followed his brother's every move. "The victim was a personal friend of mine," he said quietly. "His name was Walter Perez. He worked for me as head gardener at my house in Marin. I don't know what the Sheriff's Department is doing, and I don't care." His eyes turned colder, if that was possible. "*I* want this guy, and *I* am going to get him."

Before she could stop herself, Tabitha reached out and touched Ethan's arm, then snatched her hand away, half expecting to see burn marks on her fingertips. But the brief contact had been enough. His guilt and remorse had filtered through his bulwark of defenses, and she'd picked them up. So much anger . . . so much pain . . .

"I'm s-sorry," she stumbled, as he turned the full force of his gaze on her. "What do you want me to do?" It was all she could manage, given the way his eyes were searing her brain.

He took a piece of paper from his shirt pocket, unfolded it, and handed it to her. Her fingers shook as she looked down at the uneven scribbles on the photocopied page. She didn't need to read it to know exactly what it said.

I'm on a boat. It's very lonely out there on the water, nobody around on the flat blue sea. Then

I see another boat and a man with his line in the water, fishing. I come alongside. There is suddenly a weapon in my hand, and I point it at him. For a split second he looks at me, his expression curious, innocent of what I'm about to do. Then I see it in his eyes. He knows. He looks very sad. For no reason at all, I kill him. One shot, that's all it takes. He falls to the deck, dropping the fishing pole. His boat drifts silently away, out to sea, and is gone.

Tabitha nodded slowly. "I remember it. Peter came to me about it a month or so ago. I saw the dream very vividly, but—" Something itched the back of her brain. "What time of day was your friend killed?"

"Evening. He was heading back after spending the day fishing."

"Well, something's wrong, then. The dream took place in broad daylight, *while* the victim was fishing."

"The diary doesn't actually say anything about the time of day," Nate murmured, taking the page from her hand. Addressing his brother, he said, "What kind of weapon was used?"

"Shotgun. Both barrels."

"But that's not right, either," Tabitha rushed. "In the dream, it was a handgun of some kind. I saw it clearly."

Nate's mouth curved down on one side. "Tabby, I'm sure you think—"

"You don't believe me, do you?" She turned to face him. "You don't believe I saw Peter's dream. In fact, you don't believe I'm psychic at all."

He lifted a shoulder, pursed his lips, but refused to meet her gaze.

After what they had shared together, and he *still* didn't understand? He still had no idea who she was, what she was all about, what was important to her?

"The killings have taken place in various, seemingly unrelated locations, but it doesn't change the fact that three of them are described . . . in . . . that . . . diary." She punctuated her words by stabbing the paper in Nate's hand with her index finger.

Well, that sure proved the point. Men would have sex with anybody, anytime, anywhere, even a woman they didn't understand and maybe even thought were unbalanced.

The betrayal she felt made her chest squeeze and her throat tighten.

"Did you write down everything you remembered about the woman who visited you? Lucy Anderson?" Nate kept his eyes on the page in his hands.

From her jeans pocket, Tabitha withdrew a piece of paper and slapped it against Nate's chest. "There, Inspector. Knock yourself out. If you need my help, you know where to find me." Turning to Ethan, she said, "Would you please give me a ride home?"

Ethan looked like a shark cruising shallow water for an easy kill, but she didn't care. He shot a quick look at his brother, then his eyes narrowed on her. "Sure."

Nate grabbed for Tabitha's shoulders, but she pushed at him and stepped away.

"Tabby, listen," he said. "I can't just sacrifice evidence and logic for . . . What in the hell is *that*?"

While he'd been defending his stupidity, she'd reached into her right pocket and drew out a yellow kerchief, flinging it into the air right in front of Nate's nose. It dropped to the floor between them.

Ethan raised a brow. "A penalty flag?"

"Yes," she hissed. "My friend Rajani got it for me. For some strange reason, while men are not born with *any* comprehension of the female of their own species, all men everywhere *get* a penalty flag." Taking a much-needed breath, she said, "You've just been flagged, Inspector. Eight-billion-yard penalty for pigheadedness!"

Nate bent and picked up the cloth, crumpling it in his large hand—the hand that had delivered such pleasure to her body only an hour ago.

Blowing out a sigh, he said, "Look. You need to calm down. When you think about this ratio-

nally, you'll come to see that all your silly paranormal—"

She snatched the flag from his hand and tossed
it into the air again. It hit its apex, then dropped
to the floor, landing on Nate's big toe.

"Ow!" he yelped, bending to retrieve the flag
once more. "Goddammit, Tabby. These things are
weighted. Cut it out!"

"Not weighted enough, if you ask me," she
choked, grabbing the cloth from his hand and
stuffing it back into her pocket. "Ten-billion-yard
penalty for being a snake."

"So far you've compared me to a mule, a goose,
a pig, and now a reptile. At least I'm not a frigging
free-range escargot!"

Ethan opened his mouth, and Nate growled,
"Say one word, just one word, and I'll rip out
your tongue."

"Not a problem," Ethan said. "I was just going
to ask whether Tabitha is ready to go."

"No, she's not," Nate barked at the same time
Tabitha said, "Yes, I am."

When she got to the door, she turned to face
Nate, hating the words she was about to say, but
knowing she had to say them.

"This is for the best, Nate. You and I live in different worlds, and while I'm willing to give yours
a try, you can't even see mine. And apparently
you don't want to."

Silently, she and Ethan walked down the stairs and out to the street. He opened his car door for her, and she slid in. As soon as she fastened her seat belt, she pulled the yellow kerchief from her pocket, buried her face in the coarse fabric, and burst into tears.

"How long have you been in love with my brother?"

"I'm not." Tabitha sniffed into the water-repellent, rip-stop nylon; as hankies went, penalty flags were useless.

"C'mon," Ethan cajoled as he turned the key in the ignition and pulled out into traffic. "You don't do bullshit, and neither do I. How long?"

Dabbing her eyes with the crumpled fabric, she sighed, "I was falling for him, in a sick sort of way. But I went into remission before it became inoperable."

Laying her aching head against the headrest, she let the purr of the expensive engine lull her mind. When she felt her eyes fill with tears again, she cursed, then wiped them away and blew her nose.

Ethan shifted gears and headed up Powell. "Nate said something about a woman coming to see you. A woman who knows Peter."

"Yes," she sniffled, then coughed, then blew again. Taking a fortifying breath, she said, "She claimed to be a close friend of Peter's. She also said something about him being powerful, and that becoming involved in a scandal would ruin him."

"Anything else?"

"She said his father had died recently and that he, Peter, was under a lot of stress. Then she said she had to head back north because she had a long way to drive."

He seemed to mull this over for a moment. "What did she look like?"

Tabitha described Lucy Anderson, what little of her she'd seen that hadn't been obscured by her outfit. "I got her license number, um, sort of."

She watched as they drove by house after house. This early in the morning, everybody was still asleep. She wanted to be asleep, too. Longed to be—with Nate. Wrapped in his arms. She fought off another round of tears. How ridiculous it was to cry over Nate Darling. After all, she'd only been in love with him for a few minutes before she'd come to her senses.

Oh! Her bouquet of sweet peas. She'd left them in his car.

Burying her face in the penalty flag, she burst into tears again and sobbed until she thought her heart would break.

Next to her, Ethan growled some sort of profanity and slammed the wheel with the palm of his hand. "Hey. No man is worth it, okay?"

He sounded like he meant it, so she lifted her head and wiped her nose. Looking over at him, she said, "I thought Nate might be worth it, but I was wrong. He's a dunderhead."

Checking his rearview mirror, Ethan changed lanes, then turned left. "Are you really psychic?"

"Yes, but only when I touch people, and occasionally when I touch an object. But that's rare for me to do."

Pulling up in front of her house, he put the car in neutral, then leaned over and opened the glove compartment. "Here's a pen and paper. Write down the license number and a description of Lucy Anderson's car for me."

As she scribbled it all down, she said, "I've already given this to Nate, but he told me . . ."

She let her words drift off as she lifted her eyes to Ethan. He had a curious expression on his face.

When he took the pen from her hand, their fingers touched, and for an instant, an image blasted its way into her head.

"Ethan?" she whispered. "You live in Marin. You don't happen to know anyone who drives an expensive white convertible and who is close to a wealthy and powerful man named Peter whose father has died recently . . . do you?"

Chapter 17

*If a groom falls asleep first on his wedding night,
he will be the first in the marriage to die; if it is
the bride who falls asleep first, it will be she who
dies first.*

FOLKLORE

"Peter?"

At the sound of his name, Peter stumbled
around to face his sister. Rubbing his tired eyes, he
tried to focus on Zoey, but his vision just wouldn't
cooperate.

She stood a few feet away, more of a ghost than
a woman. Though he couldn't see her face clearly
in the darkness of the hallway, the disapproval
was plain enough in her voice.

His vision cleared a little, and he realized he
was standing just outside his bedroom door. Was
he coming out, or going in? What time was it?
Was it the middle of the night, or nearly dawn?

"Peter?" Zoey's voice was softer now, curious,

concerned. "It's five-thirty in the morning. Are you ill?"

He shook his head, but that just made his vision worse. Blinking at her, trying desperately to see her clearly, he said, "I'm fine. Just restless I guess."

"You, uh, you haven't been . . . out, have you?"

Had he? Why was he so confused? He looked down at his T-shirt, pajama bottoms, and bare feet.

"No. I've been asleep. Something woke me, I think."

"Was it . . . another nightmare?"

He searched his memory. Yes, he'd been asleep, very soundly, thanks to Zoey and her stocked-with-every-sleep-aid-under-the-sun   medicine cabinet. But no dreams, no nightmares had come. Still, something had wakened him, he was sure of it.

Maybe a gull, or a ship's horn, or the crash of a powerful wave had roused him to consciousness. His bedroom faced west and the sweeping grandeur of the Pacific Ocean. He always slept with his bedroom windows open, welcoming the sharp smell of the sea, along with the rhythmic sound of the surf crashing on the rocks at the foot of the bluff on which the mansion stood. The combination never failed to lull and soothe him to sleep—until the last few months, of course.

"Listen, Zoey," he said. "I, uh, I have a ten o'clock in the city, so I'm going to try to get a few more hours of sleep."

In the shadows of the hallway, Zoey nodded. She may have smiled, but Peter was still too out of it to tell.

"We can talk later, if you like," she offered. "You're sure you're okay?"

Turning the knob on his bedroom door, he nodded. "Yeah. Thanks."

He closed the door behind him, then went into his bathroom to pee. No need to turn on the light. Above his head, the domed skylight allowed the full moon to bathe the room with a cool, silvery glow. Flushing the toilet, he turned to wash his hands, and tripped over something.

Crouching, he examined the bundle on the Spanish tile floor. He recognized his old athletic shoes, a crumpled pair of jeans, and his favorite black and red flannel shirt. Except the red from the shirt had somehow bled onto his pants and shoes.

He stared at the garments for a moment, not quite comprehending what he was seeing. Letting the shirt drop from his shaking fingers, he held his palm in front of his face. His hand was sticky, and . . . red. Blood. Fresh blood on his clothing.

Grabbing the nearest towel, he frantically wiped all traces from his hands. He choked like a drowning man going down for the third time, frantic to breathe, gasping for air, air that failed to fill his lungs and relieve his suffering.

Not knowing what to think, how to feel, where to turn, he fell to his knees and covered his face with his hands.

"No," he sobbed. "*No*, not again. Please, God. Not *again*."

He should go to the police, tell them everything, at least what he knew, what he remembered. Except he didn't *remember* anything. They'd laugh their asses off, or lock him up in a high-security mental institution and freaking throw away the key.

Unless, of course, he really was a murderer. Then the penalty would be far greater.

He shook his head. No. *NO*. He was *not* a killer. It just didn't fit with the man he knew himself to be. He'd never had psychotic dreams in the past. As a kid, he'd never torn the wings off butterflies or tortured puppies. Hell, he was as nice and as easygoing a guy as anyone could meet. A party animal. He rarely got angry and when he did, he was pretty reasonable in sorting things out.

Yet the nightmares . . . and the blood. If there just wasn't any blood, he could write the whole damn situation off to some kind of bizarre cosmic coincidence. But as things stood, he just didn't know what was real from what was in his screwed-up head. What other possible explanation could there be?

No. No police. Not yet. Not until he *knew*.

He forced himself to focus, to concentrate. Yes, there was a way. There *was* a way, but it would have to be a secret, and in the end, he would know the truth.

Feeling a sense of control he hadn't felt in months, Peter rose to his feet and looked at his reflection in the dark mirror. Was that the face, were those the eyes of a psychotic murderer? He didn't used to think so, but if he was wrong, if it turned out he was a monster . . .

Slowly shuffling into his bedroom, he went to his nightstand and pulled open the drawer. With his thumb, he eased aside a notebook and some papers to reveal the revolver, its blue-black barrel glinting in the moonlight.

He took in a deep breath and let it trickle out of his lungs, then closed the drawer again.

If it turned out he was a monster, he may not know how it had begun, but he knew how it would end.

Nate sat on his bed. His cold, empty, disheveled bed—the bed that still held the scent of seduction and sex, and Tabitha. Though morning light filled the room, it did nothing to ease his unhappiness.

As long as he lived, he'd never forget the sight

of her reaching for those iron bars, stretching out her body underneath him, offering herself to him with everything she had.

Gazing down at the pillow next to his, he let his eyes wander over the blue-striped sheets and tousled navy spread. Funny how his bed had never seemed so big and lonely before.

He'd wanted her there the whole night. He'd wanted her up one side and down the other. Under him, above him, bare-breasted and bare-bottomed over the arm of his favorite chair, on his lap, on his knees, every which way from Sunday—and Monday, and Tuesday, and April and August and December, and this year and next year and the year after that . . .

But she'd flown out the door the moment she'd gotten the chance, and it was his fault.

He took off his glasses and rubbed the bridge of his nose, wondering if she realized just how much she was asking of him. It's not that he wasn't willing to change the beliefs of a lifetime, but that kind of shift took time *and* a desire to change, and for him, the jury was still out. Were psychic abilities real, as Tabby claimed, or were they just so much hogwash based on finely tuned intuition and lucky guesses?

He used to think he knew the answer, but since meeting Tabby, he wasn't so sure anymore. Yeah, he'd seen her do some interesting things, but seeing wasn't necessarily believing, and he wasn't as gullible as a lot of people were. Where was the proof that psychic abilities were real? Where was the scientific data backing it up? Just because lots of people believed it worked didn't make it so. Lots of people used to believe the earth was flat, too, but enlightenment and physical evidence proved them wrong.

Ah, Tabby. His arms ached for her to be in them again, his body ached to lose himself in her. He hadn't felt this way about a woman since Lorna, and that had been well over a year ago. Yet even as much as he'd cared for her, it didn't come close to what he felt for Tabby.

He needed to work it out with her. Somehow. Get her to see reason. They'd be okay if she could just overcome her ridiculous attitude about being able to read people's minds and admit it was simply that she was very good at reading *people*.

As he gripped the papers in his fist, a sense of urgency needled his brain. Not only did he need to change her thinking, he needed to find a way to protect her.

It had taken him two hours to decipher the wretched handwriting on most of the pages in the dream diary, but when he finally did, his skin prickled and his heart went numb.

She's so pretty, with her silky hair and innocent eyes. She looks at me, and I can see the quality of her soul. She means well, wants to help me. How can she know what's in my heart? How can she know her trust is dangerously misplaced?

It's easy. She's so surprised, she doesn't even struggle. The knife slides between her ribs like an oar through water. Blood gushes from the wound. She makes a sound in her throat and blinks up at me, so sad. So terribly sad, and disappointed, too.

'Bye, nice lady. 'Bye, Tabitha. Truth be told, I think you were my only friend.

Nate rubbed the back of his neck. Worry and fear tensed his muscles. He glanced at the bedside clock—ten-thirty. It was Saturday, and he had the weekend ahead of him. Picking up his cell, he started to key in her number, then stopped. He had a better idea. Leaping out of bed, he set his plan into motion.

Just after three o'clock, he knocked on her front door, but instead of being greeted by the woman of his most passionate dreams—and several anxiety attacks—he was met by two identical white-haired ladies dressed in identical outfits. Behind two pairs of identical gold-rimmed glasses, two pairs of identical blue eyes twinkled, making the women look like twin fairy godmothers in pink pastel pantsuits.

"Good afternoon, ladies," he said. "I'm Nate Darling. I'd like to speak with Ms. March."

The one on the left said, "I'm Eden, and this is my sister . . ."

". . . Flora," finished the one on the right.

In unison, they announced, "We're the Ichabod sisters."

They were sweet old gals with little rosebud mouths and round faces and a wee too much rouge on their soft, wrinkly cheeks.

"May I come in?"

Flora said, "Well, if you're looking for Tabitha, she's . . ."

". . . not here," Eden finished.

They nodded simultaneously.

Okay, this was cute, but a little nauseating.

"Do you know when she'll be back?"

"Is this an official call, Inspector?" a woman's voice intervened.

The twins parted like the Puce Sea to let Tabitha's mother navigate between them.

"Ma'am." If he'd been wearing a hat, he would have tipped it. Instead, he adjusted his glasses. "I need to speak to Tabby. Do you know where she is or when she'll be back?"

He watched as Victoria seemed to consider the question. Then, with a long, high-pitched sigh, she said, "She went away for the weekend. To think."

"Look," he said in his best grovel voice. "I owe her an apology, sort of, but I can't deliver it unless I know where she is."

"Sort of?" Victoria slipped her hands into the pocket of the floral apron she was wearing.

Eden snickered. "That's a very male thing to . . ."

". . . say," Flora accused.

The ladies gave him a *tsk-tsk*, in stereo.

"Help me out here, will you?" he implored. "I just want to talk to her."

On either side of Tabitha's mom, Eden and Flora wrinkled their button noses, looking like ancient Barbie doll bookends. "We vote to tell him," they chirped.

Biting her lip, Victoria gave Nate the once over. Then, to the twins, she said, "Eden, Flora, would you excuse us, please?"

Arm in arm, the ladies toddled off down the hallway, glancing over their shoulders at him just before they went into the kitchen.

With her head slightly bowed, Victoria said, "I'd love to tell you where she is, but I've been sworn to secrecy. If you show up there, she'll know I'm the one who ratted her out."

"I'll tell her I threatened to arrest you." He arched a brow and kicked up one end of his mouth. "Have your car impounded? The building condemned?" He nearly gave her his most charming smile, but then he remembered it hadn't worked on Tabitha and probably wouldn't work on her mother. "Please?"

"You plan to be around for a while, don't you, Inspector." It wasn't a question. "As in, for decades."

Without hesitation, he said, "Yes."

She nodded. "Then you need to know this." Looking deeply into his eyes, she said, "Just before her fifth birthday, Tabby accidentally got locked in the trunk of my husband's car. They said she was clinically dead when we found her, but the paramedics revived her and she came back to us."

He knew about the trunk incident. Ethan's report hadn't missed a thing.

"She had been conscious for a long time," Victoria continued. "Judging from the bruises on her little knuckles, arms, and knees, she fought and kicked with all her might. She must have screamed and screamed, because her voice was so raw she couldn't speak for two weeks."

Nate shut his emotions off against the agony of what Tabby had gone through. He couldn't bear to think about it just now. "Why didn't anyone hear her?"

Victoria tucked a strand of hair behind her ear. "My husband was mowing the lawn. The noise of the electric mower drowned it out. By the time he was finished . . ."

She gave a rough laugh and wiped moisture from her eyes.

"You simply cannot imagine, Inspector," she whispered, "the panic we felt when we realized what had happened. Every parent's nightmare. Ever since then, for obvious reasons, she's been terrified of dark, closed-in places."

"Why are you telling me this?"

"Because I want your assurance, Inspector, your promise that you'll always give her lots of space and room to breathe."

His heart clenched for a moment, skipping right over a couple of very important beats. He swallowed. "I promise."

They gazed at each other for a few moments, until she nodded. Lowering her lashes, she said, "Her . . . ordeal seemed to trigger a latent psychic ability, at least that's what they told us at the institute. When she was eight, we had her tested, and again at twelve. Her abilities are genuine, Inspector." She stabbed him with a piercing glare. "It's important that you accept that about her."

"I'm trying, ma'am. I swear, I'm trying."

Reaching into her apron pocket, she pulled out a small card and held it out to him. "I wrote this down when I saw you drive up. When she asks, I'm going to deny everything."

A little over an hour later, Nate found himself walking along a wooden dock in Sausalito, looking for a two-story cedar houseboat with a chimney pipe and a porch. Checking the number on the card Victoria had given him with the numbers painted on the houseboat, he walked across the slightly arched bridge, its railings covered with pink jasmine in full bloom, past a planter box of red geraniums, and knocked on the door.

It opened.

She simply stood there in a long yellow sleeper T-shirt thing, gaping up at him, tissues in one hand, a carton of ice cream in the other. She looked so adorable—like a swollen-eyed, red-nosed beauty queen—that he nearly forgot how mad he was at her for deceiving him.

Removing the spoon from her mouth, she choked, "Fuck *off*."

As she started to slam the door in his face, he wedged his body into the threshold, and she had no choice but to open it again.

"I read Griffin's diary," he growled. "Why didn't you tell me he'd dreamed about killing you?"

"I didn't think it was imp—"

"I bought you a cell phone," he snarled. Reaching into his pocket, he grabbed it and thrust the damn thing at her. She ignored it.

"Welcome to the new millennium and the world of modern technology, Tabitha. Now, if you pull some other stupid-assed stunt, like meeting a psychotic bozo late at night in a park, you'll be able to call for help, or at least conk him on the head with it."

"You have no right—"

"My number is already programmed in!" He was shouting, but he didn't care. "I'm sorry I'm having trouble believing in your voodoo woo-woo California touchy-feely claptrap. Hey, skeptics have rights, too, and I'm exercising mine!"

"No you—"

"Yes. I. Do." He emphasized his remarks with a jab of his forefinger to her chest. Then, gesturing to the nearly empty container of ice cream, he drawled, "I was going to invite you to dinner, but I see you've already eaten. I'll bet that's free-range chocolate frigging chip!"

The spoon and half-empty carton fell from her hands to land at her feet. Her blue eyes narrowed and she crossed her arms under her breasts. "Listen, you—"

"No, *you* listen," he plowed on. "I care about you. Okay? I don't just like you, I don't just find you attractive, I don't just have a nodding acquaintanceship with you. I *care* about you and what happens to you." He took a breath and gestured with his hand; the one with her new cell phone in it. Quietly, he added, "And . . . stuff."

Her eyes widened, and her arms fell slowly to her sides.

Scratching his jaw with his thumb, he said,

"More than that, even, I care *for* you. Not like a kid cares for a puppy," he mumbled, "but like, well, you know."

He reached down and took her free hand, placing the cell phone in her palm. She curled her fingers around it and held it to her chest, looking up at him as though he'd just given her a treasure trove of jewels.

"It, uh, takes photographs, has e-mail and text messaging. Lots of ring tone downloads. You can even use it like a phone." He lowered his head and gave her a shy grin.

She swallowed and stared at his gift. "I'm so mad at you . . . I . . . I don't know what . . . I don't know how to—"

"Shut up," he said, stepping toward her. Looking into her eyes, he whispered, "Just shut up. You had me at *Fuck off.*"

She laughed, a little squeak of a sound. "Nate, I—"

His kiss ended the argument. Wrapping his arms around her, he backed her inside the houseboat. The hinges screeched as he kicked the door closed.

Bending, he lifted her easily into his arms, breaking the kiss just long enough to growl, "Where in the hell's the bed?"

Chapter 18

*It is bad luck to get out of bed on the opposite side
you got in on.*

FOLKLORE

They got as far as the oak stepladder leading to
the loft. Tabby slid her arms around Nate's neck
and laid her head on his shoulder. Her tousled
strawberry blond hair fell over one eye, making
her look dreamy and sexy. Her nipples pushed
against the thin fabric of the sleeper T-shirt she
wore.

Shoving her up against the ladder, Nate
wrapped her legs around his waist, opening her
to him. He yanked up the hem of the T-shirt as he
bent to kiss her, thrusting his tongue deep inside
her mouth. She tasted like sweet-salty-chocolate-
ice-cream Tabitha.

God, he'd been waiting all day for this . . . all
night and all day and all week and forever.

He hiked the T-shirt up higher and stared at

her naked breasts, fondling them, so perfect for his hands. Her nipples were like berries, ripe for his hungry mouth. Bending, he licked one, then nibbled on it, then suckled hard.

She let her head fall back against the ladder as she murmured his name.

Moving his hands across her skin, he grasped her bare bottom and tucked her into his groin, feeling her against him, torturing himself with her heat.

Then her fingers were at his belt buckle, and seconds later she pushed his jeans down far enough for her hand to curl around his shaft. She brought the tip against her, and she was warm and wet and they both gasped at the contact.

He kissed her again, ran his tongue along her teeth, sucked her bottom lip. He felt her fingers stroking him, and his brain begin to spin. The sensation of his head against her soft flesh made him quiver and want to thrust.

Against her parted lips, he huffed, "Condom. Pocket. Quick."

She made a laughing sound deep in her throat and rocked her hips against him. Again he fought the urge to plunge into her. She had to know what she was doing, tormenting him like this. Her hand slowly made its way over his hip to his back pocket, then took its time reaching inside. Finally, she slid out the foil packet.

He was panting, barely able to catch his breath. The need to thrust into her was just about killing him, and he was damn sure she knew it.

With her arms around his neck, he waited, his every breath an excruciating labor as she tore open the packet, then moved her hands between them to sheath him.

"You're going to have to pull back a little," she whispered against his open mouth, swiping his tongue with her own. "C'mon, baby," she breathed. "Just a little."

She wiggled her hips, teasing him again, making him nearly lose it right then and there. But he bore down and held on. God, she was hot.

Easing away from her, he watched as she rolled the condom on him, then eased her hips forward again until he was partially buried inside her. With one long glide, he finished the job, sinking in to the hilt. Her back arched, and she sighed in sweet satisfaction.

Bending his neck, he watched himself thrust into her once more, and then again. He reached up and grabbed a handful of her glorious hair, tugging her head back while he kissed her deeply, then ran his tongue down her neck, across her collarbone, down to one nipple.

Around his waist, her legs tightened until he could barely move, and he felt her go still. Every muscle in her body tensed. She stopped rocking against him, while her breath became a raspy saw of sound.

Her head fell back, her eyes drifted closed. He bit her neck and she sighed, a high-pitched sound in rhythm to his thrusts. Finally, she went silent, then a soft gasp escaped her throat and her hips bucked wildly against him.

Thank God. He didn't think he could hold out much longer. With three hard thrusts, he came, his panted breaths turning to grunts of satisfaction.

After a few moments, he pulled out of her, then reached for her waist and turned her away from him.

"Up," he ordered breathlessly, and she finished climbing the wooden ladder to the loft. His eyes never left the round globes of her bottom as he followed her up the rungs. When they reached the platform, he wrapped his arms around her and fell with her onto the wide bed that dominated the space.

He held her close, looking down into her happy, sleepy eyes, stroking her hair, and letting his mind go where he'd feared it might since the day he'd met her. Her lips were swollen and she was still a bit winded from what he could only assume was his ardor. She smiled up at him and played with his hair. He felt the tips of his fingers against his skull, and her soft caresses at the nape of his neck.

Moving quickly, he shucked off his clothes, then tugged her T-shirt up her body and off. She lay there, incredibly beautiful and naked and inviting, and he knew he'd never be able to get enough of her.

As he ran his finger along her jaw, he looked into her eyes and saw birthday parties with pinto ponies and red balloons, Thanksgiving dinners, Christmas trees, a blue-eyed girl with red hair, a blond boy and a yipping puppy, car payments, mortgages, college funds, cold nights and hot sex and a white dress and a gold ring . . . and love.

"Are you okay?" Her eyes were filled with concern. With a wry grin, she said, "You look a little green around the gills. Was it someone you ate?"

He all but yanked her to him, cupping her head in his hand, burying his face in the warmth of her neck.

Her arms came around him and he felt her breasts against his chest. Mmm. Woman. Soft. Warm. His.

Snuggling closer, Tabby slid her legs through his and he trapped them, locking his ankles, imprisoning her against him.

"Nate," she whispered. "I have to get—"

"You're not going anywhere." He edged his hand up to cup her breast. Bending his head, he placed a tender kiss on her soft lips, then murmured, "You're not going anywhere for a long, long time."

"*Who* wants to see me?" Ethan said, unable to keep the shock out of his voice. From behind his desk, he stared at his admin as though she had announced that the Grand PooBah of the Federation of Planets was waiting just outside his door.

"Mr. Peter O'Hara," she drawled, her native Georgia accent softening the edges of her words. "You know, as in Scarlett? He says y'all are neighbors and that his daddy was a friend of yours. He'd like a itty-bitty pinch of your time."

Ethan eyed the woman. Shayla Tanner, thirty-something, blond, beautiful, with a genius IQ. He crossed his arms over his chest. "They teach you that helpless siren routine at Vassar?"

She grinned, and the deep dimple in her right cheek worked its magic. "Hell, no," she said, the silk suddenly turned to industrial-grade emery cloth, abrasive enough to shred a man's skin. "But a girl's got to use what God gave her to get ahead in this world." She lowered her dark lashes, and her voice. "Are you *in* for Mr. O'Hara?"

He nodded, anticipation tightening his gut. "And make sure the equipment's working. I want every word recorded."

"Video, too?" she said, turning to leave.

"Yeah."

Ever since he'd dropped Tabitha off last night at two A.M., he'd spent the last eight hours investigating the hell out of Peter O'Hara. Exhausted and in need of sleep, he had damned little to show for his efforts.

Maybe this was just plain stupid and there was no connection between what he'd read in the dream diary and the murder of his gardener.

But his instincts told him there was. Too many coincidences; there had to be a link.

Before he had a chance to sort through his tangled thoughts, the glass door silently swung open again, and O'Hara shuffled in. His skin was pale, pasty. His hair needed cutting and he hadn't shaved in days. In rumpled jeans and a faded Stanford sweatshirt, he looked like he'd just crawled out from behind a Dumpster.

Had a year at the helm of his father's company wrung the life completely out of him, or was he busy wringing the life out of innocent victims? More importantly, had Walter Perez been one of them?

Ethan stood and extended his hand, and O'Hara shook it in a brief, lifeless clasp.

Keeping his voice even, Ethan said, "I haven't seen you since your father's funeral."

The other man nodded, then took the seat Ethan offered.

"Can I get you something? Coffee? Water? I have some excellent scotch . . ."

"Nothing," O'Hara said absently. "Thanks."

Before the elder O'Hara died, the son had been nothing more than a playboy, a partier of the first degree. *Spend the old man's money as fast as possible* had been his motto. But this Peter O'Hara was a far cry from the youthful, grinning, easygoing womanizer Ethan had met in college.

Had the weight of responsibility done this to him, or was it the guilt of being a murderer?

Ethan eased into his own chair behind his desk. How interesting that O'Hara should show up here, today of all days, when he'd planned to pay his Marin neighbor a visit that afternoon.

Out of the corner of his eye, the tiny green light shining from the eye of the ornate Buddha adorning the top shelf of his bookcase told him the camera was recording.

"What brings you here today, O'Hara?"

"I, uh . . ." He stopped and cleared his throat. "I want to upgrade my security system at the house in Marin." He lifted his eyes to Ethan's. "Right now it works on sensors, but I want to add video. Can you do it?"

"The servants stealing you blind? Or has somebody been trying to break in?"

O'Hara shook his head and averted his eyes.

"No. Nothing like that. Uh, listen, Darling. I need to ask you for a favor."

"I make it a policy never to do favors."

O'Hara eyed him with a mixture of desperation and hope. "I remember you from college. We didn't run in the same circles, but I heard about you all the same. I went to school on my old man's bank account while you earned a football scholarship. Star quarterback, right?"

Ethan shrugged.

"Yeah, well, see, my father followed your career. He followed mine, too, if you call sex and drugs and rock and roll a career."

"What's your point?"

O'Hara leaned forward, clasping his hands in front of him. "You were honest. Straight-arrow. Hardworking. My father liked that, and when you needed a break, he loaned you the money to start up your firm. Now I need a break. I've turned my life around only to find . . ." His voice faltered and he stared at his hands. His knuckles stood out in white relief. "I need your help. I have nowhere else to turn, nobody honest, straight-arrow, hardworking I can trust."

"What about your sister? She—"

"Nobody can know. This *has* to be a secret, just between you and me. It *has* to be. At least until I get to the truth." He looked into Ethan's eyes, misery and despair plain to see on his haggard face. "For the sake of my father who helped put you where you are, help me."

Ethan thought of Walter Perez, shot to death for no good reason. He thought of a woman in a dotted dress, and an old bum in an alley. As unconnected to each other as numbered balls in a lottery barrel. Was the man sitting across the desk from him the common denominator?

Only one way to find out. With a curt nod, he said, "All right."

Chapter 19

*If a dead friend or loved one appears in a dream
and asks you to go with them, don't go!*

FOLKLORE

She stood looking at herself . . . but not herself. The
image was distorted in some way, as though she were
staring at her own reflection in moving water.

A hand reached for her, touched her, caressed her
cheek, and the image cleared. She knew now who she
was, where she was, and what. She was the dreamer.
She was the dream.

His thumb stroked her bottom lip. She raised her
face to him, and he kissed her. Beneath her palm, she
felt the steady beat of his warrior's heart.

She heard him laugh inside her own head and felt his
happiness, his confusion. Stepping back, she gauged
the length of his strong body, his wide stance, the gun
he gripped in his fingers.

He spoke to her, but the words bounced against her
own thoughts and she missed what he said. Somehow

she knew the words were important, so she closed her eyes, trying to recapture them. When she opened her eyes again, he was a teenage boy. His weapon was gone, and in his fist he held an iron key.

"It's not enough," he said to her, flinging it to the floor. "It's useless."

He turned and walked toward a table where his mother and Ethan and Andie sat, deep in conversation. The table was heaped with foods of all kinds, but instead of joining his family, he stood to the side and watched, staring, but not uttering a word. He waited for them to acknowledge him, but they never did.

And still he waited. . .

Tabitha's eyes fluttered open as she slowly became aware of where she was. Nestled in Nate's arms, her head on his shoulder, their hands clasped, she heard the steady rhythm of his breathing, watched the rise and fall of his bare chest. He was still in the throes of his dream . . . the dream she had seen as clearly as if it had been her own.

As she eased her hand from his relaxed fingers, the images began to fade and her own thoughts started to tumble back into her head like autumn leaves drifting one by one to the ground.

She curled in closer, and his arm came around her, pulling her snugly against him.

Saturday's daylight had faded, and they had made love again, and then again. Throughout the night, he had sought her, gently roused her from sleep, and she had eagerly complied. In the wee, quiet hours just before dawn, he pulled her on top of him and she'd come the moment she straddled him. Now spears of bright sunlight stabbed through slits in the drawn shades, announcing Sunday had broken and was well on its way toward afternoon.

"We've been in bed for nearly twenty-four hours," she said sleepily. "What exactly do you eat? Is there some special soy concoction . . ."

He opened one eye. "You tired? Because I don't have to be to work until nine tomorrow, which gives us plenty of time for at least ten more rounds—"

She placed her fingertips over his mouth and laughed, "Hush. I think it would be a good idea to pace ourselves."

Letting her smile fade, she lowered her hand and traced the taut muscles of his flat abs with her fingertip. She hesitated only a moment, then, "Tell me about your family, Nate. About your mom, and Andie and Ethan. Why are you and your brother so . . . unfriendly toward each other?"

Nate took a deep breath and blew it out slowly before he answered. "We flipped a coin when we were kids. Heads got to be the easygoing fun brother, tails became the SOB."

"And you got tails?" she chided.

He snorted and tickled her ribs until she giggled and shoved his hand away. Pressing onward, she said, "What about your sister?"

"Girls don't flip coins. They pick a number between one and ten."

Giving it a moment's thought, she said, "Huh. You're right. Because guys have coins in their pockets and girls generally have to go hunt one down."

Lifting his head from the pillow, he looked at her. "Precisely. I'm hungry. Let's go eat somewhere."

"Don't change the subject. Tell me about your family."

He let his head fall back onto the pillow and made a face. "Is this the part where we tell each other our life stories?"

How can I fall utterly and completely in love with you if we don't?

"You're right," she mumbled. "It's silly."

He shot her a glance. With a quick lift of his shoulders, he said, "Look, mine's really not worth mentioning. My parents had a bad marriage. When I was thirteen, they finally called a halt to the hostilities and got divorced. We kids were all supposed to live with my mom, but my dad seemed so, I don't know, dejected. The odd man out. I hated to see him go off all by himself, so when he left San Francisco to take a job in Olympia, I went with him."

"Was he a cop, too?"

"Police officer. We prefer police officer, and yes, he was."

"Your leaving—didn't that upset your mom?"

Sighing, he said, "Yeah, I guess. I don't really know. My mom and I, well, we're very different. I suppose I'm more like my dad. She was probably happy not to have to deal with me all the time."

"I'm sorry." Tabitha placed her hand over his heart and snuggled a little closer.

"I love my mom and she loves me," he assured her, "but we don't see each other very often, and it works for both of us. She's very dramatic, very *femme fatale*. Ethan deals with her a lot better than I ever did."

Twirling her finger around his taut belly button, she said, "How did your going with your father affect your brother and sister?"

"Andie was too young to really get what was happening, but it sure pissed Ethan off. He'd never gotten along with Dad, so he didn't understand the choice I made. He accused me of abandoning Mom and Andie. I guess he's never forgiven me."

"But you were just kids, right? Teenagers, and the victims of your parents' divorce, not the cause. You were both forced to make choices that were hard and painful." Edging up onto her elbow, she looked down at him. "When you grew up, didn't you want to reunite or something? Establish a better relationship?"

He closed his eyes for a moment. When he opened them, he said, "Yes. And no. Being apart physically only reinforced that we were apart emotionally. Family reunions were few and far between, and never long enough to mend any fences, even if we'd known how. Besides, in the last twenty years, Ethan learned how to take the meaning of hard-ass to the wall. He's so rigid, I don't think he knows how to compromise anymore, and I'm tired of trying."

"You know, it's possible it hurt him that you chose your father over him; at least, that's how he may have perceived it when he was a kid. Maybe he's afraid that if he attempted to reconcile with you, you'll reject him again. It could be he's just afraid."

"Ethan's not afraid of anything."

Stroking Nate's forehead, she brushed a lock of stray hair back into place. "I can see how you'd think that, but maybe if you tried looking at things from his point of view . . ."

"I'm willing to do it, but he's not going to reciprocate, so there you are."

"You assume."

"I *know*."

"Now who's being rigid? Sounds like you two boys are a lot more alike than you'd care to admit."

"Thank you, Dr. March," Nate snorted.

"Okay, what about your sister?"

"Andie grew up not really knowing me at all, and I guess you could say I don't know her, either. She used to write to me when she was a kid, but after a while the letters sort of dwindled down to a card at Christmas, and maybe one on my birthday." He paused for a moment and slid one arm under his head. "Andie's a police officer, too. Wants to be a detective. Must be something in the water."

"What happened to your father?"

"He died about five years ago. Cancer."

"I'm so sorry. Do you miss him?"

Nate swallowed hard. "Yeah."

Silence stretched between them. Tabitha settled back down next to him and pulled the sheet up around her chin.

A moment passed, then another.

"I had a sister," she said softly. "But you probably knew that."

He made an angry noise in his throat.

"Yeah. Look, Tabby, about that background check thing. I didn't know you then, and—"

"Ellie was beautiful," she interrupted, closing her eyes. "That probably wasn't in the file. Daddy had opened the trunk of his car to get something, and left it open. I thought it would be fun to climb inside and close the lid and scare him when he came back. Boo! Like Halloween. So we did, we climbed inside. Ellie and me. She was a couple of years younger, and did whatever I did."

Nate went very still. Against her ear, she heard the steady, stalwart beating of his heart, and hearing it gave her courage.

"The trunk had only seemed big because we were so small," she whispered, "but the air went fast. We were in there, like spoons in a drawer, my arms around my little sister. And she . . . she fell asleep. I tried to wake her up so she wouldn't miss surprising Daddy, but she wouldn't wake up."

Growing more terrified by the moment, she'd kicked and pounded and screamed. For a long time. Forever.

"It was so dark in there, and hot. I remember the darkness and how it seemed to clutch at me. Then I went to sleep, too, and I dreamed of white lights and gentle ladies, and Grandma was there and Uncle George. And then I woke up and my mom was holding me and sobbing so hard . . ."

But Ellie didn't wake up, and all Tabitha knew for sure was that it had been her idea. Ellie had gone to sleep forever and always, and it was Tabitha's fault.

"I wondered if Ellie had dreamed, too," she whispered. And if she had seen Grandma and the gentle ladies and Uncle George, and if she had liked it so much, she decided to stay with them. When I discovered I could see other people's dreams, I thought maybe it was Ellie, forgiving me, letting me know it was okay with her, that she had stayed. That maybe helping people understand their dreams was what I was meant to do, because I knew what it was like to wake up and not understand, like on that day, that day I woke up, and Ellie didn't."

He made love to her again. Tenderly, with the utmost passion and care. How could he not? What she had said, the stark look in her eyes, the torment in her simple words. Making love to her didn't nearly begin to soothe the heartache she felt, but he did his damnedest to try.

When they were finished, he held her in his arms and rocked her, and she cried a little. And with her head against his chest, and her eyes closed so she couldn't see, he did, too.

A million thoughts jumbled together inside his head. A million scenarios formed. A million words he wanted to say. Not a million. Just three. But he knew she wasn't ready to hear them, so he rocked her, and stroked her hair, and swallowed down the grief he felt for her.

After a while, she raised her head. "I need to go wash my face," she said, and pushed herself away. Wiping tears from her eyes, she gave him a watery smile, then padded into the bathroom.

As he lay there with his hands folded behind his head, letting his mind work on what he was going to say to her next, his cell phone vibrated.

"Not yet, goddammit," he mumbled, reaching for it on the nightstand. Pressing the button, he growled, "Nate Darling."

"Where are you?"

Ethan. Shit.

"It's my day off," Nate snarled. "What's so important—"

"Meet me at my office in an hour. And bring your girlfriend." The line went dead.

"Bastard," Nate muttered as Tabby came out of the bathroom.

"Do you have to go to work?" She was wearing a silky white robe and had washed her face and combed her hair. She looked sweet and vulnerable and beautiful, and, again, those three words clamored inside his head to be spoken.

"Not work," he said, tossing the sheet off his hips and standing. "Let me take you to dinner in the city. Someplace real fancy."

Smiling, she said, "What's the occasion?"

He reached for his clothes. "It'll be your reward for enduring a stuffed-shirt meeting with my dickhead brother."

An hour later, he and Tabby walked through

the unlocked double glass doors of Paladin Private Investigations.

The reception area was furnished more elegantly than most penthouses. A U-shaped mahogany desk, complete with computer and gigantic bouquet of fresh flowers, dominated the space. The carpet was thick, the sofa made of fine fabric. Nate had seen the place a couple of times before, but Tabby hadn't, and next to him, she stood looking around, her eyes wide, her mouth open.

"Nice paintings," she said, gesturing to the original oils displayed on the walls. "I'm assuming your brother serves a particular clientele, and not just your average Joe looking for his fugitive Yorkie Poo."

Behind them, Nate heard a *snick*, and realized the locks on the glass doors had been thrown. A moment later, Ethan's voice came over the intercom.

"The door to the inner offices is open."

Escorting Tabby through the heavy mahogany door, he raised his head to see Ethan standing above them at the top of the wide landing, a coffee mug in one hand, a remote control in the other.

"Hello again, Ms. March," Ethan said as she and Nate climbed the steel and glass stairs and took a seat at the table in his office. "Nate."

Their eyes met and locked. Ethan was the first to look away.

The private office was large and tastefully decorated. In mahogany and chrome, it was all polish and sharp edges, just like Ethan. Nothing of a personal nature had found its way into Paladin's inner sanctum, except for one small, curious item on the desk. Nate couldn't recall having seen it there before.

It was a photograph of two little boys sitting close together on a couch, grinning broadly for the camera as they held a crying baby girl awkwardly in their arms.

When Ethan caught Nate staring at the photo, he moved a stack of files in front of it, obscuring the small portrait from view.

"You work on Sundays, big brother?" Nate asked as Ethan walked to the conference table to settle in a chair across the table from him.

"I work every day." Turning toward the big-screen TV that took up the entire far end of the office, he said, "I think you'll be interested in this."

The tape started, and a face appeared. Next to him, Tabby caught her breath. Her fingers flew to her mouth as she stared at the screen.

"You recognize him, then," Ethan said to Tabby.

Nate watched her nod her head, her blue eyes shocked and filled with what appeared to be sympathy.

"That's Peter," she choked. "Dear God, he looks awful. Where did you get this, Ethan?"

"He paid me a visit."

Nate shot a look at his brother. "*He* came to see *you*? Where is he now?"

"I let him go home."

Nate felt his temper start to rise. "You had him, and you let him go? What in the hell, Ethan? You waiting for him to buy a one-way ticket to Timbuktu before you contacted me?"

Ethan's hazel eyes narrowed as he relaxed back into his big, fat, expensive chair. "It's complicated."

"Well, if it's so frigging complicated, why did you even bother bringing us down here? The SFPD is interested in talking to this guy, and you *know* it. Why didn't you hold him here? If you couldn't stomach talking to me, you could have called Stocker."

Ethan shrugged. "I could have done a lot of things, but what I did was, I let him go. Like I said, it's complicated." Leaning across the table, he narrowed his gaze on Nate. "I want him more than you do, so quit your bitching. I'm handling it."

Nate placed his palms flat on the polished surface, and leaned toward his brother until they were nearly nose to nose.

"*How* are you handling it? Who is this guy, and why did he come to see you? Enlighten me, Ethan, or I swear to God, I'll arrest you for obstruction."

* * *

It was like watching two gladiators in the arena, and Tabitha was terrified they'd come to blows. They were both big healthy men, well muscled, fit, equal in every way. It would be a disaster.

She watched as they glared at each other across a chasm of years too deep, too difficult, too painful to span, especially when their only bridge was the anger they shared.

"He tried to hurt Tabby," Nate bit out between clenched teeth. "He names her in his diary. He describes murdering her. *Tell me who he is.*"

Ethan flicked a glance at Tabitha, and she saw an instant flash of compassion there, then hard resolve. He would never tell, not if he didn't want to, no matter what.

"I'm sure Tabitha is well protected," Ethan said casually. "Besides, do you have any evidence against Peter? Can you connect any of those homicides with physical evidence you can hand the DA? Got any witnesses? Do you have *anything* that points to him as a killer, other than his dream diary?"

"We have a partial on a shard of glass—"

"Not good enough, and you know it."

She watched as Nate's chest rose and fell. He stood, his fists curled at his sides. "You're not going to help me out here, are you? You just wanted eyewitness verification you had the right guy."

"I can see all that time you spent in detective school paid off." With a click, he turned the TV off.

"Shove it up your ass, Ethan." Turning to Tabitha, he cupped his hand under her elbow. "C'mon. I owe you a dinner."

Tabitha looked at Ethan, assessing him, trying to figure out who he really was underneath all the bitterness and stoicism. There was a way, if she could pull it off. He was very smart; she'd have to catch him unawares to make it work because if he suspected, he'd shut down and she'd get nothing.

"All this is very upsetting," she said, giving her voice a bit of a tremble. "I thought you two were going to hit each other. I . . . Give me a minute, would you Nate?"

She slumped into her chair and put her head in her hands as though she were dealing with a severe case of nerves. "Do you think I could have some water, Ethan?"

Though he said nothing, he rose and walked to the wet bar behind his desk, filled a tumbler, and brought it to where she sat. As he placed the glass on the table, she reached out and touched the back of his hand.

A woman . . . face down, floating in the bay. Her long hair swirls around her head like golden seaweed. He reaches for her, panic choking him. Inside his chest, his heart is bursting. No, no, no, no! He yells for help, but the water is tinged pink, and he smells the blood and death, and knows it's too late . . .

Tabitha yanked her hand away. Ethan looked down at her, his hazel eyes confused at first, then they came into bright focus. He glanced at the back of his hand, then at her fingers.

"Very good," he mumbled. "Aren't you clever."

She swallowed. "I'm sorry," she whispered. "I didn't understand . . ."

"What are you talking about?" Nate said, flashing a look between them.

Without answering, Ethan walked toward his desk and dropped into the chair. "I don't care if you think I'm a bastard, Nate. I have to do this my way."

Nate's eyes flared with anger. Stalking to the door, he yanked it open and stepped into the threshold.

"Things were bad between us before, Ethan," he growled. "You've just made them a hell of a lot worse."

As Tabitha followed Nate out the door, behind her she heard Ethan murmur under his breath, "Yeah. I know."

Chapter 20

If you dream of attending a wedding, you will soon attend a funeral.

FOLKLORE

"You wouldn't really arrest your brother, would you?"

As they drove out of the darkened parking lot beneath Paladin's Embarcadero offices, Nate risked a glance at Tabby. Concern shone in her beautiful eyes, misguided distress for a man who didn't deserve it.

Which man's soul was she worried about, he wondered—his brother's, or his?

"No," he said finally. "I wouldn't arrest him, but I might beat the shit out of him."

"Hmm," she mused. "He might give you some trouble. He looks capable of holding his own."

"So we beat the shit out of each other," he growled. "I'm up for it."

Downshifting, he turned at the corner and

headed up the hill toward his apartment. "Besides, even if I did arrest him, he'd be out on bail in fifteen minutes and I still wouldn't have any answers."

He gripped the steering wheel, letting his fingers curl around the unyielding leather, imagining it was his brother's neck.

"Nate," Tabitha said softly. "I saw the photograph on Ethan's desk. There was no mistaking it was the two of you as boys, holding Andie when she was a baby. Don't you find that . . . interesting?"

He shrugged. "No."

"Oh, don't pretend it didn't surprise you, and that you didn't wonder about it. Want to know what I think?"

"Not really."

"Good." She smiled over at him, her pretty lips curved in gentle sympathy. "I think he loves you. I think he misses you. You're his only brother. A man his age doesn't keep a photograph of his brother and baby sister on his desk like that for no reason. It's his only connection to you."

"Ethan loves me," he scoffed. "Well, he sure has a warped way of showing it."

"Yes, he does, but maybe it's the only way he knows. Give him time, Nate," Tabitha urged. "He'll find a way to show you how he feels. Just give him some time."

Neither agreeing or disagreeing, he simply grunted.

"What happened back there, when you touched him? Did you see something?"

Tabby's brows shot up and her lips parted. A heartbeat later, she sent him a sarcastic look. "I thought you didn't believe in all that psychic voodoo hocus-pocus—"

"Did you see something or *not*?"

"Give me a minute," she said silkily. "I need to compose an adult response to your question, but first I have to overcome my initial urge to gloat in triumph."

"Gloat away, baby. Just don't take too long. This is a limited-time offer." He scowled over at her, letting her know he meant business.

After a moment, she looked down at her hands folded neatly across her lap. "I did see something."

"Tell me."

"I really can't." She shook her head, sending her gold dangle earrings swinging. "It's not my story to tell. Why don't you ask Ethan? A little open communication between you would—"

"Yeah, right." Nate blew out a long, weary sigh. "Okay, how about you just tell me whether what you think you saw has anything to do with this case."

She considered that for a moment. "Only indirectly. Only insofar as it affects his personal code of ethics, which, from what I can tell, are insanely high and completely unyielding."

"No kidding."

Nibbling on her bottom lip, she said, "I can tell you this, but only because I think the two of you need to mend those fences you were talking about . . ."

"Like that will happen."

"If you'll stop complaining and make an *effort*, Nate," she said, exasperation sharpening her words. "You're just as stubborn as your brother. *One* of you is going to have to give a little, don't you think?"

When he didn't respond, she said, "Touching him, well, it wasn't what I'd expected, and it surprised me, but I think I understand him better now. What I saw was the reason he left the SFPD when he did, and what drove him to start Paladin."

"What *drove* him? I thought he was just tired of bad coffee, bad hours, and shit for pay."

"No, that's why *you* would quit. I think Ethan loved his job, but I suggest you ask him about it. Ask him about . . . Cathy."

"Who in the hell is Cathy?"

"Ask him, Nate. He might just tell you."

Nate snorted. Uh-huh. If he and his brother had any chance of repairing their fractured relationship, Ethan's refusal to reveal his client's name pretty much put an end to it. As far as Nate was concerned, Ethan was every bit the coldhearted SOB he'd always been, maybe worse, because Ethan knew Tabby was named in the diary, and unless he was completely stupid, he also knew she was important to Nate. Ethan's silence could be putting her at risk, and that was something Nate was going to have a very hard time reconciling.

A few blocks before they reached Nate's apartment, the dark, heavy sky opened up, so by the time he parked the Accord on a secluded side street, it was raining buckets.

Setting the e-brake, he said, "I need to change, then we'll go out for that dinner I promised you."

Next to him, Tabby was shrouded in shadows. Fat raindrops assailed the roof and struck at the windows, making it sound like he'd parked under a rushing mountain waterfall.

"You know what?" Tabby said softly, snuggling down in her seat. "I'm not really hungry, but . . . there's something about the inside of a car at night during a rainstorm . . . " She looked over at him. "It just *does* something to me, you know?"

His mouth went dry.

Reaching to her right, she pulled the handle, and her seat slowly reclined. She unfastened her safety restraints and stretched her arms above her head, lengthening her body, giving him a good look of what she had to offer. Sleepily turning her head toward him, she murmured, "Lock the doors." Then, sliding her hands up her rib cage, she lifted her sweater, cupping her breasts. With her thumbs, she circled her nipples through the silky fabric of her bra. "Come here."

He didn't need to be asked twice, not when she made a soft little come-hither groan as she proceeded to unhook her bra and push it out of the way.

Suddenly he was so hard he could barely breathe. He practically snapped a femur leaping over the gearshift. With a little concentration, a few giggles, and a lot of hard work, they switched places, putting him on the bottom. She straddled him, her skirt hiked up to her thighs, her bare breasts inches from his hungry mouth.

She made a little cry in the back of her throat when he kissed her, thrusting his tongue deep, taking complete possession of her. His thumbs grazed her nipples, and she wiggled her hips against him, as eager as he was to get on with it.

"I've always wanted to do it in the car in the rain," she whispered against his open mouth.

"Happy to comply," he growled, then eased her higher on his body to take a taut nipple into his mouth.

"Oh, God," she breathed. "Oh, yes, oh, God, oh yes . . . please . . ."

Fumbling like a horny teenager, he managed to get his pants open. Thank God she was wearing that skirt.

"Do you have any condoms left?" she breathed as she moved against him, rubbing hard against his crotch, easing her hand under the waistband of his shorts. She pulled him out and placed the tip against her damp, heated flesh.

"Back pocket," he said. "Lift up a little."

She did and with one hand on her breast and the other sliding under his own butt, he reached into his pocket and pulled out the small packet.

Unbuttoning his shirt, she rubbed her nipples over his chest, and he choked, trying to get his arms around her to open the foil packet.

Finally, it opened.

"Shit."

"What's the matter?" She was panting, sliding her body over his, driving him crazy with lust.

"It's not a condom," he breathed heavily. "It's an Alka-Seltzer tablet. I guess I got the wrong packet."

She kissed him then, her open mouth over his, her tongue tangling with his, her laughter mingling with his.

"Guess you'd better go back for seconds," she chuckled, then kissed him again.

As she drove him higher and higher with her passion, he lifted his hips and shoved his hand into his pocket again. Ah, there. Yanking it out, he tore it open.

"Fuck." He groaned in frustration.

"More Alka-Seltzer?" she snickered.

"Vitamins."

She pressed her body down on his and wiggled. "If you don't have a condom, I guess we can use one of those packets."

"I'm going in again," he warned. "If I'm not back in five minutes, call for backup."

"Yes, Inspector," she cooed.

With a thrust of his hips, he lifted them both while he jammed his hand into his back pocket, found the damn packet, and tore it open.

"Ease back, baby," he growled. "If I don't get this thing on now, I'm going to come all over you."

Quickly sheathing himself, he tugged the crotch of her panties aside, slid his finger along her wet flesh until she choked his name, then impaled her. She gave a soft, high-pitched cry, arching over him so he could suckle and tongue her nipple.

"Oh, God . . . Nate . . . oh, Nate . . . yes . . ."

Her back arched and he thrust into her again, barely able to hang on. He hoped to hell she was close, because he didn't think he could last long.

With the rain pounding the roof in a wild, savage beat, his head spun, and the only thing he could feel was where his body met hers.

His universe collapsed down into this small dark space where the cold rain hammered out a hot rhythm and the night air was vanquished by the warmth of the woman in his arms.

In all his life, nothing had ever felt so perfect, so complete. Nothing.

Tabby found her release, sighing a high sound that electrified him to the core. Burying his face against her neck, he thrust again, and again, his climax harder than he would have believed possible.

A moment passed, an hour, a lifetime. Finally, she moved, resting her head on his shoulder, lightly fingering strands of his damp hair.

"I don't know why," she said, swallowing, her breathing still unsteady, "but this reminds me of something out of Dr. Seuss, the one about green eggs and ham."

He chuckled. "Would you do it in a car?"

She giggled. "I would do it in a car."

"Would you do it in a bar?"

"I would do it in a bar."

"Would you do it here or there?"

She purred, "I would do it anywhere."

"Would you do it on a boat, by a moat, with a goat?"

"Ewwww!"

"Sorry," he snorted. "It rhymed." Lifting his head, he kissed her, a long kiss, a slow kiss, a thank-you kiss. Inching back a bit, he looked into her eyes. "Would you do it . . . tenderly?"

She ran her finger along his bottom lip. "As long as it's you making love to me. I would do it, yes, it's true—"

"I love you."

Her breath caught. Pellets of rain bit the windshield like tiny rocks tossed against the glass. Even in the watery shadows, he could see her eyes searching his.

Okay, it had been abrupt, unplanned, all of it. She didn't have to say it back. He was an adult. She didn't have to say it back. Really. She didn't. Have to say it back.

She lowered her lashes and set her jaw. Suddenly the silence had lasted too long. He took a deep breath, flicked the locks, and opened the door. Easing himself out from under her, he stepped onto the street, then quickly closed the door.

By the time he reached the driver's side and slid behind the wheel, his clothing was back in order.

Cranking the ignition, he said nothing as he released the e-brake and headed down the street.

"Nate," she said, but he ignored her. She'd repaired her own clothing and brought the seat back up. "Nate, please listen."

"Later," he said, too casually. "I just remembered I have early shift tomorrow. Let's take a rain check on that dinner." Since it was conveniently pouring outside, the metaphor worked. "Oh, and your sweet peas are in the back seat. Little wilted. I can toss 'em if you like."

Without a word, she turned and grabbed the sorry bouquet, now dry and limp from lack of water for days.

He pulled up in front of her house. She stepped out of the car and closed the door behind her. When she reached the porch steps, she turned to face him.

Behind a curtain of rain, standing in the circle of the porch light, holding the dead flowers to her chest the way a woman would cradle a baby, she looked lost, vulnerable.

He knew he should do something about it, but he couldn't. Not after what had just happened.

She lifted her hand and gave him a weak smile and a wave, yet he did nothing but shift hard into gear and pull away from the curb.

The interior of his car still smelled like sex, so he rolled all the windows down. Rain splashed inside, wetting the upholstery. Cold air slapped his face, but he deserved the punishment. Maybe enough fresh air would obliterate the stupidity of what he'd done.

He adjusted his glasses, wiping bits of spray from the lenses with his thumb. When would he learn to think *before* he said something as explosive as *I love you*?

And he did . . . love her. The thought of losing her scared him.

But not losing her absolutely terrified him.

He didn't know how to be a married man, a man with a wife and family. What if he screwed it all up? What if she got tired of him or was bored by him? What if . . . damn, a million things.

He hadn't even been able to properly pull off telling her he loved her. He'd blurted it out in a car after having sex. Boy, that probably really impressed her. She deserved roses and a candlelight dinner, and all the free-range fricassee she could handle.

And a ring. Shit. How could he have been so stupid? He'd caught an episode or two of *Oprah*; he knew women needed all that romantic stuff that went with a declaration of love. And now he'd ruined it for her.

Not to mention she obviously didn't love him in return. Her eyes had widened and she'd stared at him like he'd just admitted to stealing candy from babies instead of making a confession of love.

If she'd blurted it right back, maybe it would have been okay, but she hadn't, which meant she didn't, and now he'd gone and ruined everything by not taking his time and doing it right.

He needed to think about this, about how to fix this, if he could. He'd never told a woman he loved her before, not even Lorna. This was uncharted territory and it left him feeling a little queasy.

Had he lost her now? Had his unbridled idiocy put her off and out of reach? Damn, love sucked.

What he really wanted to do was punch something, but instead he blew out a harsh breath and decided to move past the incident for now. He'd turn his attention to the case, to finding out who his brother's client was. Familiar territory. Work. *That* he knew how to handle.

Yeah, first thing in the morning he'd talk it over with his partner. There were leads there, clues. He just needed to follow them.

Besides, Tabby could still be in danger, and just because she didn't love him didn't mean he was going to abandon his commitment to protect her. Far from it.

Damn, love sucked.

Between bites of cheese omelet, Tabitha sensed her mother's close scrutiny. She knew Victoria was waiting for her to say something about her weekend at the houseboat, and how she'd gotten home without her car, but so far no direct questioning had occurred. But this was Tabitha's mother, after all. It was only a matter of time.

Pouring hot water into her teacup, Victoria said casually, "Get everything all sorted out this weekend?"

Tabitha swallowed. *No. It's worse than ever.* "Mm-hmm."

Her mom set the steaming kettle back on the stove and took the seat across the table from Tabitha. Fiddling with a tea bag, she said, "Inspector Darling came looking for you. He said it was police business, so I told him where you'd gone. I hope that was okay."

Her eyes glued to her plate, Tabitha mumbled, "Mm-hmm."

"I played cards for a while with Eden and Flora, then hit the hay pretty early."

Stabbing at an innocent glop of cheese, Tabitha kept her lashes down. "Good."

"I didn't hear you come in."

"I came. Uh, in," she corrected. "I came in. Late. It was late, but I definitely came . . . in."

Victoria chuckled as she raised her teacup to her lips. "I assume so, since you're sitting here now." Cocking her head, she said lightly, "How did the police business work out—"

"Well if you're going to *grill* me like this, I guess I'll just have to tell you!"

She let her fork fall from her fingers. It made a clattering sound as it hit the porcelain plate, and bits of omelet splattered the blue-and-white-checkered tablecloth. Thumping her elbows down on either side of her plate, she let her face fall into her hands. "I'm sorry, Mom."

With a motherly kind of look, Victoria said softly, "I take it you and Nate slept together."

Tabitha nodded. Miserably.

"If you don't mind my saying so, he looks like he'd be pretty damned good."

Tabitha nodded again. Enthusiastically.

"So what's bothering you, honey? Didn't you use protection?"

"Yes and no," she choked. "I did use protection, but the wrong kind."

Her mother's pretty eyes grew somber. Setting her teacup on the table, she said, "I see. You used protection for your body, but not your heart."

Tabitha nodded once more. Slowly.

"And you've been working so hard at not falling in love with him." She stared down into her teacup. "You've been so determined to never let another man into your life, this one just sort of snuck up on you. You were angry at being out of love, and now you're angry about being in it. It won't come as any shock to learn you can't have it both ways, sweetheart."

Tabitha lifted her lashes to look into her mother's eyes. "He told me he loves me, but I couldn't say it back. Oh, Mom. I just couldn't say it. He was so hurt. He drove away without even saying good-bye."

Reaching for Tabitha's hand, Victoria covered it with her own. She curled her fingers over her daughter's and squeezed gently. "I wouldn't worry too much, honey," Victoria soothed. "If Nate really loves you, he'll come around. He just needs to figure a few things out first."

"He does? About what?" She sniffled and willed herself not to cry.

"About you. Something inside him must know you love him in return, which is why he felt safe telling you how he feels. But men have very fragile egos, my dear. A little rejection goes a long way. In the meantime, you have some thinking of your own to do."

Tabitha gazed across the table at her mom. With a wry smile, she said, "You're the best mother I've ever had."

Victoria stood to take her dishes to the sink. A plate in one hand, her teacup in the other, she said, "Just remember *that* when it's time to put me in a home, kiddo."

"Mom?" When her mother turned to face her, eyes wide with curiosity, Tabitha decided it was time for a full dose of the truth. "First, can you drive me over to Sausalito to get my car?"

"Sure, but it'll have to wait until after work."

She checked her watch. "I've got to leave in about ten minutes."

"Thanks. And, um, on the way, I need to discuss some stuff with you. I haven't said anything because this case didn't seem to be going anywhere, but I think it's time I told you everything about it, and about Nate, and his brother, and Cal, too—"

"Cal?" Victoria's attention seemed to snag on her former son-in-law's name. Her brow creased and her mouth curved down. "What in the hell does that loser want now?" she growled. Her eyes took on an angry glint. "I swear, I'm not a violent woman, but if he's said or done *any*thing to hurt you any more than he already has, I'll strangle that little bastard with my own two hands!"

Chapter 21

> *If you place a few sprigs of fresh rosemary in a vase next to your bed, you will have pleasant dreams.*
>
> FOLKLORE

"Peter," Nate grumbled. "Dammit. Peter *who*?"

Across the small conference room table, Nate's partner shuffled through a stack of papers. "Okay, well, you got your Peter Peter Pumpkin Eater, Peter Rabbit, Peter Pan . . ."

"I think we can rule them out."

Bob snorted.

Scanning Tabby's handwritten notes, Nate said, "Apparently this Lucy Anderson looked and acted rich, maybe even powerful. Since she thought this Peter guy drove a Jag, we can tentatively assume these are people who move in high financial and social circles."

Bob grabbed his mug of coffee and took a gulp. "So we have a rich guy named Peter Something who would be plunged into scandal if his name was connected with a homicide investigation. That could narrow it down."

"And he probably works in the city, but doesn't live here, as noted by the remark that Lucy Anderson had a long drive north to get home. Maybe Peter does, too, like Sonoma, Mendocino, Marin, or Napa . . ."

Bob stood and walked to the white board and added that fact to the list of others the two detectives had already noted.

"According to what this Anderson woman told Tab—Ms. March," Nate corrected himself, "Peter's father died recently, which put a great deal of stress on our guy. So we're going to need a list of obits for men over the age of say, fifty, in the last eighteen months. Maybe one of them has a son named Peter."

Rubbing his jaw, Bob said, "Going to take some time to assemble that kind of data."

"Then we'd better talk to the lieutenant and get started."

As the two men began to gather their papers, Nate said, "Did you, uh, you ever meet my brother?"

Tossing papers into his briefcase, Bob shook his head. "Ethan Darling? Not personally, no. But I heard of him. He was sort of legendary. They called him The R.C."

Nate arched a brow in inquiry.

"The Righteous Closer. He had the highest percent of cleared cases on record. The tenacity of a freakin' bull dog, and the personality to match." Bob raised his head to smile at Nate. "No offense."

Nate grinned. "None taken." Snapping the lock on his own briefcase, he said, "You ever hear why he left the force?"

"You're his brother. Didn't he tell you?"

Clearing his throat, Nate said, "We're not close."

With a tilt of his head, Bob seemed to consider the situation. "Well, there was talk. You know how it is. But I was working the Tenderloin and he was out of Central, so I don't know the details. I kinda recall that he was involved in a case where a civilian—a young woman, I think—got caught in the crossfire. Nobody seemed to have anything more to say on it than that."

Nate switched off the light and held the door open for his partner. "Do me a favor, would you, Bob? Start running those obits?"

"Sure. Listen, I'm heading for the deli at lunch. You want something?"

In the back of his mind, he saw Tabby, the dismay in her eyes when he told her he loved her . . . the jab to his heart when she'd remained silent . . . his reflection in the bathroom mirror that morning when he'd cursed himself, yet again, for being ten kinds of idiot.

"Yeah," he said. "See if they have any free-range crow."

Cal March chuckled out loud as he headed for the elevators on the eleventh floor of the posh Montecito Building.

The news from the lawyer had been good; hell, the news had been *awesome*. Tabitha's old wreck of a house was going to bring a tidy sum on the market, and he was first in line to cash in. What with California real estate prices running sky-high and no end in sight, in San Francisco even a Victorian in need of major repairs would bring a fucking fortune.

Finally, he'd have enough money to head down to Hollywood and hang for a while until the right part came along. Bay Area commercials and regional stuff were fine, but really he was cut out for bigger things. Everyone, from his agent right on down to that starstruck bimbo with the big tits he'd laid last night, told him so.

He ran his fingers through his thick hair. At thirty-four, he was prime stock. He had looks, style, a killer smile, and what he lacked in talent he more than made up for with a pair of kick-ass dimples. Yeah. Hoo-ray for Hollywood, baby.

A microscopic twinge of guilt pinched his

brain. He probably shouldn't have slept with that girl last night, but she'd given him the come-on, and he wanted to test the waters, so to speak. Hollywood was filled to bursting with babes like her, and he just figured he'd get an early start. As long as his girlfriend didn't find out, he'd be okay. Her uncle had a reputation for getting huge settlements for his clients and it wouldn't pay to piss him off. If she told him Cal had been sleeping around, it might squelch the deal.

On the one hand, he hated to do this to Tabs, but damn, the woman had a stubborn streak. If she'd taken out a loan on the house and given him his share, he wouldn't be forced to coerce her into selling, but things just hadn't been going his way lately, and, well, she *had* inherited the house during their marriage. To his way of thinking, it was by rights half his. According to his attorney, they stood a better-than-fair chance of a judgment in their favor.

Cal pulled the cell phone from his pocket and pushed speed dial. She answered after one ring.

"Hey, babe. You up for a night on the town?" He laughed, feeling like he was walking on freakin' air. "My treat this time."

The connection wasn't good, but he thought he heard her say, "Sounds . . . great . . . ere are you?"

"I just left your uncle's office and I'm heading down to get my car. Can you hear me okay?"

". . . hear you most . . . cutting out . . . uncle say?"

He pushed the button for the elevator.

"I'm about to go down to the parking garage, so I have to make this fast before I lose the signal. Your uncle says we can pull it off. Half of whatever my ex-wife has belongs to me, and I'm suing her for it. If I'm lucky, I should clear at least a million on the deal."

The elevator door opened and he got in and pressed the button for the parking garage. "Can you still hear me?"

". . . bad, but it's . . . me up?"

"Yeah, I'll pick you up. Can you be ready in twenty minutes?"

She said something, but it was faint and distorted by static.

"I'm losing the signal. Listen, I'll see you in twenty. And dinner tonight's my treat. You've been paying for everything, and I think it's time I took a turn, okay? Hello? Hey, baby, you there?"

The signal was gone, so he flipped the phone closed. When the door opened, he stepped out, trying to remember where he'd parked his car. As he moved away from the elevator, he heard a noise behind him, a slight scuffling, then a popping sound.

Something stung him between his shoulders, and he dropped the cell phone from his hand. Searing pain began making its way from his back to his brain, driving him to his knees.

He was having trouble breathing, and as he put his hands to his throat, he looked down to see a red stain growing on the front of his white shirt.

Jesus. What in the hell . . .

He slumped over, his strength easing itself away from him as though he were drugged and going into a deep sleep. Unable to remain upright, he slid to the cold concrete floor of the garage, his eyes focused on his cell phone lying only two feet away.

What was happening to him? Had he been shot? Yeah, yeah. That was the only explanation. But why didn't it hurt? The pain had been great at first, but now it was diminishing, fading like music from a slowly passing car.

He closed his eyes for a moment, too weak to keep them open. Seconds ticked by, or was it minutes? The sound of footsteps caused him to lift his heavy lids.

His cell phone was gone. Blinking rapidly, he tried to focus on the retreating figure, but his lids were too heavy, and he closed his eyes again.

He heard a car door slam; an engine hummed to life. Using every ounce of strength he possessed, he opened his eyes in time to see his killer's car roll through the garage and head for the street.

No way. Son of a bitch . . .

Running his tongue over his dry mouth, he tried to form words, but his lungs didn't have enough air to propel them from his lips. He stared vacantly at the empty, silent garage.

But I was going to Hollywood . . .

Monday drifted into Tuesday, and the rain clouds blew away, but Tabitha's heart felt as bleak and heavy as if it were encased in permafrost. Wednesday, she did a lot of work for Dooley, Chissom and Hall, which helped keep her mind on legal tomfoolery and off Nate Darling. By Thursday she was thoroughly depressed and ready for her dream interpretation class. Interacting with her students always made her feel better, and she was hoping this week's session would have that same effect.

As she tossed her briefcase into her car and slid behind the wheel of her Civic, she thought about how much she missed Nate. Her throat ached all the time, not to mention her heart. Whenever the cell phone he'd given her chimed, she expected it to be him.

She could call him and apologize, but what could she say? *I'm sorry I hurt your feelings because I wasn't ready to say the words you thought I should say just because you said them first?*

But the better question would be, why *had* she bit her tongue rather than confess her feelings? Her mom had been right—Tabitha had to ask herself some hard questions, soon, or she risked losing a man she'd grown to love from the very center of her being.

It wasn't love itself that was the problem, it was her trust *about* love. She knew full well that a man could love you fiercely one moment, and the next the fire that warmed your relationship was gone. And so was he.

She was sure her parents had once had that kind of love, but look what happened to them. After thirty-five years of marriage, her father had up and left to "take the road less traveled," was how he'd blithely put it. What had been wrong with the old road, except that it didn't include love for her mom—and apparently Tabitha—anymore?

And Cal had done the exact same thing.

God, how she had loved Cal. And she'd been convinced he'd loved her. But he'd begun to stray whenever his actor's ego needed a boost, and when she came home unexpectedly that fateful day, to find him in bed with not one, but two women from his theater company . . .

Turning the corner a block short of the school, she let a soft "jerk" past her lips.

And now that lyin', cheatin' ex of hers wanted money, and he actually might get it? Why in the hell didn't he get a regular job like everybody else instead of skating by on his good looks, charm, and more confidence than any mortal had a right to have? If there was any justice in this world, it would all come back to bite him in the butt one of these fine days.

Her grandmother's house was the lynchpin of her life, her home base, the place she could go and feel safe and secure, and because of Cal she might lose it. When they'd divorced, her emotions and feelings of self-worth had shattered, and it had taken her all this time to recover. She'd put her heart and soul into her marriage and he had thrown it away. And more.

Desperately, she'd wanted a baby but for years, he wouldn't commit, saying he needed to get his career going first. Her twenties slipped by, and then she turned thirty, then thirty-one, and still Cal refused.

Then the day came, the day that shocked her to her core. The day that was the beginning of the end for their marriage.

"You did *what*?" She'd stared at him, uncomprehending, certain she'd heard him wrong.

"I had a vasectomy. Yesterday." He'd said the words with not so much as a hint of guilt, as though he were ticking off items on his auto maintenance list. *Yeah, got the oil changed, tires rotated, brake job. Oh, and finally got that vasectomy taken care of . . .*

She'd been unable to wrap her mind around the concept, and continued staring at him until the reality of his action finally began to penetrate her brain.

He'd simply done it. Without talking to her, asking her permission, or taking her feelings or wishes into account at all, he'd had a vasectomy. There would be no babies. No family of her own.

She'd been confused and hurt and angry and had cried for days. The betrayal was so great, divorce became inevitable. When she found him in bed with those two bimbos, it was simply a matter of filing the paperwork and making it official.

He hadn't wanted her to get pregnant, but more, he hadn't wanted any of his girlfriends to get pregnant, either. It was all about Cal. Forever and always, it was about *Cal*.

She couldn't fathom Nate doing something so horrible, but where was her guarantee he wouldn't simply grow tired of her? That would be the worst betrayal of all.

Pulling into the school parking lot, she slid into her usual spot, more unsettled than ever.

What she needed was a little clarity. Some time to sort things out. She'd hoped it would happen at the houseboat last weekend, but then Nate had come . . .

Heat curled through her body at the memory, and she let it warm all the dark, cold places that she didn't even know she had, until she'd met Nate Darling. He'd been so loving and tender with her after she'd told him about Ellie. It was at that moment when she realized she'd fallen thoroughly in love with him. He'd held her while she'd cried, and rocked her, and said soft, soothing words while he stroked her hair.

Oh, Nate. I do love you, but I can't risk having you walk out the way Daddy and Cal did. I just . . . can't. How can I make you understand?

Not to mention the fact that he was a cop and she was a psychic. Oh, yeah. Like *that* was a compatible mix.

Her briefcase in her hand, her mouth tight in concentration, she entered the classroom and forced herself to relax. While she wrote the lesson plan on the whiteboard, a few more people trickled in behind her and took their seats. When she turned around, her heart skipped three beats and her tongue went numb.

There he sat, front-row center, wearing boots, faded jeans, and a long-sleeved black T-shirt that stretched across his muscled chest and flat abs like a second skin. He was sprawled in his chair, his long legs out in front of him, crossed at the ankles. Behind his wire-rimmed glasses, his brown eyes blatantly raked her body, then locked with hers. Steely-eyed and serious, he surveyed her like a gunslinger preparing for a showdown.

And she knew exactly who he was gunning for.

Chapter 22

It is bad luck to sleep with your feet pointed toward the door.

FOLKLORE

Tabitha forced her mouth into a smile. "Welcome to class, everyone." She glanced at Nate. *Not too sure about you, though, cowboy.*

He pursed his lips and crossed his arms high over his chest—which only served to emphasize the width of his shoulders and show off his bulging biceps, which in turn only served to make her nerves do the jitterbug.

Instead of her usual casual dress, Tabitha had chosen a pair of jeans and a jade knit top. If she'd known Nate was going to show up, she'd have worn a suit of armor and a chastity belt.

But she could and would rise above her hormones, her hesitation, memories, regrets. Clearing her throat, she said, "As usual, we'll begin with a discussion and analysis of a student dream. Anybody have a dream they'd like to—"

Nate's hand shot up.

"—share?" she finished. Ignoring Nate and his long, perfect arm, she glanced around the classroom. "Anyone? Anyone at all?"

But his was the only hand raised. He wiggled his fingers, then stretched his arm higher.

"Anyone," she stated. "Any . . . one . . . at . . . all. Hmm." Looking over his head, past his shoulder, out the window, she let her gaze roam everywhere but over Nate Darling.

Because she was bent on ignoring him, all eyes turned to Nate and his childish bid for attention. Kismet, sitting just behind him, snorted a little laugh.

Sliding her hands into her back pockets, Tabitha plastered a cheery smile on her face. "Okay, well, if nobody has anything to share—"

"Scaredy-cat," he mumbled, loud enough for the class to hear.

Her eyes narrowed on him and her jaw tightened.

With a smirky curl to his lip, he lowered his hand. "I had a dream I'd like to share with the class, Miss March."

Tapping her toe, she said, "I find that surprising, Nate, since you once informed me that you don't remember your dreams. Unless, of course, you plan on making one up. Again." *Heh. Gotcha.*

"No," he drawled, lengthening the word to five syllables. "It's a real dream, and I remember every detail. Vividly." His voice was low, throaty, and a warning bell chimed inside Tabitha's head.

The other students watched the exchange with growing interest. Most of the women kept their gazes on Nate, the look in their eyes one of undisguised longing.

If they only knew what a pill he is.

There was obviously no getting around this situation. She had no choice but to cave. "All right, Nate," she said on a long, labored breath. "Make it snappy. Tell us your dream so we can get on with the class."

A look of wry satisfaction shone in his eyes as he straightened in his chair.

"I guess I should warn everyone," he began. "It's sort of R-rated."

Titters and sighs emanated from the women in the class.

"In that case," she began, "perhaps you shouldn't—"

"Oh, let him tell it, Ms. March," Lois Sherwood begged. "We're all adults here. I'm sure we can handle whatever Nate has to say with . . . maturity, and an open mind." Then she blushed and grinned at him like a lovesick seventh-grader.

Several other women nodded in agreement.

"Fine," Tabitha said in a tone of irritated capitulation. "Nate, you're on."

Leaning forward, he placed his elbows on his knees and looked into her eyes. She steeled herself for what she was sure was coming.

"I dreamed I was in my car with my girlfriend."

Tabitha's foot ceased to tap. Her heart ceased to beat. Her brain ceased to function.

"Yeah, and it was cold and windy and raining."

She swallowed.

His lids looked sleepy. Softly, he said, "But we were in the passenger seat of my car, having absolutely phenomenal sex."

Her blood froze, but her cheeks burned. She crossed her arms under her breasts.

"Actually, it was her idea," he continued. "It was raining hard, and the windows got all steamed up. A little soft jazz on the radio."

There was not! Not unless you consider the occasional SFPD ten-code melodic.

"She was so hot and seductive, I went for it. Who wouldn't?"

He looked around the classroom. Heads nodded, throats cleared, students swallowed and murmured affirmative responses. Tabitha was mute, but kept her eyes glued on Nate.

"It was a very passionate encounter," he insisted, "and when it was over and we were relaxed and having a nice little conversation, I, well, I told her that I loved her."

A couple of the women actually sighed out loud. Tabitha glared at Nate, her cheeks like living flames, her throat tight in embarrassed fury.

He cocked his head and tented his fingers in front of him. Her gaze dropped to his hands. He had such great hands, and he knew just what to do with them, the bastard.

"But she just stared at me like I had two heads, and didn't say it back. *That* was when I woke up. What do you think it means, Ms. March?" he asked with an innocent lilt to his voice. "Why do you think she didn't tell me she loves me?"

The whole class stopped breathing while all eyes turned to Tabitha.

Licking her lips, she paced in front of the class for a moment, then swiveled to face him. "What do *you* think it means, Nate?"

His gaze narrowed on her. "You're the expert. *You* tell *me*."

"But it was *your* dream."

"But *you're* a woman. When a man tells a woman he loves her, why wouldn't she say it back?"

"Class," Tabitha rasped, ignoring his challenge, "what type of dream did Nate just describe— prophetic, release, wish, or problem-solving?"

Elderly Mr. Franklin mumbled, "Erotic." For a moment he looked like he wanted to cry.

Curly-haired Beverly Adams piped up. "I think it was a classic wish dream," she said, then looked at Nate as though that's exactly what she was doing.

"Seems like a classic release dream to me," Nate muttered, running his gaze over Tabitha's body.

Everyone but Tabitha giggled. "Perhaps," she began, "*in your dream*, your girlfriend was, maybe, caught off guard and didn't know what to say. Your getting angry and sullen certainly didn't open the lines of communication, which is, I assume, what you did—get angry and sullen, that is?"

"Yeah, I was pissed. But not at her." He tilted his head and relaxed back in his chair. "Don't women *want* to hear a man tell them he loves them, especially after she's given her body to him so many times in so many ways?"

Beverly Adams choked.

"S-sometimes," Tabitha stumbled. "But maybe, *in your dream*, your girlfriend had some trust issues she's dealing with and simply didn't know how to respond."

"Trust issues?" He snorted. "I'm a decent guy. I've never intentionally hurt—"

"Yeah, trust issues, buster." She balled her fists at her hips. "With men. Like a father who just up and walked out one day, or an ex-husband she caught in bed with two women and who now wants to sue her for about a million dollars that she doesn't have. And maybe your girlfriend, *in your dream*, is a teensy-weensy bit upset because you deny part of what she is, who she is, and it hurts her feelings."

His brows shot up. "It wasn't my intention to hurt her feelings, but—"

"Well, you did! Um, probably. *In your dream.* And maybe if you hadn't let your ego get all bent and taken off in a huff, and maybe slowed down a little and asked her what she was thinking and feeling, and maybe held her in your arms and made her feel safe, and let her know that, even though you're not sure you believe her about her special gifts, it's okay, you're willing to keep an open mind, you might have come to understand that the real reason she didn't tell you she loves you is because . . . because . . ."

As a unit, the students leaned forward, their eyes wide with curiosity. Nobody moved; nobody even breathed.

Smacking her forehead with her open palm, she laughed. "Oh, shoot. I left your corrected homework assignments in my car. I'll be right back."

She grabbed her keys from her open briefcase and bolted for the door. When it looked like Nate might follow her, she said, "Nate, while I'm gone, please lead the class in a discussion about the importance of penalty flags in dream relationships."

With that, she hurried down the hall and out the double doors that led to the parking lot.

Tears burned her eyes and her throat ached. Her cheeks felt hot and she wanted to throw something or kick something . . . or someone.

Her head down, her emotions a jumbled mess, she reached her car and jammed the key into the lock, flinging open the door.

Damn him, damn him, *damn* him! Did he have to be so public about their private affairs? Did he think this little stunt was going to get her to reveal her innermost feelings to him—in front of a classroom full of students?

Grumbling under her breath, she reached for the stack of papers she'd tossed onto the front seat of her car. When she heard the footsteps behind her, she realized that, instead of doing as she'd asked, he'd followed her.

Damn him *again*. This was neither the time nor the place to hash out their relationship problems. When she finally decided to tell him how she felt about him, she wanted it to be special and meaningful, not part of some angry battle of wills in a high school parking lot.

Turning, she watched him approach, but, thanks to the track lighting over the locker rooms behind him, all she could see was his silhouette. As he moved closer, he emerged from the shadows and into the light, and she realized that it wasn't Nate at all.

"Oh, it's you," she said, as her heart stammered over its next beat. "What are you doing here?"

Just as Tabitha's delectable little ass disappeared out the door, Nate's cell phone vibrated. Trying to bring his frayed emotions back in check, he yanked it from its holster on his belt and flipped it open. "Darling."

"Nate?"

"Yes, ma'am?" He recognized Tabby's mother's voice. "What can I do for you?"

"I've been trying to reach Tabitha, but she must have her cell phone turned off. Do you know if she's all right?"

"I'm here at class with her. She's just gone out to her car to get some papers."

Victoria made a sound of obvious relief. "When she gets back, would you please tell her to call me? It's an emergency."

He glanced at the empty classroom doorway. "Is there a problem?"

"Yes. I mean, no. I mean, here's the thing. You know Cal, her rat-bastard son-of-a-bitch creep of an ex-husband?"

"I've met the rodent in question, ma'am."

"Yes, well, apparently three days ago somebody shot him! He's in stable condition now, and they're pretty sure he's going to make it. He didn't have any ID on him, though, and it took a couple of days for the authorities to figure out who he is and contact his mother. Now the police want to question *Tabby* about the shooting."

"Bullshit," Nate snapped. "Tabby's not capable of that kind of thing."

"Well, this Inspector Nakamura came to the house, and he was cordial, but I got the feeling they think that Cal's suing Tabby over the house is a pretty good motive for killing him."

"Where was he shot?"

"Geographical location or body part?"

He half grinned. Now he knew where Tabby got her sense of the absurd.

"The first one."

"They said he was in a parking garage downtown, the Montecito Building. Somebody shot him in the back as he stepped off the elevator, but a maintenance guy just happened to show up for work right after it happened, and they got him to the hospital."

"Was he able to identify the shooter?"

"He's in a coma," she said. "He'd lost a lot of blood and was unconscious, and then went into surgery for hours. His mother lives in Daly City, and she's at the hospital with him now."

"I don't know Nakamura," he said, glancing

again at the doorway, "but I'll get in touch with him. See what he's got to say. I wouldn't worry about Tabby, Ms. Jones. There's no way she's involved in this."

Victoria choked a little, and Nate realized she'd been crying. "Just have her call me when she comes back, okay? I'll feel better when I can talk to her."

As he flipped the phone closed, he began walking toward the door. Where was she? It had been five minutes. Where in the hell had she parked? Maybe she'd taken the opportunity to stop by the rest room to piddle. Women and their itty-bitty bladders. That and she was upset about his little dream stunt, so she was probably cooling off.

Still . . .

Moving out into the hall, as he walked toward the rest rooms, his cell vibrated in his hand.

"Yeah. Darling."

"Good news. Your hunch paid off, boy-o," Bob said. "I just picked up the computer printout and with the search criteria you came up with, we have a hit. One perfect hit. Everything fits, from the recently deceased father to the money to the fact he lives in Marin."

The back of Nate's neck began to itch. "His name?"

"Peter O'Hara. Pulled up his photo ID, and it matches the description your lady gave us. I just sent it to you, so you should be able to see it on your LCD screen."

"Hang on." Nate pressed the appropriate buttons on his phone, and there, staring back at him, was the man he'd struggled with in the park that night; the man who'd gotten clean away. Slick bastard.

"Affirmative for a positive ID," he said. "Listen, do you know an Inspector Nakamura?" Quickly he explained about the attempt on Cal March's life.

"Yeah, I know Stan," Bob said. "Good cop. He's not going to jump to any conclusions, if that's what you're worried about."

Rapping his knuckles on the door of the women's rest room, Nate waited for a reply, but none came. Pushing it open, he peeked inside. All three stalls were empty. He let the door swing closed. She really should have been back by now.

He picked up his pace as he rammed through the doors that led to the parking lot.

"Listen, Bob," he said as he scanned the area, looking for her car. "I'm at Merced High School. Can you meet me here ASAP?"

Whatever Bob said was lost on Nate as he spotted Tabby's white Civic. The passenger door was open and the overhead light was on. Checking inside, he saw the stack of papers—the papers she'd come out to retrieve—sitting on the seat. As he shifted position, he stepped on something and looked down.

Her car keys lay in a heap at his feet.

As he straightened, he yelled her name, frantically taking in every inch of the large parking lot. He spun on his heel, did a three-sixty, and continued calling for her. In his ear, he could hear Bob's voice asking what was wrong.

"She's gone," Nate panted. "The SOB's got her."

"Listen," Bob said. "I got a handle on that partial on the diary—"

True panic thickened Nate's brain, numbed him, paralyzed his muscles. In his ear, he heard Bob yell, "Did you hear what I said? Nate?"

As he lowered the phone from his ear he felt a breeze blow in from the bay, chilling him to the bone. Along the busy street, cars moved at a steady pace. Behind him, students finished with their classes began meandering out to get into their cars, chatting and laughing, looking forward to going home to their loved ones.

He barely heard them. The words in O'Hara's journal came back to him with haunting clarity . . .

It's easy. She's so surprised, she doesn't even struggle. The knife slides between her ribs like an oar through quiet water. Blood gushes from the wound . . .

He narrowed his eyes and gazed into the night.

"It's not going to happen," he said through clenched teeth. "I'll find you, Tabby. Hang on for me, baby. Hang on."

Chapter 23

To ensure dreams of a future lover, place a blade-bone under your pillow.

FOLKLORE

The moment she came to, Tabitha realized where she was. Exactly . . . where she was.

Pressing her lips tightly together, she swallowed the scream that wanted to form, the tears she wanted to cry, the panic that had begun rising in her throat.

She fought down hysteria, fought it with everything she had. She wasn't five years old anymore. She was a grown woman, and if she kept her head, she could handle this. She *could*.

God, how could she have been so blind, how could she not have realized? It all made sense now. She would have laughed at her own stupidity, but it would have used up too much precious air.

Forcing herself to calm down, she slowly inhaled. The air inside the trunk was hot and thick, musty, smelling of motor oil and grime. Something rigid dug into her hip, but she couldn't imagine what it was. She lay on her side, slightly curled, her knees bumping against the spare tire.

Reaching up, she let her fingers move along the inside of the lid. Then forward, then behind her. The trunk was only slightly bigger than she was, but she did have a little wiggle room.

How long had she been in there? How much air had she breathed up; how much remained? How long before it would run out and she would drift off to sleep and not wake up?

Doubling her fists, she pounded on the roof. With each strike, her panic increased until she hit harder, and harder, until she was pummeling the metal like a street fighter flailing an enemy.

Gasping for air, she began kicking, thrashing around, letting her fear and anger out, venting her rage and humiliation and terror on the space that confined her.

Tears slicked her face and long sobs escaped her. She closed her eyes and kept kicking and hitting and crying, until her rage was spent, her lungs empty, her flame of hope diminished to a tiny, fragile flicker.

With one final blow to the roof, she let her hands fall to her chest, holding her bruised knuckles against her throat, sobbing until she could barely breathe.

Finally, she lay still and quiet, her muscles nearly spent from the exertion.

"*Nate*," she choked. Her voice sounded tired, strained, but somehow talking out loud made her feel not so alone. "I love you, Nate. Why didn't I have the courage to tell you when I had the chance? Life *is* too short. Sometimes even shorter than we expect. I should have told you . . . I should have let you know . . ."

Her voice trailed off into soft cries and throaty whispers. "I love you, you silly, arrogant, macho, funny, tender man. I *love* you . . ."

Closing her eyes again, she saw her mother's face. How would Victoria bear another daughter lost in this way? How ironic and cruel were the Fates to do this again?

Tabitha's heart jumped. What if they *never* found her? What if the car was parked in the woods somewhere, abandoned to time and the elements?

No. That wasn't right. It didn't fit Peter's journal. In the dream log, he had used a knife and stabbed her. It wouldn't work if she simply suffocated in the trunk of a car. No. Her fate wasn't sealed quite yet.

She swallowed, and wiped away the tears. Doubling her fists again and steeling her spine, she prepared herself for battle.

The scent of chloroform still clung to her

clothes, making her feel lightheaded, or maybe it was from lack of oxygen, but she fought not to go under again. Time was of the essence. She had work to do if she expected to save her own life.

Ethan's mansion in Marin County had been built just after World War II, amid towering redwood trees, and offered a panoramic view of the wide-open Pacific all the way to the edge of the world. When he bought the place two years ago, he'd left the decorating to a professional. He liked what she'd done well enough, but it had that showroom quality about it that made it clear he'd had little to do with the final outcome. Since he rarely entertained, and his mother and Andie didn't visit that often, as long as he had a kitchen with food in it, a bed at night, and a housekeeper to make sure everything worked and the bills got paid, he didn't care.

Though the rest of the place was comfortably furnished in relaxing colors, his home office was every bit as high-tech as his glass-enclosed enclave in San Francisco.

As he eased back in his chair, his eyes never left the surveillance screens on the far wall. Three rows across, three down. Nine views from which to choose, and nothing happening on any of them.

Something was going on, though. He could feel

it in his gut, but thanks to a four-car pileup on the Golden Gate Bridge, he didn't know what it was.

Three hours ago he'd watched as screen number five flickered to life. A car pulled out of the garage and headed down the long drive. It was the move he'd been waiting days to capture. Immediately he'd contacted his field agent, Lucas Russell, and set the tail in motion. All had gone as planned, but as the subject drove across the Golden Gate Bridge, the car in front of Russell's had spun out, slammed into three other cars, and stopped traffic dead. He called Ethan right away, but by the time he'd edged his way past the wreckage, the trail was cold.

Ethan glanced down at the cell phone sitting on his desk. Maybe he should call Nate, warn him. But warn him about what? Going for a drive in the city wasn't a crime, and maybe that's all this was.

Flicking aside the cell phone with his thumb, he returned his attention to the screens.

As he watched, the same car that had driven away three hours ago turned onto the long drive, pulled into the garage, and cut its engine. He narrowed his eyes on the screen. Everything looked normal, but it wasn't. He *knew* it.

Hell, anything could have happened in San Francisco in those three hours—another lady in a polka-dot dress, another bum in an alley, another old man fishing quietly in his boat. The authorities wouldn't know about it until somebody found the body.

Damn, talk about rotten luck.

The cameras he'd installed on O'Hara's property were well hidden. Unfortunately, a little clarity had to be sacrificed in the name of secrecy, and the garage camera didn't yield up the detail he'd been hoping for.

As he peered at the screen, the car door opened. Nothing amiss, as far as he could tell. As the driver began walking to the house, there was a slight pause at the trunk, then a gloved hand reached out and patted the fender.

When the kitchen door opened, the interior camera picked up the action. Again, nothing out of the ordinary.

No staff tonight. The house was empty. Convenient, Ethan thought. He suspected it had been that way on the other nights, too. The other nights when a lone figure had slipped out of the O'Hara house, gone for a drive, and come back a murderer.

On the console to his right, a red light flashed. Somebody coming for a visit. Switching on the monitor that displayed the entrance to his driveway, he recognized his brother's Accord.

By the time Ethan reached the front door, he could hear fists pounding on it as curses filled the air. Throwing the safety locks, he yanked the door open to face his furious brother.

Nate lunged over the threshold, grabbing Ethan by the collar. Shoving him up against the doorframe, he snarled, "What kind of security cameras did you install at O'Hara's, and how do I get past them?"

Without moving a muscle, Ethan said quietly, "Let go of me, or I'll take you apart."

Nate shoved harder. "Later, big brother. I'm going to enjoy beating the shit out of you, but right now I want to know how to get into Peter O'Hara's house undetected."

Ethan cocked his head. "So you figured it out."

"Yeah, I figured it out, no thanks to you."

Nate pressed his face close to Ethan's. Behind his wire-rimmed glasses, his brown eyes were hard with fury and purpose. "Listen, smart-ass, and listen good. Tabitha's missing. Kidnapped. According to the diary, O'Hara kills her with a knife. If anything has happened to her, I'll hold you personally responsible, got that?"

"Fuck." With a twist of his body, Ethan thrust his hands between them and broke the death grip Nate had on his collar. "Come with me."

As they ran through the house toward the office, Ethan shouted, "I've been monitoring the surveillance cameras. I can get us past the security system, no problem. But what if she's not there?"

"She's there."

At the door of the office, Ethan stopped. "How do you know?"

"Because that's got to be the plan. That's where the murder will take place, in O'Hara's room. Her blood on his hands. It'll be the final blow and it's what will put him away for good. He'll either get arrested or turn himself in. Either way, he's history."

Ethan pointed to camera three. "That's O'Hara's bedroom. He's in bed. Been there since about ten."

Nate's eyes narrowed on the screen. "He won't even know what happened until he wakes up with blood on his hands and Tabitha's body on his floor. How far is it to O'Hara's place from here?"

"Five miles over very winding roads. They're a bitch to navigate in the dark."

"Then we'd better get going."

Tabitha scooted around until her feet were pressed against the interior wall of the trunk. She knew something about cars now that she hadn't known when she was five, not that it would have made any difference back then. She'd been too little to kick out the back seat—but she wasn't little anymore.

Her head was spinning and she felt weak. Her

skin was wet and clammy, her breathing labored.

It was now or never.

Bringing her knees up, she thrust out, kicking the interior wall of the trunk. It didn't budge. She pulled back and kicked again, harder. Something gave. Encouraged, she kicked again, and it gave a little more. A few more well-placed kicks and the back seat broke away from the frame. Writhing around, she used her hands to shove the seat forward a couple of inches. Immediately she put her face to the opening and took a deep breath. Then another, and another. Relief eased her panic. She wasn't out of the trunk yet, but she wouldn't suffocate, not today, anyway.

Turning so she was on her side, she put her shoulder to the seat, planted her feet against the spare tire, and shoved as hard as she could. The seat move forward a few more inches. Just as she felt it begin to give way, she heard a click.

The trunk lid popped open and the interior light flickered on.

Raising her hand to shield her eyes from the sudden brightness, she blinked several times, trying to assess the person standing before her, car keys in one hand, a gun in the other.

Her captor smiled. "I'm happy to see you're still alive. Sadly, that's a condition that won't last much longer."

As Tabitha uncurled her body and climbed out

of the trunk of the car, she held on to the fender to keep from falling. The chloroform, combined with lack of fresh air, not to mention screaming and kicking, had weakened her considerably. But her brain still functioned, and that was all she needed.

Raising her head, she looked into the deadest blue eyes she'd ever seen.

"When you touched me, before the chloroform," she said, appraising her captor, "I saw it all. Everything."

"Really."

Tabitha nodded slowly, buying as much time as she could. With each passing second, her strength was returning, and she was going to need it.

"I know what you have in mind, and it's never going to work," she warned. "The police aren't stupid. There's no way you can get away with this, Zoey."

A dense midnight fog had rolled in off the Pacific, slowing their progress to a near crawl. All Nate could think was that Tabby was in the hands of a murderous madwoman, and may already be dead for all he knew—

No ... wait ... stop. If she were dead, he'd know it. He may not have fully accepted her abilities, but if being psychic was akin to a sense of finely tuned intuition, *that* he understood.

Tabby was alive—he'd know if she weren't.

But she could be suffering. That alone was enough to break his heart and fire his blood.

Just then, he felt something of her move through his body, her life force, her energy, her thoughts, her soul, for all he knew. The two of them were connected to each other in some way he never had been with another human being, and he relaxed his death grip on the steering wheel a little, as certain as could be about anything on this earth that she loved him. Maybe she hadn't said it back, and maybe that was okay, but it was there all the same. He knew it.

"Turn here," Ethan said, gesturing to a road that veered off to the west. "It doesn't look like it leads anywhere, but about a half mile farther in, there's a wrought-iron fence. I'll tell you where to park so the cameras won't pick us up."

As they drove along the smoothly paved street, the headlights reached out in front of them, illuminating tufts of gray mist blowing over the road. No houses, no lights, just tall trees with thick red bark and the bone chilling fog.

"Talked to my partner," Nate said. "The lab went to bat for us and got a match on a partial we found on the diary."

Ethan nodded. "The sister."

"Bingo. She was hauled in on a DUI a few years ago. Her big-shot uncle lawyer got the charges dropped, but not before she'd been printed."

Ethan nodded. "O'Hara began to suspect it might be her, so we set up hidden cameras to monitor her activities. She's been slipping him knock-out drops, reading his journal, and mimicking the murders he'd dreamed about."

"Bitch," Nate snarled.

"That would be my— pull over here," Ethan ordered. "There's a cipher-locked side gate next to the garages, but I know the code."

A moment later, letting the gate close quietly behind him, Nate pulled his weapon and moved silently through the shadows to the garage. He could see a black Jag parked there, and next to it a white Bentley. The trunk was open. It looked like somebody had kicked out the back seat.

Panic hit him right between the eyes.

Dear God, Zoey had locked her in the *trunk*. His eyes closed for a moment and he felt nauseous. What had she gone through, locked inside the trunk of a car . . . again? What kind of terror had she endured? If Zoey had tried to, she couldn't have come up with a better way to torture Tabby than to lock her inside that small dark place.

On the floor of the trunk lay a crumpled rag. Judging from the lingering scent, it had been doused with chloroform.

He let the anger roll through him, chill his blood, strengthen his resolve.

Ethan had drawn his weapon and sidled up next to Nate. Glancing into the trunk, he said quietly, "No blood. She's okay, Nate. She got up and walked out. She's smart and resourceful. We'll find her."

Nate lifted his gaze, and the two brothers locked eyes for a moment. For the first time, he saw worry, maybe even fear, on his brother's face.

Simultaneously, they glanced at the house, at the partially open kitchen door. Though they stood only thirty feet from the porch, the thick fog obscured much of the house's façade, and since few lights were on inside, Nate hoped they could make their way upstairs without being detected.

"As soon as we get in," Ethan whispered, "I'll disable the security system. It's in a small room just off the kitchen."

Nate nodded. "I'll head upstairs. Follow me when you're done."

As the two men silently moved through the fog to the kitchen door, the night was shattered by the sound of a gun blast. Upstairs, a window splintered, and a woman screamed.

"*Tabby.*" Nate mouthed her name, unable to find any breath in his body to give it voice. A second later he broke into a run, his brother hard on his heels.

Chapter 24

*To dream of winding yarn into a ball symbolizes
romance and domestic bliss. This is especially
true if the yarn is pink, purple, or white.*

FOLKLORE

Tabitha flattened herself against the bedroom
wall, her heart racing. While her bones had frozen
stiff, her muscles had turned to Jell-O. Against her
heaving ribs, she felt the hard barrel of a gun.

"That was a cute move, Tabitha," Zoey said
sarcastically. Thrusting out her full bottom lip,
she chided, "But it only works in the movies. Try
knocking the gun out of my hand again, and I
won't care how I kill you, I'll simply do it."

Judging from the masculine décor of the room,
and the man lying prone across the bed, this must
be Peter's bedroom. Gesturing toward him with
her chin, Tabitha rasped, "Is he dead?"

"Now, what good would killing him do? If I'd
wanted him dead, I'd have done it months ago."

Zoey gave a little shrug. "If I'd killed him, suspicion would have fallen on me. This way, he's convicted of murders even *he* thinks he committed, and I get all the sympathy and none of the blame."

Tabitha tried to find some moisture in her mouth. Licking her lips, she said, "You've been drugging him so he'd be asleep on the nights you crept out to commit the murders."

Zoey laughed as though Tabitha had just told a great story. She was dressed all in black—boots, leggings, sweater, cap. Her gun was black, too.

"How else could I make sure he didn't have an alibi? I'll tell you, that dream log of his was a stroke of genius. When I read it, I felt like it was the answer to my prayers. And it was fun, too, a real test of my skills."

"Your *skills*?" Tabitha stared into the eyes of the woman who held her life in her hands. "Killing innocent people is a *game* to you?"

"No," she said. "Of course not." Her lovely blue eyes sparkled now, not with joy or happiness, but with a menace so astonishing, Tabitha wanted to look away. "I have an infinite capacity to compartmentalize. I set aside my human feelings and focused on the job. In order for the plan to work, people had to die. I'm sorry for it, but that's just the way it had to be."

Stepping back, Zoey lowered the gun a little as

her expression changed from anger to regret.

"You have to understand, Tabitha," she said, her expression sincere, her voice soft. "I worked my ass off for my father. I got the highest grades in every school I attended, I graduated with honors, I even ran the company when Dad got sick. I did it *all*, while Peter played, gambled, partied, and screwed everything in skirts."

Taking a breath, she gazed around the large room, but Tabitha was sure she wasn't seeing her brother's bedroom, but a whole different world, a world in which Zoey O'Hara ruled.

"I drove myself, night and day, with board meetings and data analyses, trips all over the world to talk to our subsidiaries and our customers. I *made* that company work."

Her eyes filled with tears, but she swiped them away angrily, as though they were burning her flesh. Taking another breath, she raised the barrel of the gun to Tabitha's chest.

"I expected to inherit the company," she choked. "I adored my father, and I know he loved me. But he never saw *me*, saw what *I* did, the contributions *I* made. He only saw the pampered, beautiful trophy daughter he had created. That truth came home to me the day he died and I discovered he'd left everything to Peter. It was as though I'd literally been stabbed in the back."

Tabitha tried not to look at the gun, but her eyes

kept drifting down to it, wishing it would point in some other direction.

"So you decided to eliminate Peter, one way or the other."

Zoey sniffed, then blotted her nose on her sleeve.

"Killing Peter outright would have raised all kinds of suspicions. I tried to get him to step down, convince him I was better suited to run the company. He could still party on . . . but no. No, he decided it might be fun to stand at the helm of my father's empire, the empire *I* should have inherited."

Tabitha glanced around the room. The door through which they'd entered stood open. Behind her, there was another door, but who knew where that led . . . right into a closet, for all she knew. The door next to the bed was probably a private bathroom. Of course, there was always the broken window.

". . . slipped things into his drinks and food to make him sick, give him nightmares, sleepless nights," Zoey was saying. She kept talking, as though she needed to tell somebody the whole sordid tale. She'd been holding all this in for a year, and now she literally had a captive audience. She could unburden herself with impunity, since she probably figured Tabitha would be too dead to pass the information along.

"I tried to convince him it was the stress of taking over the family fortune, but instead of breaking him, it made him stronger. He worked harder, got better at running things. Imagine that! Who would have guessed my brother even had a spine, let alone known how to straighten it?"

She paced the room for a moment, then turned again to Tabitha.

"It started getting really good when he found the shoe. He was utterly *convinced* he'd killed her."

Tabitha's pulse jumped. "Iris Reynaud's shoe, from the Conservatory of Flowers."

Zoey moved to the window, drew the heavy curtain aside with the barrel of the gun, and looked out into the darkness. "From then on, I began getting more creative, making sure he had blood on his hands or clothes when he woke up. I made certain he saw the newspaper articles about that old bum in the alley and the guy in the fishing boat. I thought he'd crack any second, but he never did. *Sit*," she ordered suddenly. "There," she said, gesturing with the gun to a plush chair in front of the massive flagstone fireplace that took up the entire far wall of the bedroom.

Never taking her eyes from the gun, Tabitha eased her trembling body into the chair. As soon as she'd settled in, Zoey moved to the desk by the broken window, opened a drawer, and with a gloved hand removed a long, thin blade.

"My brother uses this as a letter opener," she said with a laugh. "It has his prints all over it."

"Why'd you come to my house that day, Zoey?"

"So you'd follow me, get my license, and give it to the police. Hell, I gave you every clue, practically drew you a map."

Tabitha raised her chin. "You *wanted* me to get your license number. Wanted me to give it to the police so they'd find Peter."

"Exactly. I drove away slowly enough for you to get my license number, but when nobody put two and two together, I decided to move things along a little more quickly. I think the professionals refer to it as *escalating*."

Tabitha tried to get a line on Zoey, a weakness, something she could use against her. Looking her in the eye, she said, "Where is your humanity, Zoey? Even people who are bad to the bone have some redeeming qualities."

"Maybe I used to," she said on a high-pitched sigh. "A long time ago, but I lost it somewhere along the line, and I don't care to get it back. When we were kids, I loved Peter. I guess I still do, but there are more important things in life than love. Love never got *me* anywhere, now, did it? Only money. Only power. And one day I decided I'd do anything to have as much of both as I could get."

"And now you think killing me will bring all

this to an end. They'll find me here, assume Peter murdered me, and you'll get everything."

Instead of answering, Zoey glanced at her watch.

"Look, it's been lovely chatting with you, but it's getting late. I need to kill you so I can leave. When the servants arrive in the morning, they'll find your dead body on my brother's bedroom floor, your blood on his hands." She glanced at Peter's prone form. "He should be awake by then. He'll think he actually killed you, so I'm sure he'll go willingly—"

"No, Zoey, I won't."

Tabitha spun around in her chair in time to see Peter sit up on the bed, a revolver in his hand, rage in his eyes.

As Zoey stared in shock at her brother, Tabitha leapt out of the chair and bolted for the open bedroom door, slamming the light switch as she ran, plunging the room into darkness.

The sound of a gun blast made her cover her ears and scream as the wood in the doorjamb next to her face splintered into a thousand pieces. Another shot exploded behind her, but she didn't stop to see who'd fired it or whether it had found its mark. She just kept running.

Nate finished calling for backup and shoved his cell phone into its holster on his belt. Two more shots exploded from somewhere upstairs. Running for the wide staircase, he and Ethan reached the bottom step at the same time. Without so much as glancing at each other, weapons drawn, they started up the stairs, taking two at a time.

As Nate reached the top step a little ahead of his brother, a shadow appeared in the darkened bedroom doorway about ten feet down the hall to his right. He caught a glint, and realized the figure in the doorway was armed.

"Police!" he yelled. Clutching his .38 in both hands, he raised it straight in front of him. "Drop your weapon!"

His eyes glued on the figure in the doorway, he began to inch forward when he felt fingers coil hard around his collar. Ethan jerked him off balance, then stepped in front of him.

From the shadows at the opposite end of the hallway, a shot exploded, and a split second later, Ethan lurched against Nate's shoulder, knocking him down, trapping Nate's gun hand between them.

Another shot from the shadowy hallway went wide. Ethan raised his arm and squeezed off a shot, then slumped against Nate.

As Nate wrestled himself out from under his brother and stood, the figure in the doorway stepped into the hall—Peter O'Hara. A gun dangled loosely from his limp arm, a wash of red blood smeared his shoulder. His face was pale and haggard as he slid to the carpet.

"Zoey. The back stairway," he managed. Raising his arm, he pointed down the hall. "There."

Nate spun to face his brother.

"Goddammit!" he shouted, grabbing Ethan by the arm, yanking him up, shoving his back against the wall. "What in the hell were you doing—"

Instead of glaring back at him, Ethan blinked slowly, his eyes gone dull and sleepy. As Nate watched, Ethan's lips curved into a smile, then faded as his legs seemed to go out from under him.

Nate caught Ethan in his arms just before his body hit the landing. Easing his brother onto the rug, he drew his hand away and realized it was sticky with blood.

"Ethan? Shit, *no* . . . God, what . . ."

Ethan's eyes pinched opened. "You didn't see her. I did."

"So you stepped in front of me to take a bullet, you stupid son of a bitch! *Why?*"

His voice harsh, his breathing labored, he whispered, "You're . . . my brother."

The two men stared at each other for a long moment, then Nate blinked.

"I've gotta go," he rasped. "You gonna be okay?"

"Sorry, pal. I'll live."

Nate squeezed his brother's shoulder. "Asshole," he choked.

"Prick."

On the floor in front of the bedroom doorway, O'Hara let out a long moan.

"I'll take care of him," Ethan said. With a flick of his gaze down the hall, he bit out, "Go get that bitch for me, will you?"

Tabitha knew she had a good head start, but the house was so dark, she was losing valuable time just trying to figure out where she was and not bump into any of the furniture—or Zoey's gun.

Having been brought onto the estate inside the trunk of a car put her at a disadvantage. She hadn't seen the road, landscape, or even what the house looked like until she'd walked into the back of the house from the garage.

After fleeing Peter's bedroom, it had been just pure dumb luck that she'd found a staircase leading down to what appeared to be a workroom just off the kitchen.

Keeping low, she crept along as quickly as she dared, heading toward what appeared to be a door. Light coming from somewhere else in the house eased the shadows a little, helping her find her way. All around her it was deathly quiet; any noise she made could bring Zoey down on her in an instant.

When she reached the door, she turned the handle and opened it only as far as she needed to inch through, then silently closed it behind her.

She stood on some kind of deck surrounded by gigantic redwoods. The already dark grounds were made even darker by the branches swaying high overhead and the dense fog that lay on the earth like a damp blanket. Faint moonlight tried to shine through the fog, but it was a losing battle.

A few feet away from the deck, she caught sight of a lighted path that led away from the house and into what looked like a garden, but beyond that the mist obscured everything. She could be running into an open field, or off a cliff.

She knew what lay behind her; what lay ahead couldn't be any worse.

As she plunged into the fog, she heard the door through which she'd just exited being flung open. Glancing over her shoulder, her eyes were met with only gray mist.

She quickened her pace, keeping her attention focused on her feet, hoping the brick pathway would lead to some kind of safety.

She considered trying to make her way back to the garage to get a car, but it was unlikely any of the cars had their keys conveniently dangling in the ignition. Besides, that was something Zoey would probably anticipate. Best steer clear of the garage.

As she stumbled her way along, her eyes grew used to the darkness. Throwing another glance over her shoulder, she left the path and slid behind the trunk of an enormous redwood, flattening herself against its rough trunk.

Slowly, she eased herself down into a crouch as far as she could, held her breath, and listened.

Nothing. Zoey must be doing the same thing.

It was so cold, she was afraid her teeth would begin to chatter and she'd give herself away. Rubbing her arms, she tried to warm up a little, but it was no use. The mist dampened her hair, her skin. Her clothing felt wet and uncomfortable.

Shifting her position a little, she felt something in her front pocket dig into her thigh. What in the world . . .

She extended her leg, then shoved her hand deep inside until her fingers curled around the cell phone Nate had given her.

My God, she'd forgotten all about the damned thing! She'd turned it off for class and had absently stuck it in her pocket.

Her heart raced for a moment, then hit a wall.

Okay, she had a cell phone, but if she turned it on, it would make that little musical noise, which would tell Zoey exactly where she was. There must be some way to mute it. Oh, *why* hadn't she read the whole owner's manual Nate had left her? She'd only read enough to learn how to make calls.

Well, the minute she got home, she was going to dig that thing out of her junk drawer and read the whole damn thing!

The snap of a twig a few feet away made her heart jump. She wasn't wearing white, but her jade-colored top was light enough to be seen in the fog, and Zoey was dressed all in black, rendering her nearly invisible.

She looked around. Eerie shapes, tree branches dipping low to the ground, rocks, thorny bushes, all became barriers to her freedom.

In the distance she could hear the sounds of waves crashing hard against the shore, and the mist had a briny snap to it. She couldn't be too far away from the beach. Maybe the hillside rolled gently down to the shoreline. That would be good. Once she hit the wet sand she could run until she came to another house.

But if the estate stood on a cliff, she was trapped.

"Tabitha-a-a-a," Zoey's voice taunted her from a few yards away. Dammit. She was much nearer than Tabitha had anticipated. Staying put was the only option now until Zoey either moved off in another direction or walked by.

Footsteps in the dark, receding, it seemed, in the opposite direction.

She shivered, but whether it was from the cold or sheer terror, she couldn't have said.

Clutching the cell phone, she decided to risk turning it on. Even though it might do that little musical start-up tune, at least it would be on, and she could punch the autodial and talk to Nate one last time . . . just in case Zoey got off a lucky shot.

But first she needed to put as much distance between her and Zoey's gun as possible.

Easing herself into a standing position, she backed away from the tree and headed toward the sound of the ocean.

As soon as she got far enough away, she flipped open the phone. Taking a deep breath, she pressed the button. Musical notes trilled loud and long, sounding like a tinny version of the San Francisco Philharmonic on opening night.

Damn. Tabitha rolled her lips together. Zoey had to have heard that, but if she moved quickly enough, she could be somewhere else by the time the woman reached this spot.

She stepped back, her goal still the shoreline and as fast a getaway as she could manage. As she rounded a large, leafy fern, she skidded to a halt.

"Don't you just love cell phones?" Zoey cooed. The gun she held was pointed straight at Tabitha's heart. "You know, you can download all kinds of tunes for them, even dirges, I'll bet. I think a dirge would come in pretty handy right about now, don't you?"

Tabitha let her arms drop to her sides. There

was nowhere left to run, and they both knew it.

"Change of plans, Tabitha," Zoey said, moving quickly forward. "Unexpected company. Instead of killing you, I need you as a hostage. C'mon." She gestured with the barrel of her gun. "This way."

Tabitha felt for the button on the phone, the button that would send a call to Nate. Wherever he was, he'd be too late to help her, but at least he'd be able to hear what was going on and know she'd gone down fighting.

She pressed the button. A moment passed, then another, then, from the mist behind Zoey, the twinkling sounds of "Take Another Little Piece of My Heart" filled the air.

Zoey turned in the direction of the music and fired.

Tabitha curled her fingers around her cell phone and leapt forward, slamming Zoey in the temple as hard as she could.

The woman screamed and fell to her knees. A moment later, Nate emerged from the fog, grabbed Zoey's arm, and flipped her onto her stomach. Pressing his knee into her back, he relieved her of her weapon. From his belt he yanked off a pair of handcuffs and snapped them first on one wrist, then the other.

Out of the mist, uniformed men with flash-lights swarmed the area. Floodlights came on, washing the darkness with bright light. Blinking rapidly, Tabitha covered her eyes and turned her head away.

When she looked back, Nate had risen to his feet and was coming toward her. Before she could move, his arms were around her, his mouth on hers, his fingers gliding through her damp hair.

Grabbing her shoulders, he held her away from him and looked her up and down. "Tell me you're all right." His breath was gone; he was panting, sounding like he'd just run a thousand miles and more.

Tabitha swallowed. "'T-take Another Little Piece of My Heart?'" she choked as tears ran down her cheeks. "When I call you, that's what plays?"

He adjusted his glasses. "Only because I couldn't find a download for 'Witchy Woman' or 'The Battle Hymn of the Republic.'"

She laughed, and started to say something, but no words came out.

Then she looked up at him, at his smudged face, his rumpled hair, his glasses, his grin, and she threw herself into his arms. As he wrapped his arms around her and placed his cheek against her hair, she sobbed, "I love you! I love you! Oh, Nate. I should have told you before, but I . . . I . . . I—"

"Tabby, sweetheart," he soothed. "You don't have to—"

"Yes, I do!" she cried. "I love you. I've loved you for days and days, but I didn't know how to tell you. I was so afraid—"

"It's okay. Everything's okay now. You're just in shock—"

"No, I'm not!" she yelped, lifting her head. "I *love* you. I *love* that you put a song on your cell phone just for me!"

He chuckled, then lifted her face with his knuckle. His eyes grew serious. "Tell me the truth. Are you really all right? I'm so sorry about the trunk, Tabby. It must have been—"

"I *loved* being in the trunk," she sobbed, grabbing a fistful of his shirt in her fingers. Hot tears ran down her cheeks and into her mouth and under her chin, but she didn't care. "I fucking *loved* it! I finally dealt with the last three decades of pain and remorse. I kicked my way *out* of the trunk this time, Nate." The air all gone from her lungs, she squeaked softly, "I didn't go to sleep and not wake up. Ellie would be so proud of me. I would have gotten away, too, but Zoey—"

"Tabby," Nate said, his voice warm and mellow. "Marry me. Please. I know it's kind of soon, but I can't imagine loving anyone else the way I love you. I want to spend the rest of my life trying to figure you the hell out. Please don't deny me the opportunity. Marry me."

Her arms slid around his waist, and she lay

her head on his shoulder. Closing her eyes, she squeaked, "Yes. Oh, yes."

As the ambulance carrying a patched-up but definitely alive Ethan headed down the long drive, Tabitha and Nate stood in the quiet of the mists and shadows, listening to the waves crash against the shore somewhere over the horizon.

It was done. It was done, and now that it was, she wanted nothing more than to spend the rest of her life in this man's arms, bearing this man's babies, walking by this man's side.

Pulling back from him a little, she said, "Do you finally believe I'm psychic and can see other people's dreams?"

He looked down at her for a long time.

"This is one of those *Does this dress make me look fat* questions, isn't it?" He rubbed his jaw for a moment, then, with a wry smile, he curled his fingers around hers.

"Perhaps one more little test is in order."

"What test?" she said warily.

"Close your eyes and tell me what I dreamed last night. If you get it right, you'll have made a believer out of me. Deal?"

"Deal."

She curled her fingers around his, lowered her lashes, and almost immediately raised them again.

"Oh!" she choked, looking deeply into his eyes.

"Oh, my! Oh, God! Well, I . . . I had no idea you could even . . . oh, my!"

He grinned, then bent his head.

As his mouth claimed hers, she murmured, "I didn't even know you owned a hammock."

Epilogue

Victoria was in the kitchen, clearing away the dishes from her late Friday dinner of homemade lasagna and salad, when the doorbell chimed.

Immediately Winkin scurried out from under the table to tear down the hall, barking up a storm.

"Who on earth can that be at this hour?" she muttered, drying her hands on a dish towel.

She checked her hair in the mirror in the foyer, decided she was presentable, then scooted Winkin away and opened the door.

"Good evening, ma'am."

Her breath, along with her power of speech, seemed to disappear for a moment. When she recovered, she said, "Inspector Stocker? What a pleasant surprise."

And boy was it. He looked great in his tailored gray suit, which matched the color of his hair perfectly. The detective was a very handsome man, and he'd drifted across her mind on more than one occasion over the last couple of weeks.

"Inspector Darling and Tabitha are still at the hospital with Ethan," he said. "They should be done soon, but I thought I'd bring you up to date on the situation. If you have a moment?"

"I do," she rushed. "I mean, what I mean is, well, please come in. Tabby called me earlier from the hospital to say that Nate's brother had been injured, but that she was okay. God, I'm just so happy this whole thing is finally over."

Stocker walked through the door to stand next to her. She loved how tall he was. His broad shoulders were impressive, and even for a man his age, he seemed so wonderfully fit.

"Ethan took a bullet in the ribs," he said as they walked side by side toward the parlor. "He's going to hurt like hell for a while, but the prognosis is good."

When they entered the room, she sat on the sofa, but instead of taking a chair, he sat next to her. Not too close, but not too far away, either.

Inside her chest, her heart gave a decidedly heavy flutter.

"As for the others," he said, "it looks like Cal March is going to make it. When he woke up, the first thing he did was identify Zoey O'Hara as the one who shot him. Peter O'Hara's been treated for a superficial gunshot wound and released."

Victoria shook her head, then looked down at her hands in her lap. "That horrible woman did so much damage. I'm just so grateful she didn't harm my daughter."

Stocker smiled sympathetically. He had a wonderful smile, very open. His whiskey-colored eyes crinkled in the corners in an attractive way.

She really should stop thinking about him like this. He could be married, for all she knew, or in a serious relationship.

"The O'Hara woman confessed to everything," he continued, casually leaning forward and resting his elbows on his knees. "She not only committed the three homicides to emulate her brother's dream log entries, she pushed Tabitha in front of the cable car."

"But why on earth . . ."

"Anger mostly, I think," he said. "She's a pretty nasty specimen. Vindictive as hell. She felt Peter should have talked to *her*, and not gone to a dream interpreter. She wanted him out of the way, but she also wanted him to acknowledge her as the head of the family. It only came to her later, after she'd read about his dream of killing Tabitha, that she decided to hold off until the timing worked to her advantage."

Victoria settled back into the plush cushions on the sofa and let herself relax a little. "But why did she shoot Cal?"

Stocker looked into her eyes, and she felt her cheeks warm. "After she'd discovered Peter was seeing Tabitha, she tracked Cal March down and began an affair with him. I guess she was hoping to get some insider information on your daughter. Zoey O'Hara seems to be a very controlling, manipulative type. Maybe she just wanted all the bases covered so there wouldn't be any surprises. When she found out March was sleeping around on her, she got mad and took retaliatory action."

An awkward silence stretched between them for a moment, then Victoria smiled and sighed. "Well, I guess that about wraps everything up? What happens now?"

"What happens now is Zoey O'Hara gets indicted on three counts of aggravated murder, plus a whole passel of other offenses, including kidnapping. There's no way she's ever going to harm anybody ever again."

Licking her suddenly dry lips, Victoria said, "W-would you like some coffee, Inspector, or do you have to get back to work now?"

He straightened and returned her smile. "Well, actually, I, uh, I'm off duty as of about twenty minutes ago. I just wanted to come by and, uh, you know, tie up those loose ends. Answer any questions you might have, you know, about the case."

"How thoughtful of you. Thank you."

More silence. Why wasn't he leaving now? He was off duty, but he'd come to see her? And he seemed so nervous.

"Um, so," she ventured. "You're *off* duty."

He looked into her eyes, then looked away. "Yes. Off. So maybe you should call me Bob."

"Bob," she repeated. "And I'm Victoria."

He grinned. "I know." Clearing his throat, he said, "Uh, as a matter of fact, Victoria, I, uh, was on my way to get a bite to eat. I know it's short notice, and nine o'clock's kind of late for some folks, but if you don't have any other plans—"

"I don't," she rushed. "I mean, I'm starving. Haven't had a thing all day." Her stomach was still groaning from having had a few bites too many of lasagna, but he didn't need to know that.

"Great," he said as he rose to his feet.

She excused herself to go upstairs for a moment to check her makeup, grab a sweater, and get her purse. When she came down, he was waiting for her at the bottom of the stairs.

"You look very pretty," he said, grinning into her eyes.

"Thank you," she breathed, trying not to sound

as overwhelmed as she felt. "And you look quite handsome."

He took her arm and walked with her to the door.

"I was thinking," he said as he turned the knob. "After dinner, maybe we could spend some time together. Relax a little and get to know each other."

Her heart fluttered again, several times, and she thought she might actually giggle. Instead, she said, "That would be very nice."

Placing his hand at the small of her back, he escorted her down the steps.

"Maybe we could play cards," he said. "Do you like to play cards? I was thinking about maybe a nice game of Hearts . . ."

Next month, don't miss these exciting new love stories only from Avon Books

Claiming the Courtesan by Anna Campbell

An Avon Romantic Treasure

Called "different and intriguing" by Stephanie Laurens, Anna Campbell's debut novel is the darkly emotional tale of how far the Duke of Kylemore will go to claim his bride—London's most notorious courtesan.

Be Still My Vampire Heart by Kerrelyn Sparks

An Avon Contemporary Romance

Emma Wallace has made it her mission to get revenge on the monsters who killed her parents. But when Angus MacKay appears, the Scottish vampire throws all of Emma's plans into a tailspin. Angus is strongly attracted to Emma, and while overcoming the CIA member's demons won't be easy, Angus is sure it will be more than worth it.

Mistress of Scandal by Sara Bennett

An Avon Romance

Francesca Greentree wants nothing to do with her courtesan mother's life—and that includes passion. But when the handsome and dangerous Sebastian Thorne arrives to protect Francesca from a villain of the past, the young woman must decide if she can give up the fears of her childhood for the possibility of love in her future.

When Seducing a Spy by Sari Robins

An Avon Romance

No one in London knows that Lady Tessa is a spy for the government. But when her childhood friend Heath Barlett suddenly resurfaces, it becomes clear he is investigating her! Tess fears for her future and her country—but as passion overtakes good sense, the pair is forced to choose between love and duty"

Avon Romances

the best in

exceptional authors and unforgettable novels!

NO MAN'S BRIDE
by Shana Galen
0-06-112494-X/ $5.99 US/ $7.99 Can

THE PERFECT SEDUCTION
by Margo Maguire
0-06-083732-2/ $5.99 US/ $7.99 Can

DELICIOUSLY WICKED
by Robyn DeHart
0-06-112752-3/ $5.99 US/ $7.99 Can

TAKEN BY STORM
by Donna Fletcher
0-06-113625-5/ $5.99 US/ $7.99 Can

**THE EARL OF
HER DREAMS**
by Anne Mallory
0-06-087295-0/ $5.99 US/ $7.99 Can

**TOO GREAT A
TEMPTATION**
by Alexandra Benedict
0-06-084794-8/ $5.99 US/ $7.99 Can

**FOR THE LOVE
OF A PIRATE**
by Edith Layton
978-0-06-075786-1/ $5.99 US/ $7.99 Can

**CONFESSIONS OF
A VISCOUNT**
by Shirley Karr
978-0-06-083412-8/ $5.99 US/ $7.99 Can

**WILD AND WICKED
IN SCOTLAND**
by Melody Thomas
978-0-06-112959-9/ $5.99 US/ $7.99 Can

DESIRE NEVER DIES
by Jenna Petersen
978-0-06-113808-9/ $5.99 US/ $7.99 Can

**NIGHT OF THE
HUNTRESS**
by Kathryn Smith
978-0-06-084991-7/ $5.99 US/ $7.99 Can

GOOD GROOM HUNTING
by Shana Galen
978-0-06-112496-9/ $5.99 US/ $7.99 Can

Avon Romantic Treasures

Unforgettable, enthralling love stories, sparkling with passion and adventure from Romance's bestselling authors